I0727285

Published by:
Powder River Publishing LLC
1014 Black Mountain Road
Thermopolis, Wyoming 82443

Copyright © 2024
ISBN: 978-1-956881-41-7
Printed in the United States of America

www.powderriverpublishing.com

*For all the families missing a loved one
who has disappeared and are praying for their safe return.*

CHAPTER ONE

Alex was washing her face when the lights went out.

Her dog Maisie, sitting patiently next to her on the bathroom floor, gave a soft woof in the dark. Alex put her hand on the dog's back to assure her nothing was wrong.

Alex was certain nothing was wrong. Besides the fact that she was in a log cabin in the middle of the mountains of Wyoming on a stormy night, there was nothing to be concerned about. She fumbled for a towel and used the flashlight on her cell phone to make her way out of the bathroom.

A flash of lightning briefly lit her way into the main room that was connected to the kitchen by a breakfast bar. Alex played the light of her flashlight around. The cabin was small and cozy with two bedrooms located on one side, along with the bathroom that also acted as a laundry room. Was there an electrical box somewhere? Would that do any good? She found it in the laundry room, but it looked like everything was in order. She walked back into the living room and looked out the front window. The lights of the office and yard light on this remote guest ranch were also off. The power outage was not isolated to her cabin, she realized.

"What do we do now?" Alex asked Maisie. "I feel like this is a bad sign and now I'm rethinking that whole get-back-to-nature idea. Sure, I wanted to be alone, and visit somewhere new, but we could have gone to the beach, right?"

The dog softly woofed again as Alex shined her light around the living room.

One side of the room featured a huge stone fireplace, but it was dark and cold without a fire. She looked around and saw no wood and quite frankly, didn't know if a fire was allowed in the cabin, so that wasn't going to help her now. The walls were knotty pine and the entire cabin was decorated in moose. That was also not helpful. A larger flashlight would be nice, Alex thought. Maybe there were some candles somewhere. She looked around again.

Alex could live here, she thought. The views from the front porch and the back deck were breathtaking, the porch looking out towards the mountains to the west and the deck overlooking a small lake. At the moment, there was no view. Rain was pounding the roof of the cabin and Alex jumped at the flash of lightning and the immediate clap of thunder that followed.

"What do we do now?" she asked the big dog standing next to her. "There are no candles to be found."

Maisie wagged her tail. Storms didn't bother her and Alex knew the dog was ready for bed. She was too and since the electricity was off, they may as well call it a night. It had been a long day, Alex decided. Her whole body ached. They had driven from Kansas City to Laramie, Wyoming, before driving west into the Snowy Range to this little cabin on the Bar CG guest ranch. It had been a long drive and had taken several days. Even now, she thought she should have stayed in Laramie tonight since it was nearly dark when she left there about forty-five minutes ago. The last mile of driving in the dark had been a challenge. Alex found that being in a vehicle for long periods of time made her legs hurt. She was also paranoid. Other drivers made her very nervous. She hoped one day she would get over that, but so far she tended to treat every other driver like they were out to get her.

There was no one in the office when she checked in, which didn't surprise her since she was so late, but there was an envelope with her cabin key on the desk. Alex had unpacked and relaxed with a murder mystery until her eyelids started to droop.

She looked around the cabin again, lit up by another flash of lightning. There was no television and Alex was okay with that. The brochure had said there was a television in the Commons, a room separated from the office by a patio, that guests could use, but none in any of the cabins. Wi-Fi was also available...in the Commons. Alex didn't care. It wasn't fancy, but she wasn't looking for fancy. She was looking for a place to heal and decide on a future.

The car accident more than a year ago that left her with a badly broken leg and broken ribs had taken the life of her fiancé. It took everything she had to get through the grief and the knowledge he was gone. Surgery had repaired her leg, but that was followed by therapy, and despite months of grueling work with the physical therapists, Alex's left leg was still weak. Even now, she walked with a slight limp that was worse when she was tired. Maisie, a Bernese Mountain Dog, was a big help, adding companion- ship and helping her keep her balance getting out of chairs and up and down stairs.

Before the accident, she worked as designer for an outdoor gear com- pany in Kansas City, and at first, they said she would have a job to come back to, but as the months went on, she was told they had to fill the position. Maybe they could find other duties for her, they said, but Alex was a de- signer and that's what she wanted to do. She still didn't have any leads on a designing job although she had signed up on a job recruiting site and sent resumes to every company she could think of. She loved her job and she loved Kansas City, but the memories there were still raw and suddenly it was too crowded and too noisy. Was she running away? Maybe. But there really wasn't anything in Kansas City for her now. James was gone and his family had moved on with their lives without her. Alex had taken a risk coming out here, just for a vacation, with no job and no place to live, but, well, lots of people started over. She could too.

Alex's parents lived in Arizona and her only sister Bree lived in southern California with her husband and three children. They all had lives and right now, Alex thought her own might be on shaky ground. So, she decided to take a vacation and think things through. She and James had planned on coming out here after they were married, so the mountains were a perfect choice. Alex could hike to build strength in her leg, and had brought a good selection of books to read. Maybe she would learn how to fly fish. The ranch's brochure offered that, along with off-road adventures and horseback riding. She didn't know how her leg would react to riding a horse, but the off-road adventure might be fun if she had someone with her.

For now, though, Alex needed to remember which lights she had on when the power went out, so if it came back on in the middle of the night... and she was certain it would...the cabin wouldn't be completely lit up. She headed toward the front door and caught a glimpse of movement outside the window. She gasped. There was someone out there. Her imagination jumped back into high gear and she took a step back.

"Stop being silly. There are no ax murderers outside your window. It's just the trees blowing." Maisie cocked her head as if she didn't believe Alex.

As she reached for the light switch by the front door, Alex jumped. Outside, someone was banging on the door. Alex put one hand to her heart and instinctively reached for Maisie, who growled at the door and whoever was behind it. Ax murderer came to mind and Alex shook her head. No more reading murder mysteries before bed.

"Hello?" A muffled male voice called out from behind the door. "It's Cole from the office. Everyone okay in there?"

Alex sighed with relief. Ax murderers didn't usually announce themselves. She set her phone on the table next to the door and turned the doorknob. She kept one hand on Maisie as a precaution. She opened the door a crack and saw a tall, lean figure in a soaked raincoat dripping onto her little porch. Another flash of lightning turned him into a silhouette.

"The electricity is off," he announced, pulling off his hood and shining a flashlight in Alex's eyes. She immediately raised her free hand to shield them. He moved the beam away from her face, allowing Alex to see a hint of his features in the dimness. His dark hair was curly from the rain, and Alex could see a hint of beard on his lean, angular face. He was too good looking to be an ax murderer, she decided, and almost laughed out loud. She was sure there were good-looking ax murderers out there. She opened the door a little wider and Maisie poked her head out. Maisie had stopped growling but was pulling on her collar.

"Pipe....?"The man stopped in mid-sentence. Alex saw him shake his head and turn back to her. Alex looked at him watching the dog. Maisie was brown and black with white on her chest, paws and down her nose, Alex always felt like Maisie's fur was the same color as her own hair, not quite brown and not quite red. Alex felt her face flush as she realized she had her hair pulled up in a little pony tail that was only about three inches long.

She looked up at him, and Alex knew the minute he realized she was waiting for him to say something.

"I'm Cole Gilchrist, owner of the Bar CG. I missed you this afternoon when you checked in." He offered a hand. "Is everything okay with the cabin?"

Alex smiled as she opened the door wider and took his hand. She noted he shook it gently, a gesture she appreciated. "It's wonderful, except we don't have any electricity. I'm Alex Bennington and this is Maisie."

Maisie thumped her tail on the floor and Cole bent down to ruffle the fur behind her ears. "Hi there," he said to the dog. Cole looked up. "I saw on your reservation that Maisie is a certified service dog."

Alex nodded. "She is. I don't need her help as much as I have in the past, but I still rely on her for balance. I injured my leg in an accident," she explained as they both glanced at her leg, "but it's getting better."

Cole straightened up. "I can get a generator for you if you want. It's hard to say how long the electricity will be off."

Alex shook her head. "We don't need a generator. We were just going to bed." Now why did she say that? He didn't need to know her plans.

"Well, welcome to the Bar CG. If there's anything you need while you're staying here, stop over at the office and I'll be happy to help."

"Thanks. I'll do that."

Cole knelt to give the dog another scratch under her neck and in the light of another flash of lightning, Maisie lunged out the door and onto him, pushing Cole off balance and knocking both of them off the porch. They ended in a heap of dog and man in a puddle of water. Alex stood still, completely mortified, then raced down the two steps to them.

"Oh my God, Maisie, get off of him," she shouted, entering the melee, and trying to pull the big dog away. "Maisie, stop!"

Maisie did stop for a moment, then went back to licking Cole's face. Cole finally managed to get himself untangled from the dog as Alex commanded Maisie to sit. She did, but looked at Cole with something like love on her face as she thumped her tail up and down in the muddy water. Alex was appalled. She imagined the freezing water was soaking into his clothing and bent down to the muddy man covered in muddy dog slobber.

"I'm so sorry, are you all right?" Alex offered a hand to help Cole off the ground. He tried to get up but Alex slid, sending both of them back to the muddy ground. Cole absorbed the additional weight, and Alex felt his arms go around her waist. For just a moment she felt the hardness of his muscles and they were still, looking into each other's eyes, the dog and the storm forgotten. Alex leaned down and gently touched her lips to his. Maisie saw it as a game and jumped back in, licking both their faces.

"Maisie, stop." Alex could feel the man beneath her shaking. Oh no, he was hurt. She pushed the dog away and looked down at Cole. He was laughing. Alex couldn't help it, she started to laugh too. The kiss was forgotten. Maisie joined the pile on the ground and tried to squeeze between their two bodies.

"Argghh. Maisie, no." Alex nudged the dog back again and pushed herself off Cole. "Maisie, here." The dog remembered her job and stood for Alex while she got back to her feet.

Cole, still laughing, followed on his own this time and stood up. All three were wet and muddy and Maisie, with her tongue hanging out, was still sitting, thumping her tail and acting very pleased with herself. Alex could feel the cold seeping through her wet pajama pants and t-shirt. She folded her arms across her chest in an effort to get warm. She could not believe what had just happened.

"I'm so sorry, are you okay?"

Cole nodded, rubbing his hands on his jeans. "I've been a lot worse, but I feel a little silly at being knocked over by a dog. I just wasn't expecting that. She weighs more than I anticipated, and packs a pretty good punch, doesn't she?"

"I don't know what got into her, she never does that. Never." Alex turned and limped back onto the relative dryness of the porch. Her leg ached from the encounter on the ground and she was soaked, muddy and freezing. And yet, there had been a moment there when she hadn't wanted to be anywhere else except with this man. There was a spark of attraction there she hadn't felt for a long time. Alex shook her head. No, she couldn't think about that.

Both the dog and the man followed her. Maisie gave a big shake, spewing muddy water everywhere. Cole followed, shaking the water out of his hair.

"Are you sure you're all right? I swear, I've never seen her do that, not even to someone she already knows. She's usually very well-behaved."

"I'm fine." Cole reached down to pat Maisie's head. "And it's okay. I like dogs. They aren't usually that affectionate, but..." He shrugged. "What can I say? She likes me. And the question is, are you all right? I noticed you limping."

"I'll be fine once I get warm." Alex turned toward the door and opened it. The electricity had come back on while they were outside and a lamp near the sofa bathed the main room in warm light. "Maybe we should get inside. I can get us some towels." She turned back to Cole and the dog and found Cole right behind her. Maisie squeezed past them and into the cabin. "Not on the furniture, Maisie."

Cole stood by the door and held Maisie's collar until Alex came back with a stack of towels. She had one draped across her shoulders and handed one to Cole before wiping down the dog. Maisie had enough fur not to feel the cold, but Alex didn't want her to get mud all over the cabin. It took special permission to allow Maisie to stay here, and now the owner was in the cabin with them. On the first night. She sincerely hoped he wouldn't make them leave.

Alex shivered again and looked down at herself. Mud was everywhere, and she was going to need a shower before she could go to bed.

Cole looked up from the dog, followed her gaze, then quickly looked away so he wouldn't get caught staring. He shifted his stance and let Maisie go.

The dog trotted over to her owner and sat down at her feet. Alex was visibly shivering.

"You're probably going to need a shower." Cole handed her a very wet and muddy towel. "Do you have enough towels?"

Alex nodded. "I think so, but I may need a new supply in the morning."

"Why don't you hop in the shower and I'll go back to the office and grab a couple more for you?" Cole turned to leave. "I can put them inside your door if you leave it unlocked for a few minutes."

"That's not necessary." She didn't want to bother him with towels, especially since he was going to have to take a shower himself. "I can pick them up in the morning."

There was an awkward silence. "Well, I'll be on my way then. Maybe I'll see you tomorrow." He backed out the door and stopped. Alex was holding Maisie by her collar this time, allowing Cole to get out of the cabin without getting jumped on again.

As the door shut behind him, Cole could hear Alex scolding the dog about her manners. He smiled. He liked them. Both of them. They had made a pretty picture, woman and dog softly lit by the light from the lamp. She was muddy and disheveled, but that didn't stop Cole from admiring the view. Her pajamas had been stuck to her body in all the right places. He whistled to himself as he loped back through the rain to his own cabin just down the lane and attached to the office. She was here.

"That was interesting," he said out loud as he let himself in. "Alex Bennington. I like it." He thought she had reserved the cabin for three weeks. Yep, it was going to be interesting, and if Cole had his way, he was going to get to know Alex Bennington better. There was a moment there when they were lying in the mud that it just seemed right.

"That was interesting."

Alex let the hot water of the shower warm her. She thought back to the unexpected encounter with Cole Gilchrist. She hung her head and admitted there had been a spark of attraction. With a man she had just met. In those few minutes of chaos and when she was lying on top of him, her body reacted in a way it hadn't reacted to male attention since James had held her. And then Alex remembered, and groaned. She had kissed him and she didn't even know him. Alex's eyes widened as guilt rushed through her. He wasn't James.

James. The love of her life. They had been together since high school. They went to the same college and had the same friends and their lives had been perfect. They planned to get married once they were established in their careers and were on schedule for that. They set the date for their wedding, Alex had purchased her dress, they had the church reserved and had decided on a cake.

Then one Saturday afternoon, when they were driving across Kansas City to meet with the caterer, a drunk driver drove across the median of the four-lane highway and crashed head on into them. That was just over a year ago. James was killed instantly, and Alex was left with a broken leg, three broken ribs, a punctured lung, and bruising that took months to heal. She had spent weeks in the hospital, part of it sedated and on a ventilator until her ribs had healed enough to allow her to breathe. No one was able to tell her that her life-long friend and lover was gone.

James had been buried and grieved for by his family during Alex's time in the hospital, leaving Alex with an empty place in her heart and her life. When her parents finally told her, Alex couldn't even react. She already knew, in her heart, he was no longer there. The date for her wedding day had come and gone while Alex was trying to get well. Their first anniversary should be next week, but the wedding had never happened.

And here she was, in a strange place thinking thoughts about a man she had just met and knew nothing about.

"I'm sorry, James." She raised her face to the water. "I miss you so much. How do I get through this?" There was no answer, except for a rumble of distant thunder as the storm moved off to the east.

CHAPTER TWO

"It's her."

"You're sure?" Cole's housekeeper Mary Louise asked for the third time as she sipped from her coffee mug. Mary Louise was Cole's rock, and he was closer to her than his own mother. She was shorter than him by a foot and loved brightly colored skirts and blouses. They reminded her of growing up in New Mexico, Mary Louise always said. Her black hair streaked with gray was long but pulled back into a low bun most of the time. Eyes that were nearly black reflected her Hispanic origins but were slightly hidden by the gold-rimmed glasses she always wore. Mary Louise was almost always smiling, and this morning was no exception.

The two were sharing an early morning cup of coffee. Mary Louise's husband, Buck, took care of the stables at the Bar CG, and had taken his mug to the horse barn. He liked to get an early start and make sure the horses were ready for the morning rides before riders started showing up.

Cole nodded. "I'm sure. It took me by surprise, but after our encounter last night, I'm sure. And she kissed me. She's the one."

"She kissed you? Right when she met you?" Mary Louise asked with surprise.

Mary Louise didn't argue with him. They had similar conversations many times over the past few years, but he had always been adamant that this woman or that woman wasn't the one for him. Cole wouldn't accept blind dates, he hadn't looked at one woman who had stayed at the Bar CG since he bought it, and as far as she knew, he hadn't dated much in high school or college.

When she asked him about it, Cole said he already knew who he would marry even if he didn't know her yet. When he met her, he told Mary Louise, he would know. And now she was here. Alex had literally fallen into his arms and if he had a say in it, she would stay in his life. Now all he had to do was convince her.

"You're going to have to get to know her first," Mary Louise cautioned. "And you can't be weird about it, you know, you can't spook her."

"The same goes for you."

Mary Louise nodded in agreement as she rose to get the household chores started. She glanced back to see Cole staring into his offee and smiled. Yes, his heart was taken. Now, she hoped the young woman wouldn't break it.

Someone was breathing on her.

Alex sat straight up in bed. It took everything she had to hold back a scream as she pushed her hair back from her face and spotted Maisie at the edge of the bed, sitting and waiting patiently for Alex to notice her. She fell back against her pillow and closed her eyes, willing her breathing to slow.

"That was crazy," she muttered to herself. "There are no ax murderers in this cabin and these mountains. If you don't pull yourself together, you're never even going to get to see said mountains. You're going to have a heart attack and have to go to the hospital."

She turned her head and opened one eye to look at Maisie. The dog took the opportunity to put her big paws on the bed. Alex put a hand out to pet her.

"I guess it's time to get up. Is it even morning?" Maisie licked her hand. "It looks light out, so I guess it is." Alex rolled over to get up and Maisie stood still to allow her to use her as support.

"Thanks, sweetie. Let me get a jacket and some slippers and I'll let you out." Maisie raced out of the bedroom to the patio doors. Alex followed a bit slower and opened the doors to the deck. Maisie pushed by and went out ahead of her. Her leg was no worse for the incident last night. No, don't think about that, Alex lectured herself. It didn't mean anything.

"It is absolutely beautiful here." Alex breathed deep. The air was clear and clean after last night's rain. The sun was just peeking over the tops of the pine trees and the lake was smooth. It was a little chilly, but Alex predicted that by afternoon it would be warm enough to be without a jacket. The cabins were at an altitude where the air stayed cool, but the sun was warm. "We should definitely go explore. Come on Maisie, let's get some breakfast and then we can go for a walk."

Maisie padded back up the steps to the deck and into the cabin behind Alex, who shut the door and went to the coffeemaker. She could use some coffee and maybe she would make some scrambled eggs. She had stocked up on groceries before she left Laramie. She would have to make another trip or two back down the mountain, but that was for another day. Today, she just wanted to enjoy the moment.

After brushing her teeth, Alex looked at herself in the mirror. The late night shower had her hair sticking out at odd angles this morning. It was a mess. She rewetted it, dried it and brushed it back into the long, bobbed style she wore. Just below chin length, parted on the left side and cut so it curved around her face in layers, the style suited her, Alex thought, and was easy enough to care for. After the accident, she couldn't handle her long hair so she found a style that worked for her.

Alex dressed in her favorite hiking pants, made of black knit material, and added a teal tank top and a lightweight teal button-up shirt. She put some sunscreen on her face and added a light coat of mascara to bring out her brown eyes. She was never going to be a movie star, Alex thought, but then again, she didn't really want to be, so it worked out. Enough pampering, she decided, and didn't look back as she walked out of the bathroom.

She made scrambled eggs and toast for breakfast and added a bowl of fresh fruit. Maisie sat patiently while she cleaned up the kitchen. Alex helped Maisie put on her service vest and they got on their way.

Alex had studied maps of the area and knew where the trails were, but for today, they were just going to walk around the lake behind the cabin. This trail wasn't on the list of trails in the area, but it looked easy enough, so she took only one hiking pole. She wore her hiking boots and had picked out a neon green jacket...one she designed...and a wide-brimmed hat made to stay on her head and protect her face and neck from the sun.

"Let's go, Maisie." They started down the path, Maisie on her leash just to the left of Alex, ready to help if she needed it. Maisie was trained to be allowed off leash, but on a trail in the mountains, Alex knew she was safer on the leash. Wild animals were unpredictable and if Maisie went to investigate, she could be injured. Or worse, in Alex's opinion, lost. She didn't know what she would do without Maisie. It was unimaginable, so Alex kept her safe.

It wasn't long before Alex was out of breath and her legs started to hurt, not from her injury, but from exertion. This area looked pretty level overall, but there were places where she had to hike up inclines and down again. She sat down on a rock and decided the high altitude was getting to her as well. Maisie sat next to her, also panting a bit. Alex knew they would get used to the altitude, but was glad they were just taking a short, easy hike. Okay, maybe not easy, but not hard either.

"Look at that." Alex pointed out a bird on a branch of a nearby pine tree. She wasn't a bird watcher, but the bird's blue and black feathers caught her attention. She stopped and pulled out her phone, snapped a couple of pictures. It looked like a blue jay, but larger and much more elegant. She would have to look it up later. Maybe she should buy a bird book. Alex could do that the next time she went to town. A little farther on, they stopped to watch a deer wander across a meadow and listened to the bubbling of a nearby stream.

Alex slowed to cross the little stream and they maneuvered around a few rocks along the trail and continued along the edge of the lake. As the sun got higher and the breeze picked up, Alex realized the lake was larger than it looked or the maps showed. Her pace slowed and Maisie looked at her with head cocked.

She looked around. Except for the wind in the trees and the occasional chatter of a bird, it was quiet. There was no sign of human life here, it was just her and the dog. It was absolutely beautiful, but daunting. Alex wondered if she should turn around.

"What do you think?" she asked Maisie. "Plow forward or turn around and go back? I should have packed a backpack with water and snacks, and you know, I should have been smart enough to think of that before we left. I work in the outdoor gear world, for heaven's sake, and I'm always telling others to be prepared. I even designed a great backpack which at this moment is sitting next to my bed." Alex shook her head as she looked around. "And yet, here we are."

Alex checked her phone. She didn't have a signal, but her clock showed it was nearly lunchtime. They had been gone about an hour and that meant it would take another hour to get back to the cabin. She had no idea how long it would take to complete the trail. She sighed and admitted defeat.

"Okay then, we turn back, and we try again another day." They turned around and retraced their steps, trying to move a little faster than they had been going. The mountain air was clean and fresh, but with the increased pace and the altitude, Alex's breathing became labored, and she had to stop to catch her breath several times.

"This was a bad idea," Alex muttered to herself as she sat down on a rock. "I'm hot, hungry, thirsty and my leg hurts. I was not prepared for this." She checked the time. She should be almost there, but the trees revealed nothing.

She sighed in relief as the cabins came into view a few minutes later. Alex limped up the steps to the deck. "First things first, we need water. Come on, Maisie."

Maisie panted as she entered the cabin. She noisily gulped down the water Alex got for her. Alex did the same and found two granola bars and a treat for Maisie. "Let's go sit on the deck."

They sat on the steps and ate their snacks. Alex looked out at the lake. They would try again tomorrow, but they would be better prepared. It couldn't be more than three miles around, Alex thought, and she had hiked before, hikes much longer than three miles. Alex and James had loved hiking in the Ozarks in Missouri and had hiked several times near Denver. Once, she and James had hiked rim to rim and back in the Grand Canyon. It had never been this difficult.

Thoughts of James led to thoughts of the encounter from last night. Alex groaned at the memory. She had kissed a complete stranger. What was she thinking? Hopefully, he had forgotten about it. Alex sighed as she acknowledged the attraction, but she wasn't ready for anything else. She probably wouldn't even see Cole again on this trip. She was sure he was too busy to bother with a renter.

Alex untied her hiking boots and pulled them off. She placed them both beside her on the step and wiggled her toes in her wool socks. It had been a while since she wore the boots, but her feet felt pretty good. She rubbed her leg. It actually didn't feel too bad either. Alex considered that a win as long as it didn't stiffen up later. She patted Maisie's head. The dog reached up from where she was resting and licked her hand. They sat in silence and watched the lake and the clouds moving across the bright blue sky. Alex and Maisie were still sitting there when a couple came out of the cabin next door.

"Hello," the woman called to Alex. "We saw you come back from a hike. How was it?"

Alex and Maisie lifted their heads and Alex waved back. The man was about six feet tall and thin with brown curly hair that was pulled back in a little man bun. It looked like his hair would explode if the band holding it broke. He had a scruffy beard and a ready smile. He waved back at Alex.

The woman was shorter by a few inches and had long brown hair that hung over her shoulder in a loose braid. They were both dressed in baggy shorts and t-shirts and were wearing tennis shoes. His were the old-style Converse canvas high-top tennis shoes. They both looked like they were in high school.

"It was good." Alex stood and walked over to the deck's rail, leaned on it. The cabins here were set up so two were close together and the next two were separated by places to park. Her cabin was on one end of the row of cabins and closest to the office so she wouldn't have a neighbor on the other side of her. "It's absolutely beautiful here. Have you been out hiking too?"

The couple looked at each other. Alex felt a flicker of unease. It was gone in a second, so quickly she must have imagined it.

"We've just been out exploring a little," the man said. He leaned on the deck railing. "I'm Anthony Morgan and this is my wife, Merri."

So, old enough to be married but still young, Alex thought, very young. "It's nice to meet you both. I'm Alex Bennington and this is Maisie. We're up here for a few weeks, just exploring and enjoying the area."

Anthony nodded. "Us too. We've never been in Wyoming before."

"Really? Where are you from? I live in Kansas City."

"We're from Texas," Merri replied. "We really wanted to see the mountains. It's beautiful out here, isn't it?"

There were many mountains closer to Texas than in Wyoming, Alex thought, but she couldn't fault the young couple for their choice of destinations. She also had chosen Wyoming when she might have gone to visit her parents, or the beach somewhere, for that matter.

Alex nodded. "Enjoy yourselves. I think we're going to get some lunch. I'm sure we'll see each other again."

"For sure," Anthony said as Alex took a step away from the railing. "They do this thing here where once a week we all get together for dinner at the Commons, that big building attached to the office. Potluck and all that, but the owner grills burgers. Most of us met the night before you got here."

"That sounds like fun. I haven't been over to the Commons yet, but I understand from the brochure it's a great place to get together for games and such. I'll have to check it out. I'll see you later, have a good day."

The couple nodded as one. "Have a good lunch," Anthony called as Alex and Maisie headed indoors.

"They seem nice," Alex told Maisie as she pulled containers of diced chicken and lettuce out of the refrigerator. The granola bars had taken the edge off, but she was still hungry. "I might be cynical ,but I wonder what they're really doing here. It seems odd."

Maisie, lying on the floor with her paws in front of her, looked up but offered no answers.

Alex laughed. "Maybe they eloped and haven't told their parents. And that's their business." She cocked her head to one side. "And since when did I become the busybody lady next door?"

Alex put the couple out of her mind and ate her lunch, then found her book and took it out to the deck. She and Maisie got comfortable and she opened the murder mystery she had been reading last evening. She lost track of time as she read and only raised her head when she heard the rumble of thunder.

Maisie looked up at Alex as a raindrop splashed on the deck. "I guess it's time to go in." The sky was dark, making the inside of the cabin dark as well. She turned on the kitchen light and the lamp by the sofa in the living area.

Just as she was getting ready to curl up on the sofa, another rumble of thunder sounded, immediately followed by a knocking at the door. Alex had an eerie feeling of déjà vu. This scene played out last night and that didn't end well for anyone but Maisie.

Maisie woofed softly as Alex padded to the door, her stockinged feet making no sound on the wooden floor.

"You behave, do you hear?"

Maisie sat back down by the sofa but kept her eyes on the door.

When Alex opened it, Cole was standing on her porch with a pile of neatly folded towels, sunlight shining from behind him. The little cloudburst was moving on. And here she thought she wouldn't see him again. A smile touched her lips.

"I brought you some fresh towels since we got all of yours dirty."

He was wearing canvas khaki jeans with a t-shirt and flannel shirt over the top of it, and sturdy hiking boots, a similar, but cleaner look to last night's outfit. Alex decided this was his normal attire, not that she minded, it suited him. She also suspected the t-shirt would show some pretty serious muscles if he wasn't wearing the flannel shirt.

She forced her attention back to the moment and moved aside to let him in. The encounter in the rain last night had not done him justice. Tall, lean, and muscular, he looked really good in those jeans. His nearly black hair was cut short on the sides, with those short curls she noticed last night falling over his forehead. A very short, scruffy beard covered the bottom half of his face. As he turned to her, Alex focused on his eyes. As good as all the rest made him look, his eyes held her attention. They were a bright blue, framed by dark eyelashes that made her just a little bit jealous. Alex realized she had missed a lot last night in the dark. A little flutter in her stomach made her stop as she reached for the towels.

The change in motion nearly resulted in the towels on the floor since Cole was in the process of handing them to her. They both grabbed for the stack and managed to save the towels, but they were now a big wad of fabric between them.

"I swear, I'm not clumsy," Cole said, still holding his half of the towels. He gave his towels to her and took a step back.

Alex corralled the towels and carried them to the small dining table. "I believe you." She laughed. "I'm not either. Let me get the dirty towels for you." She made it to the bathroom without falling on her face and came back with the towels, tidy in a clear tote.

"Thanks. I'll bring your tote back." His voice sounded strained to Alex.

"I really could have washed them myself," Alex said. "These cabins are great, they have everything a person could need, you know, including a washer and dryer."

"True, but I feel partially responsible, so... anyway, how was your morning?" His voice was friendly again. "Did you manage to get out and see some sights?"

Alex nodded. "A little. Maisie and I hiked around the lake. Well, part of the lake. I misjudged how far it was, so we turned around and came back after about an hour. I didn't think it would take much more than an hour. The lake doesn't look that big from here."

"It takes a little more than two hours to go around, so you were almost at the halfway mark.”

"That's good to know. The map I have doesn't give the distance.”

"Most don't. Maps, unless they're really good and detailed, don't account for the coves and the places you have to hike around, like marshy areas and areas that are rocky.”

"I suppose that's true. I was thinking about going the other way for an afternoon walk. That is, until the rain showed up.”

"That was just a little afternoon shower.” Cole smiled. "They tend to build, come across the mountains and then show off on the eastern side. It's done for today. Would you like some company? Once I take the towels over to the laundry room, I have a little bit of free time this afternoon.”

This time it was Alex who smiled as she turned to the big dog. "We would love that, wouldn't we, Maisie?”

Maisie had been sitting obediently throughout the conversation, but she was trembling with anticipation.

"We would,” Alex said, turning back to Cole. "Prepare yourself. Maisie's been waiting all this time for you to acknowledge her.”

Cole set the tote down, went over to the big dog and knelt down. "Come on then, hello.” Maisie didn't knock him down this time, but she tried. Cole laughed as she tried to lick his face. "No wrestling and no licking today. We've got other things to do.”

He rubbed her ears and the dog melted to the floor. He rubbed her belly and Maisie hung her tongue out in obvious bliss. Alex knew how she felt. Cole had only smiled at her. She wasn't sure what would happen if he caressed her neck and ears.

He stood up and picked up the tote. "Let me take this back to the laundry room and I'll meet you back here, in about ten minutes. Will that work?”

Alex nodded. She let him out and when Cole was gone, Alex put on her hiking boots and found her backpack. She wasn't going unprepared this time, even if it was for a short hike. Snacks, a little first aid kit, two water bottles and a collapsible water dish for Maisie so she didn't have to drink out of the lake. The last thing she needed was a dog sick from drinking the water.

Cole was true to his word and ten minutes later, they set out on the path from Alex's cabin, Alex with her hiking pole, Maisie on her leash and Cole walking easily at their pace. If he was honest with himself, Cole thought, he should be thanking Maisie for introducing them. He almost panicked earlier when he noticed the huge diamond ring on her left ring finger. Alex was engaged. He had immediately realized the love of his life was already in a relationship with another man, a serious relationship.

So, she had a fiancé. Where was he? Why would Alex have come all the way out here by herself,? He thought, then mentally kicked himself. The guy was probably coming later. Cole sighed. He would be friendly, he decided, as friendly as he was to other ranch guests.

As they walked, that's all Cole could think about. They discussed the mountains and the flowers they saw along the path, and he kept his tone light. Alex didn't know all their names, but she wasn't afraid to ask. She took pictures of bright red, Indian paintbrush, and the dainty little marsh marigolds that made a bouquet of yellow next to the path. There was little evidence of the limp he had seen last night.

As they walked, Alex pointed out one of the black and blue birds she had seen earlier.

"It's a Stellar's Jay," Cole said, "and look, there's a ground squirrel."

Alex handed Maisie's leash to Cole. "I'm going to try to take a picture."

Cole watched as Alex took pictures with her cell phone. He liked that she wasn't wearing any makeup. Her skin was like porcelain, he thought, her face pale with patches of pink on her cheeks. Her heart-shaped lips smiled easily and almost begged to be kissed. After reflecting on exactly what that would be like for a moment, he realized he shouldn't be thinking about it at all or it was going to happen. And she was definitely wearing another man's ring. Cole shifted his feet and turned his attention back to the ground squirrel. The little rodent darting back and forth didn't seem to bother Maisie. Alex laughed and Cole's heart pitched a bit. He didn't know why or how but had already fallen hard for her.

He was wondering how to approach the subject of the fiancé when three hikers appeared around a bend. Alex and Cole stopped to let them by, and Cole recognized them as guests staying at the ranch.

"Oh, hello, Cole." The woman smiled at the two of them. "We've been having a little hike. This is a great place to hike before we head out to the harder trails."

Cole agreed and made introductions. "Alex, this is Jackie and Steve Cooper and Jackie's brother, John Campbell. They're also staying at the ranch. And this is Alex Bennington and her dog Maisie, also guests here at the ranch."

They all shook hands, including Maisie, who lifted her paw as the three hikers acknowledged her.

The Coopers were tall and in their late fifties, Alex guessed. Steve looked scholarly with white hair cut short and wearing black-rimmed glasses. He wore a hooded sweatshirt with cargo shorts and brown high-top hiking boots. Jackie was wearing dark blue Bermuda shorts and a white t-shirt with a pink light jacket tied around her waist. She had wavy, auburn hair that fell to just below her shoulders, and she looked very glamorous.

John, like Steve, was wearing khaki cargo shorts and a dark blue polo shirt. He was slightly shorter than Jackie and was likely the oldest of the three, Alex thought. His dark hair had receded to nearly bald on top and he wore a neatly trimmed beard, streaked through with the same gray as his hair. Except for the hiking boots, they all could have been on their way to the country club.

"Are you enjoying your stay?" Jackie asked Alex, smiling again.

"So far. We just arrived yesterday and so far it's been...interesting." She looked at Cole as she spoke and the smile they shared was not lost on the older adults.

John cleared his throat and adjusted the strap of his hiking pole. "Shall we move on?"

Jackie and Steve nodded and with assurances they would see the younger couple later, moved down the path.

"They seem nice and they appear familiar with the area. Have they stayed here before?" Alex asked as they began to walk again. She got the impression they had. They were comfortable with the path around the lake and with Cole.

Cole nodded. "The Coopers are professors down in Boulder, Colorado, and John is an engineer from Indiana. They've been meeting here every summer the last few years."

"It must be interesting, meeting different people all the time and getting to know them." Alex slowed to step over a rock and Cole stopped to assist if she needed help.

"It is. All nine of the cabins are rented right now and most through next summer. Most people stay at least a week here, so I usually interact with them at some point. Right now, there's a couple of families with young children, two older guys on a fishing trip and two couples from Idaho sharing a cabin. Then there's John Campbell and the Cooper's, who each have their own cabin and a young couple from Austin, Texas."

"I met them earlier. They are staying in the cabin next to me and..." she trailed off.

Cole glanced at her. "And what?"

Alex shrugged. "I'm not sure. When I met them, I got the feeling that something wasn't quite right." She laughed. "Maybe I need to lay off the murder mysteries. My imagination has been going wild ever since I got here."

"Interesting. I thought that too, but I can't put my finger on anything specific. They haven't really done anything out of the ordinary," Cole said. "They're quiet but friendly, they leave each morning and come back before it gets dark and my housekeeper, Mary Louise, says they're very neat. I have no idea where they go every day, but I assume they're hiking like everyone else."

Alex cocked her head. "They're already back today, I suppose because it rained. I understand wanting to be private, and they're adults. At least I think they are, so they can do what they want. I thought maybe they eloped, but don't you think if they were on a honeymoon, they would want to spend all their time in their cabin?"

Cole grinned. "I certainly would." That was another path his mind couldn't take, he thought. Fortunately, they came upon a small waterfall that followed a little stream to the lake. Alex took more photos and Cole sat down on a rock to watch. Maisie sat down beside him. She made such a pretty picture herself that he got out his own phone and took a couple of pictures of her enjoying the view.

"I suppose we should start back." Alex walked back over to him. She took off her backpack and got Maisie's water dish out to give her a drink of water. She pulled out her water bottle and filled the dish, then took a drink of her own.

Cole grabbed his own bottle of water. "That's an interesting backpack. They usually aren't that colorful."

Alex lovingly ran her fingers over the pack. "Not usually, but I designed this one myself. I didn't, and still don't, understand why packs have to be boring." She shrugged. "So, I made one that wasn't."

"You designed your own backpack?" Cole asked incredulously.

"I did." Alex nodded and smiled. "And I designed my jacket too."

She stood still while Cole walked around her and inspected the jacket. It was made of neon green nylon with an equally bright yellow fabric lining. It had a hood, and pockets inside and out. There was a little whistle on the pull of her zipper.

"I like it. But...turn around."

Alex complied. "What's this? It looks like some kind of pocket." He ran his fingers along a reflective strip just below her shoulders.

"It is a pocket. There's a tent inside."

CHAPTER THREE

A tent. In her jacket. Wait. What? A tent? Alex was carrying a tent in her jacket? Who did that? Cole was taken aback.

"A tent?" he asked incredulously.

Alex turned and laughed at the look on his face.

"Well, technically, it's a tarp with ends."

"Doesn't a tarp with ends make it a tent?"

"I say it does, but you can unfold it to make a lean-to of sorts. Or it can go on the ground and form a triangular tent around you. Then you can close or open either end. It's a survival tent." She opened a pocket on the side that he hadn't seen during his inspection and pulled out tiny stakes and some nylon cord. A plastic card gave printed instructions on how to set up a shelter. She handed it to Cole.

"Using one, or two hiking poles, you can set it up like you would a tent and it'll protect you from the weather. It's also a neon color so rescuers can easily spot you, even from the air. Especially from the air."

Cole turned the card over a couple of times in his hands. He examined the jacket's back again and then went back to the card. He was quiet for so long, Alex started to get nervous. She had only known him a day but realized his opinion meant something. Although she had designed the jacket, it wasn't yet out on the global market. Alex had several prototypes with her from a test run, but the first orders were in the process of being sewn.

"This is....well, amazing. More than amazing. You're a genius." Cole handed the card back to Alex. "A shelter you can easily carry with you. In colors that can be seen from a distance. With stakes and everything. I worked for several years for the forest service before I bought the ranch and I still work for them part-time. I go out on forest fire calls and rescue calls and it's so difficult to find someone out here, especially if they think they're invincible and take few precautions."

Alex hoped her face wasn't red, because that's exactly what she had done this morning. Sure, she stayed on the path and turned back when she realized it was farther than she thought. But Cole was apologizing.

"Sorry, I get on a soap box every now and then, but I can see that this could really save lives."

"That's my hope as well. It's waterproofed just like a tent." She looked up at him. "I was looking for a lightweight alternative for a tent and I thought this would do it. It's also perfect for ultra-light hikers doing overnight hikes."

"Why hasn't anyone thought of this before?"

Alex smiled and put the card, stakes, and cords back in their pocket. She hefted her backpack onto her back and started back up the trail. Cole and Maisie fell into step beside her.

"I did think of it, years ago. I just had to come up with a design and convince my bosses it was a good idea."

"Your bosses?"

"I work for Outdoor Gear in Kansas City. Well, I did work for them."

"Worked there? As in not anymore?"

"Exactly. I'm officially unemployed and technically homeless." Alex shrugged. "I'm trying to figure out what to do with the rest of my life."

"So, you're thinking of relocating?" Cole felt his heart lift. Maybe she would stay here. Alex was going to live nearby. He wanted to hug her but kept walking. "What do you mean, homeless?"

"It's a long story, let's finish our walk and I'll tell you over a soda."

A little while later, sitting in patio chairs with sodas, and cookies Alex had brought from a bakery in Kansas City, she told her story, about James, and their plans, and then gave him the short version of the accident story.

"When I got out of the hospital, I went into a rehab center and since I shared my apartment with James, his family decided to give it up." She thinned her lips. "I paid half the rent, but the apartment was in his name so I wasn't given a choice. I only got out of the rehab center before I came here, and maybe this wasn't the best idea, but here we are."

Interesting, Cole thought, very interesting. "So, the ring on your finger?"

Alex looked down at her hand and smiled sadly. "I haven't been able to take it off. I know I should, but it's of the few things I have left from him. Except memories."

Cole was torn between wanting to jump up and dance on the railing ſand wanting to pull her into his arms. He could hear the grief in her voice, and he knew it was real. But she wasn't engaged to an unseen man. He would consider that later.

"So, you could relocate to Wyoming?"

"I suppose so, yes. That's one of the reasons I came here. I don't want to live in a big city anymore, but I could live in a place like Laramie. I drove around a bit on my way here and I like it. If that's what I decide to do, I just have to find a job and a place to live. My concern is that Laramie isn't big enough to have a company that needs a textile designer. I researched it and didn't find anything, so most of my inquiries have been in larger cities, like Denver or Salt Lake City."

Cole was silent for a moment. "Would it have to be gear designing?" he finally asked.

Alex smiled. "Technically, no, but I love textiles and I would like to stay in the field. I guess I could design boxes or something like fly fishing reels. Or maybe not, since I don't know much about either one."

"Sure, that makes sense, although there is a company here that designs fly reels. It's a pretty big deal here. I lived in Laramie before I bought the ranch. I went to college there and yeah, it's a nice place to live. I prefer it up here now, but it's not so far away I can't go in for an evening or an afternoon."

"So far, I like it up here too, but I don't think I could afford to rent one of your cabins year-round." Alex smiled. "Can you even get out of here in the winter?"

Cole grinned. "Most of the time, once the main road is plowed. We use snowmobiles and if it's not a super heavy snow, I can plow us out to the main road. There's a ski resort nearby and plenty of snow-mobiling trails up here, so we're busy year round. You can't always make it over the pass to the west, but we manage." He shrugged and stood up. "I guess I had better go check on Mary Louise and see if she needs help. Thanks for the soda."

"Thanks for the hike," Alex replied, "I'm sure I'll see you around. I want to hear all about this forest service work."

"Are you planning more hikes?" Cole turned serious. "You shouldn't really hike by yourself. It's not a safe thing to do."

"We're going out tomorrow for a longer hike, but I'll be fine. I have Maisie," Alex replied, bristling a little. She really could take care of herself despite her lack of preparation this morning. She was never telling anyone about that, she decided.

Cole heard the bite in Alex's voice and realized his mistake, so he backtracked. "You're right, Maisie is a great hiking companion. I've seen that for myself, but would you mind if I tagged along, anyway? It's been a while since I've done any real hiking and I can show you some of the best scenery in the area."

He went by his own rules and seldom went out on his own except for the well-used trails. Having said that, he had been all over these mountains, especially in the last few months, sometimes with Buck, but by himself too. He carried a two-way radio when he was out, so generally he and Buck could stay in contact. He also had a GPS unit on his watch, so he was able to track his route, even to the point of being able to backtrack if needed.

Alex let go of the bristling feeling. Actually, she liked his company, she admitted to herself, and it would be nice to have someone along who knew the area. And liked was probably an understatement, but it was too soon for that. Anyway, Cole was just being friendly and she was determined to hold James's love close. It just wasn't the right time, she told herself.

Alex smiled and cocked her head. "Could you teach me to fly fish?"

Cole grinned. "I could, and I would. We actually offer that as a service at the Bar CG. Tomorrow?"

"I saw that in the brochure." Alex smiled. "Maybe not tomorrow, I want to check out the trails near Medicine Bow Peak tomorrow, climb it myself. I was thinking of driving over there tomorrow. Do you want to come along?"

Cole's heart sunk for just a moment. He would rather take her fishing. Cole loved fishing and would love to teach Alex, but he supposed there were plenty of trails for her to explore and he would be happy to show her his little part of the world. She made a pretty picture standing there on the porch with the dog at her side. Yep. More than happy.

"Tomorrow then?" He wasn't sure about taking on the largest mountain in the area on her second day here, but if she was going, he would go along.

"That would be great," Alex said. "I'll stop by the office in the morning when we're ready to go, say about nine?"

"Maybe a little earlier for this trip, eight might be better," Cole answered. "Make sure to bring plenty of water, and maybe a lunch. This is a pretty ambitious hike, especially on your second day."

He saw the surprised look on her face. "My trail guide didn't show it as being that long of a hike, maybe three hours or so. Don't you think we'll be back by lunch?"

Cole shook his head. "I've found that trail guides generally give you the best-case scenario. They don't take into account stops for pictures and rest. This hike is a lot of going up, so you walk a little slower too. But the weather's supposed to be nice tomorrow, so it'll be fine." He waved as he walked away. Alex stood and watched him for a moment before retreating into the cabin.

"Whew, he is one good looking man," Alex told Maisie as they walked into the kitchen. "I really should stay clear of him. I'm not ready for a relationship. I'm not. I don't want to start something I'm not willing to finish." Maisie sat on the floor and thumped her tail. "I know, I know, you like him...a lot. But you don't get to fall in love with him either."

Alex stopped in the middle of opening the refrigerator door. Who said anything about love? She just met him last night. She knew nothing about the man...or very little. There should be no thinking about love or relationships. None. She came to Wyoming to finish healing and sort out her life, not to start a relationship with the owner of a guest ranch or anyone else for that matter.

"Right?" she asked Maisie. "Right. Now, let's get some supper. We can go out and eat it on the deck."

"I shouldn't have agreed to let him come along, he's a huge temptation," Alex said the next morning as she packed her backpack. She looked at Maisie and sighed. The big dog was sitting at the front door ready to go as soon as she gave the word. How could she disappoint her favorite companion? "Fine, we'll go, but it's just a hike, remember that. No slobbering over the man, and that goes for you too."

They walked over to the office and met an older woman at the door.

"Well, hello you two. I bet you're Alex and Maisie of Cabin One. We didn't meet when you checked in, but I'm Mary Louise. I take care of the housekeeping here. My family comes from Mexico, but I grew up in New Mexico. I came here about thirty years ago and I met my husband here, so I've never left. Buck and I...you haven't met him yet, have you? He runs the horseback rides here at the Bar CG. Well, most of the time anyway, because Cole likes to get out on horseback when he can, he rides like he was born to it, and he really was. Anyway, I'm sure you'll meet him soon enough, Buck I mean, you've already met Cole, haven't you? We have a little ranch down on the Little Laramie River about ten miles from here. We've raised five children here and probably should move into town....that's Laramie, I mean.....but we love it so much out here." Her endearing accent gave her heritage away without the explanation.

The rest of it Alex wasn't so sure about, but she immediately fell in love with the older woman. She was short and stocky and had what Alex decided was miles of pure black hair streaked with silver all pulled up into a bun on the back of her head.

Alex held out her hand to the older woman. Mary Louise ignored it and enveloped her in a hug. "It's so good to have you here. We've been waiting for you. How do you like it so far? I mean, it's pretty wonderful, that's why I keep working here, and Cole is like a son to me."

"It's good to be here," Alex responded as Mary Louise let go and stepped back. "Wait, what? You've been waiting for me?"

"Did I say that?" Mary Louise asked. "Well, I guess I might have said something like that, but oh, you know, I meant, well, we've been waiting for you ever since you made the reservation." She laughed nervously and glanced away. "Well, I've got to run now and straighten up the Commons, but you have fun hiking. It was nice meeting you. I'll see you later." She bustled away before Alex had a chance to say another word.

Alex stood there for a moment and considered the conversation. She only made the reservation a month or so ago on a whim and was surprised there was a cabin available for three weeks, but she never questioned it. Now, she was puzzled. Yesterday, Cole clearly said the cabins were full now, and well into the next year. Maybe she got lucky and someone canceled their reservation. She shook her head.

None of it made sense but it didn't matter. She forced her thoughts back to the present.

"Hello, Cole?" she called out as she opened the door to the office. "It's Alex and Maisie." She heard a muffled sound from somewhere in the back that might have been "I'm coming." She stepped in and looked around. There wasn't much room in here, most of it was taken up by a counter with a computer on it. A rack of tourism brochures hung from one wall and a large painting of a mountain scene hung behind the counter, next to a closed door. The other wall sported a large basic black and white clock. It was functional and that was about all Alex could say about it.

The door behind the counter opened and Cole entered the little office. Her stomach made a little flutter and she mentally told it to stop. He was dressed in the same type of canvas jeans he had on yesterday and was wearing a black t-shirt with a brown and blue flannel shirt over it with the sleeves rolled up on his forearms.

"Ready to go?" He smiled and came around the counter and the little room became even smaller. Cole stopped to give Maisie a good rub behind her ears. There wasn't room for her to flop onto the floor for a belly rub, but he was sure she would have if she could.

"We are. Lead the way."

Cole opened the door and held it for her and Maisie, allowing them to go first. Alex squeezed by and stopped on the porch.

"We just met Mary Louise. She said something about...."

"I bet she did," Cole interrupted and then grinned. "She's a whirlwind, isn't she? She has so much enthusiasm for everything in life. All of her kids are grown so she thinks she has to mother me. Let me tell you, I don't mind. She's the best cook and is always making me special treats." He put his hand on the small of her back as he guided her and Maisie over to an open Jeep.

Alex decided to drop it, but she couldn't ignore Cole's hand on her back. It felt right…and apparently, whatever Mary Louise meant, Alex wasn't going to learn today.

Maisie jumped up and into the back seat as soon as Cole opened the door, settling in as if she had ridden in it every day of her life. Alex followed and settled in the passenger seat.

Alex loved the feel of the wind on her face as they traveled out to the highway and west, higher to soak in the mountain air. Huge mountain peaks emerged, and Cole turned off the main road onto a dirt road that wound down into a valley and a parking lot next to a lake.

He pointed to the three peaks jutting from the valley floor. "That's Sugarloaf Mountain, Medicine Bow Peak and Brown's Peak. There's a trail that winds up and through them and eventually makes it around Brown's Peak and back down over by the Bar CG."

"It's so beautiful," Alex replied. "I'm excited to hike up Medicine Bow Peak today."

Cole glanced at her. "Are you sure you want to go all the way to the peak? You've only been here a couple of days, maybe we could hike to Lost Lake today and try Medicine Bow another day."

Alex heard the doubt in his voice and pressed her lips together.

"I'm sure," Alex said, as she gathered her gear. "It's not that far, according to my trail guide, only about three-and-a-half miles both ways. I did okay yesterday afternoon, so I think I've acclimatized to the altitude already."

All of the hike was above the tree line, Cole knew, which meant they would be starting at just under eleven thousand feet and hiking to more than twelve thousand feet. It wasn't an easy hike that was made worse because it was a huge elevation increase in a short distance. He didn't really think she was serious when she talked about it yesterday.

"It's pretty steep," he pointed out. "Are your legs ready for this?"

Alex's chin nudged up. "I can do this, Cole. If you hadn't offered to come along, Maisie and I would do it ourselves." She gestured to the parking lot near the lake's edge. "There are plenty of people out here so we won't be alone."

Cole couldn't dispute that, but he had a bad feeling about this. Yesterday, she was limping after walking around the lake near the ranch. He didn't want her to add to her injury. He watched her face, feeling uncharacteristically protective. He could see she was determined to do this, prove to herself that she was healthy enough to do it. He detected a stubborn streak in this woman he already loved. That wasn't necessarily a bad thing, he decided, and backed down. At least she wasn't going alone.

"Okay, let's go."

CHAPTER FOUR

Alex's legs were screaming for her to stop, but she refused to listen. She had set out on this trek to the top of the mountain and she was going to finish it. Yes, Cole had said it would be too much for her and it apparently was, but she wasn't going to admit failure.

They had started early, but for such a short hike, it was all almost straight up and grueling. It was already mid-afternoon, and they still weren't at the top of the peak. They had made a few stops, including one for lunch and a bathroom break. Alex could think of many things she would rather do than pee outdoors, squatting on the ground, but it had to be done. They hadn't talked much, but that was more because Alex was concentrating on breathing and putting one foot in front of the other.

Alex was gasping for air when they finally stopped for a break, and her head was pounding to the beat of her heart, but she wasn't going to tell Cole that. She leaned against a rock to rest. She was positive that if she sat on the ground, she wouldn't be able to get back up.

"You're not ready for this. It's too much too soon." Cole, who was not breathing heavy, crouched on the side of the trail and drank from his water bottle.

Alex would do that too. In a minute. When she could.

The last thing Alex wanted to do was argue with him, but she might have if she could breathe in enough air to do it.

"We should go back," Cole said. He looked at her face, it was red with exertion. She needed a longer rest.

Alex cut him off with a shake of her head.

"I can do it," she spit out.

Cole shrugged and offered her his water bottle. She took a drink and handed it back, suddenly remembering her own water bottle. She got it out and took several long drinks, then got Maisie's dish out.

"I'm sure you can, but what about Maisie?" He gestured toward the dog. "She's panting pretty hard."

Alex looked at the dog lying belly down on the ground. Cole was right. Maisie was having a hard time breathing, maybe harder than she was. She immediately felt guilty. Maisie would keep going for Alex's sake, but she couldn't do that to her.

"You're right, let's go back." Maisie finished drinking and Alex hooked the dish back on her backpack. Alex pushed to her feet and gritted her teeth to keep from moaning. She adjusted her walking stick and Maisie's leash and started down the path, head down and back-tracking the way they had ascended. Maisie obediently walked with her. She was so disappointed that her stomach hurt. Hiking this trail was one of the reasons she came here. She also wanted to prove to herself she was healed. She was disappointed and frustrated, but she would not cry.

"Wait. Alex."

Alex turned and Maisie stopped.

"You made your point, we're going back."

"Just stop a minute and around look around." Cole touched her shoulders and turned her.

Alex lifted her eyes, and they widened in wonder. She sucked in her breath. They were high above the lake they had started from. She could see over the trees to the east and south and lakes to the north where the mountain range curved around them. Big fluffy clouds skirted across the afternoon sky. It looked like it was raining off to the south, dark clouds making the sky a bluish gray with streaks of rain slanting to the ground. The western sky was bathed in sunlight, making the gray clouds turn to almost purple. Her anger faded.

"It's, it's beautiful, majestic. I've never seen anything like it."

"Look how far we got. Getting this high is no small feat, many hikers don't even make it this far."

Alex didn't reply. Instead, she pulled her phone out of her pocket and took several photos. If she didn't get back here, and she probably wouldn't, she wanted to remember it.

"Here, let me take a picture of you and Maisie." Cole stepped forward.

Alex handed him the phone and stood while he clicked several photos. She stood and smiled and wouldn't admit that her leg was killing her, wouldn't admit that he was right, and she had gone farther than she should have. She squared her shoulders.

"Let's do a selfie with all of us. Selfie mode, Maisie."

"Selfie mode?"

"Watch."

As Cole held the phone so the mountains to the north were in the background, Maisie stretched her neck and cocked her head.

Cole took several pictures. Maisie didn't move until he handed the phone back to Alex.

"How did you teach her to do that?" Cole asked as he bent down and ruffled Maisie's fur.

Alex smiled. "I didn't. Apparently, she just likes having her picture taken. Don't you sweetie?" She crouched to snuggle Maisie's neck, then stayed that way.

"Up Maisie," she finally said, and Maisie stood to stand beside her. It didn't help. Her legs, both of them, refused to move.

"Umm."

Cole immediately reached to help her to her feet. "You're not okay."

Alex grimaced. "It's not my leg, it's my thigh muscles. I think we stopped too long and my muscles have tightened up." She stepped away from Cole. "Anyway, I'll be fine. We should head back."

It took much less time to hike down the mountain than it had going up and they were mostly silent. The silence continued all the way back to the ranch.

"Look, I'm sorry too we didn't make it all the way," Cole finally said, "but we can try another day, truly."

Alex paused as she reached for her pack. "I know that, but I've done this before, tried something and failed and I never had the chance to try again. It's just disappointing."

Cole walked around the Jeep and she let him pull her into his arms. "We'll go again, I promise."

Alex looked up at him and their eyes met, then their lips met. It was a tender kiss that started out comforting. Alex put her hands behind his neck and pulled him closer, let herself slide into something deeper, her disappointment forgotten.

Cole finally broke the kiss and cupped her face. He smoothed her hair back from her face. "I promise."

Alex thought about the kiss as she got Maisie's supper ready. She wasn't hungry, but she ate some fruit and drank several glasses of water to replenish what she had lost hiking. She had already taken a hot shower and massaged her thighs, so they felt better, but she decided a book was in order for the evening.

"I'm not ready, I really am not," she told Maisie. "But he's so... so, I don't know, but I wanted to curl up with him and never let go. What's that about?"

She was still asking herself that as she drifted off to sleep, book finished and so tired she thought about sleeping on the sofa.

Alex came awake to Maisie licking her hand that was stuck out of the blanket on the bed. She opened one eye to see the dog looking at her expectantly, then scratched behind Maisie's ear. "I know, I know, you want to go outside."

The dog thumped her tail on the floor and Alex eased out of bed. Her muscles protested. There would be no mountain climbing today. She grabbed a sweatshirt and a pair of slippers. She was not going outside without something on her feet. The morning was chilly and the sun was barely up. As she let Maisie back into the cabin, Alex made a plan for the day. She was going to try to hike around the lake again, even though Cole thought she shouldn't hike alone. She wasn't hiking out into the wilderness, and she had Maisie. They would take plenty of water and snacks, make sure she had her rain jacket. They would be fine.

She also needed to check emails and do a couple of sketches for a new product she was thinking about. She hadn't used her phone for anything but taking pictures since she got here, she thought, and that was unusual. Maybe she would drive to town and see if she had a signal to check phone and text messages. She hadn't missed not having a phone, Alex realized, and that was interesting.

Coffee, first, though, she told herself heading to the kitchen, and then breakfast. She and Maisie sat on the deck while Alex finished the rest of her coffee. It was so peaceful here. Alex wondered what Cole was doing this morning. Stop it, she told herself. She had no business getting involved with someone on a summer vacation. She was only staying a short time and getting too close meant she was going to get her heart bruised when she had to leave.

"Hello there."

The voice drew her out of her lecture. She looked down to the trail where Steve and Jackie Cooper and John Campbell had paused.

"Well, hello there. You guys are out early."

Jackie laughed and shrugged. "We're old. We get up early every day."

"Are you heading out for a hike?" Alex rose from her chair and walked down the steps to meet them.

Jackie shook her head. "We've just walked around the lake. We're going out on a drive around the area, maybe take in the hot springs on the other side of the mountains, so we wanted to stretch our legs before we got going. What are you up to today?"

"I've got to check messages and emails, so I'm going to town." Down the mountain a few miles was the town of Centennial where she was told she could get a cell signal.

"That's the beauty of this place," John responded, and added a playful wink. "We're pretty much unlocked from technology."

Alex laughed. She was sure John was a favorite of the ladies. "Aren't you an engineer? That just screams technology."

"Well, sure, but when you work with it every day, it's nice to get away from it for a while, and this is the perfect place to do it."

Alex agreed. "I can't believe I've never come out here before." She and James had talked about it, planned it. They weren't planning a honeymoon, but maybe a trip later in the summer. That was one of the reasons she decided to come here this summer.

"The best part is that it isn't crowded like some of the national parks are," Steve said. "Sometimes we don't see anyone on the trails when we're out. You could probably live out in this area for months without seeing another person, if that's what you wanted."

Alex shuddered at the thought. "I don't think I could do that. I like this peace and quiet, but I don't want total isolation. And I like indoor plumbing."

All three nodded.

"That's how we feel too," John said. "I guess we better keep moving. Have fun with that technology." They waved and were off.

The trip around the lake was uneventful. Alex was mindful of her surroundings and had taken plenty of water and snacks. She and Maisie found a small waterfall to sit next to while they rested. As Alex watched the mesmerizing flow of water, she made a realization. "Steve Cooper was right. I've been living in a big city with people everywhere and have been pretty much isolated for the past year," she told the big dog. "I seldom left the rehab center, and certainly never went anywhere with friends. And you know what?"

Maisie thumped her tail.

"Exactly. I've been lonely."

Maisie whined and Alex hugged her. "Well, sure, I have you and you're great company. But it's been nice having someone to hang out with here who can actually talk back to me. I've probably taken up too much of Cole's time, but I'm enjoying myself."

Alex realized another thing. She was content. And happy, as happy as she had been in the last year. She pulled out her phone and flipped through her photos until she found the last picture she had taken of

James. It made her sad to look at it. His face, frozen in time, was so familiar. The blond hair parted on the left and falling to the right, neatly trimmed at his ears, made her smile. They always laughed about how young he looked. Blue eyes looked straight into the camera and that crooked grin reminded her how happy he'd been that day. They had just gotten done renting his tuxedo, the one he'd never gotten to wear. She pushed her engagement ring around on her finger. It would never have a wedding band with it, but James had given it to her. and she couldn't bring herself to take it off.

Alex supposed that's how married people felt when their partner died. She knew women who wouldn't take their ring off and, in the movies, they finally took it off when they found someone new to love. Would she be like that? She didn't know. Was it time now? If she allowed her attraction to Cole to continue, she probably should. She realized she had only known Cole a couple of days, not the years it took to fall in love with her best friend, but she wondered if she should be willing to take a bigger chance this time and quicker. After all, she didn't know what tomorrow would bring.

She and James had always thought they had tomorrow, and next week, or next year, and in reality, they only had the day, because that could be their last.

Alex shook her head to clear it. Enough of this, she told herself. She didn't want to spend the day thinking about what could have been. She stood up and started walking. "Come on, Maisie, let's go to town."

The walk around the lake had been much easier, Alex thought, once her muscles loosened up. She decided as they drove down the winding road to town that she must be getting stronger, and even though she hadn't made it to the peak yesterday, she was better for the hike.

The little town of Centennial that was just down off the mountain looked like it really only had one road and that was the highway running through it. There was a motel and a steakhouse and a couple of little shops, including a general store, but that was about it. She had cell phone service here though, and knew when it kicked in. Her phone dinged about fifteen times. Alex sighed and pulled into the parking lot of a little market that sported a sign advertising the sale of gasoline, beer, fishing licenses and souvenirs.

Alex sat in her SUV and flicked through texts and missed calls. She answered the texts and listened to voice mails and made the realization that except for one, none of them were that important. It was a sad reflection on her life, she thought. Only one caller asked her to call back and that was a company in Detroit that manufactured furniture. They would like to talk to her about a job. Alex dialed the number and after talking to a receptionist, who asked her to hold, talked to the human resources woman who had called her. Alex didn't think it was a fit for her, but she thanked the woman for reaching out. Upholstery design was a different animal from what she had been doing. She called her mom to let her know she was safe and then put the phone in her pocket, grabbed her purse and rolled Maisie's window down so she had some air, then went inside the little store.

She bought a cold soda, a carton of milk and some butter. They didn't have much of a meat selection, but she found packages of sliced ham and turkey and picked those up. She added a package of tortillas to the pile, they would work well as a wrap for her turkey and ham as well and her bread wouldn't get squished in her backpack. She looked at the souvenirs and found a t-shirt with a Snowy Range picture screen-printed on it. She looked for any history or area books, but couldn't find any, nor could she find a bird identification book She had noticed a few books on a bookshelf in the Commons, but decided she would find a bookstore in Laramie when she went there and look for a bird book.

She paid for her purchases as the clerk chatted about the weather, then headed back out to her vehicle where Maisie was patiently waiting.

Cole waved to her as Alex drove by the office. She waved back and she and Maisie got out of the SUV, and walked back to meet him. He helped her get her purchases into the cabin and stood at the open patio door to watch Maisie as she took a much-needed bathroom break.

"How was your morning?"

"It was good, and my legs feel much better." She wasn't going to squat and get back up to prove that, but he didn't press the matter.

"Do you have plans for this afternoon?"

Alex thought about it for a minute. She didn't have anything concrete planned, maybe a drive to see some of the wildlife, but she was flexible.

"Not really. What do you have in mind?" Her face turned several shades of red when she realized she was hoping he would take her off somewhere private and have his way with her. "I mean, I wasn't planning on taking on Medicine Bow again." She laid her hand on his arm, then quickly removed it when she realized what she was doing. "I shouldn't have been so snippy about it, but it was one of my goals for this trip."

Cole almost asked why but decided to let it go for the moment. He suspected she would tell him when she was ready.

"I was thinking about fishing. You mentioned fly fishing and we have a group going out his afternoon that has room for one more. We had a cancellation."

"I would love that," Alex exclaimed and clapped her hands. Maisie, who had come back inside while they were talking, immediately sat and started wildly wagging her tail.

"Yes, you can come too." Cole ruffled Maisie's fur. "Don't tell me she loves fishing?"

Alex laughed. "I have no idea. I've certainly never taken her."

Alex hadn't been fishing since she was little, but she had fond memories of going to a small lake near their home in Missouri with her dad. She had grown out of spending time with her father, choosing to take dance lessons and hang out with her friends. This could be fun.

CHAPTER FIVE

Alex and Maisie walked over to the large metal building that functioned as an office for outdoor recreation activities, including fishing and utility vehicles that people rented to drive on the many low-maintenance roads in the area. Alex thought she would like to try that sometime, but probably not on this trip. She didn't know much about them and certainly wouldn't want to go off by herself.

Cole, who was already there, helped her pick out waders and get a fishing license, which was still required even if going with a professional guide. Alex looked at it with pride. She had never had a fishing license, hadn't needed one when she was little. Maybe she would even catch a fish. She could have a picture taken and send it to her dad. As far as that went, maybe she could revisit doing more things with him. Alex took a breath. One thing at a time, she decided. She didn't know the first thing about fly fishing. It didn't look that hard on television shows, but that could be deceiving.

"We're going with Danny, one of our two fishing guides, and Grant and Deb Simmons," Cole was explaining. He made the introductions. "They'll ride together, and we'll take my Jeep, if that's okay."

Alex appreciated the extra people when they arrived at the river and actually had to try their luck. She was glad she wasn't the only one struggling to cast her line. They had practiced casting at the ranch, but it was one thing to do it standing in a grassy area and another to stand in a fast-flowing river full of rocks, with trees overhead and bushes on shore. It was beautiful though, Alex admitted, and the sound of the water running over the rocks calmed her nerves.

Cole helped her put a fly on her line and let her try. It had been easy enough back at the ranch, so she pulled out her line, flicked her wrist and arm and just like that, she caught one of the bushes behind her. She would have caught Cole, but he moved at the last second. Ten minutes later, despite Cole's encouragement that she was doing well, Alex was ready to call it quits. She couldn't get the fly in the water. It hit the bush several times, a tree branch on the river's bank and the back of her shirt. That was the final straw as far as she was concerned.

Alex could see Cole trying to hide his smile and tightened her lips as he stepped behind her and freed the fly from her shirt.

"Will you let me help?" Cole asked when he was done. He stepped into the water with her while Maisie waited patiently on shore. They worked together and finally Alex's line was in the water. He made it look so easy, she thought.

There was a yelp from Deb Simmons as she caught her own bush. Danny got it loose and they both tried again. Her husband had gotten the hang of it and was happily fishing away upstream.

"Just like this," Cole demonstrated. The line and fly fell nicely on the water. "Now let it drift downstream a bit, then twist and flick it back upstream."

He stepped away, a good thing, Alex thought, since she had a difficult time concentrating with him that close.

Twist and flick. Let it move downstream, twist and flick. "Like this?"

"I think you've got it," Cole said from behind her.

Alex stood in the knee-deep water and worked her line. The waders kept her dry, but she could feel the cold from the water on her legs and feet. The waders were clearly made for a man and the attached booties that went inside her boots were too big, making her feet slide around. She was pretty sure she was going to have blisters later. Maybe she could design a woman's version, Alex thought. Hmm. She would give that some thought, but for now she needed to concentrate on fishing.

Every now and then, Cole would have Alex pull her line back in and recast. It was a risk since she wasn't very good at it, but once she got the line back in the water, she was good to go.

Cole sat on a rock on the bank with Maisie and Alex wished she had her phone so she could take a picture. Cole did have his phone and took pictures of her.

Just as Alex pulled her line back to recast, Deb squealed. "I think I have one," she exclaimed, and as Alex looked over, she could see a fish fighting against Deb's line.

Danny gave her instructions to reel the trout in and got a net ready.

Alex stopped casting to watch them and as she shifted her feet, a rock moved under her. Despite her best efforts to regain her balance, she fell forward into the water. She came up out of the water in a whoosh as Cole was there immediately to pick her up. He carried her to shore where Maisie was waiting. It all happened in a matter of seconds. Cole set her on the ground.

"Are you okay? What happened?" There was concern in his voice.

Alex pushed her wet hair out of her eyes. Her pole was lodged up against the bank, but Cole didn't seem to care. Danny was still helping Deb, and Grant looked up but kept fishing.

She laughed. "Oh my gosh that's cold. I think my waders are full of water." She laughed again.

"But are you hurt?" He looked so concerned that she stopped laughing and gently touched his face.

"I'm fine, really I am, and I swear I'm not clumsy." She limped to a rock and sat down, trying to untangle herself from the now soaking waders.

Cole pulled the waders off her feet. "You're limping."

"Yeah, I think I bruised my knee." Alex grimaced as Cole pulled up her pant leg. Her knee had a bruise on the side of it that was already purple. "I must have hit a rock on my way down." She pulled her pant leg back down. "My leg didn't give out, I just shifted a rock. It's really nothing."

Cole didn't look convinced but offered to go get her hiking boots from the Jeep. Alex peeled off her socks and hobbled bare footed over to where Danny was taking pictures of Deb with her trout. They took care to keep it in the water and when they were done with pictures, they released it back into the river.

"That was so great, your first fish." She hugged Deb, who had admitted, along with her husband when they were practicing, that they were novices like Alex.

"I'm sorry you fell into the river," Deb said.

Alex shrugged and smiled. "It's no big deal. I was just excited for you and forgot what my feet were doing. This has been so much fun, I want to try it again so I can catch a fish too. And I'm sure I'll have another chance."

Alex fetched her gear from the bank and hobbled back to the

rock. She sat down just as Cole came back with her hiking boots. "I don't have any extra socks with me, sorry."

"No problem," Alex replied. "I can go without my socks for a while. I already took them off and they're drying as we speak." She pointed to the wool socks laid out flat on a nearby rock. She wasn't going to mention the three blisters she had on her feet.

They all gathered up gear and packed it back into Danny's pickup before heading back to the ranch. Once Alex and Cole were back in the Jeep, Alex chatted happily about the trout Deb had caught, about the huge elk they saw grazing in a small meadow and Maisie's joy to be riding in the back seat with her ears flapping and her tongue hanging out.

Cole stopped in front of Alex's cabin and came around the passenger side to help her out. She poked her bare feet out of the Jeep and he had to stop a moment to admire the pink polish on her pretty toes.

Alex had worn her boots to the Jeep but removed them as soon as she was seated. She claimed that while she could wear damp socks if she had to, but she didn't, so that was that.

She launched herself into Cole's arms, nearly sending them both to the ground since Cole wasn't expecting it. She threw her arms around his neck and kissed him full on the lips, but it was over before he could react.

"I had so much fun, can we go again sometime?" In the next second, Alex was grabbing her boots and pack from the Jeep. Maisie jumped out and waited patiently for whatever came next.

"You had fun even though you didn't catch anything, and you fell into the river?" Cole wasn't sure he believed her. She seemed happier and more animated than she'd been since she got here. Other women he had known would have cried or thrown a temper tantrum in the same circumstances.

"I did have fun. I think there's more practicing to be done, but I liked the challenge of it. There's a sort of art to it, I think. I also had an idea for a better pair of waders and rod and reel carrying case I think I want to design. In fact, that's what I'm going to do, whether I have a job or not. Well, first I'm going to have a shower, but then, design." she amended.

Cole looked skeptical.

"What?"

"I don't want to burst your bubble, but they already make those things."

Alex reached up and kissed him on the nose. "Not like mine, they don't." She turned and gingerly walked to the porch.

"Come on Maisie," she called as she turned around to face Cole. "See you later." She waved cheerfully and let herself and the dog into the cabin, leaving Cole to stand in stunned silence.

Cole was still shaking his head as he walked into his cabin. Mary Louise looked up from the carrot she was chopping and noticed his serious expression.

"Didn't the fishing trip go well?" she asked, concerned. "I wasn't sure she would like fishing, but you said she asked to go. She's such a sad girl. I hope you can help her be happier. You need to do something special for her, oh, how about a picnic? I can fix you a lunch, why don't you see if she wants to go tomorrow?"

"She fell in the river."

Mary Louise fell silent. "She fell in the river?" Another minute passed. "Ooh, that's bad, I bet she was angry."

Cole shook his head and got a soda out of the refrigerator, then sat across the island from Mary Louise. He stole a carrot from her pile and munched on it while he told her about the fishing trip.

"She wasn't angry, she just laughed it off, even though she bruised her knee. She talked more on the way home than she has since we met. And, she kissed me."

Mary Louise set down her knife and pushed up her glasses. "Really? She kissed you? Why?"

Cole shrugged. "I have no idea. Maybe it was because she was barefoot. And happy. She didn't like our waders, said they didn't fit women, so she's going to design some, and a fly rod and reel carrying case."

Mary Louise considered that.

"She's not wrong. I couldn't wear a pair of those if I wanted to. It's a great idea and I bet she can do it. Wait, I thought she didn't have a job."

"She doesn't as far as I know, but I suppose she wants to get a jump on it."

Mary Louise resumed cutting. "I had hoped she would find a job around here, but we don't have much to offer a designer, now do we?" She stopped again. "What if she leaves? What are we going to do then? Oh my, I hadn't thought of that." She sniffed a little to hold back tears.

Cole stood and walked around the island to her, then kissed her on the forehead.

"Don't you worry about it, things will work out. She's still here for a couple of weeks, but I've got to run. I left Danny cleaning gear, so I'd better go help him get done."

He stole another carrot and headed out the door.

Alex dressed in yoga pants and her new t-shirt, and decided the shower was just what she had needed. That water was cold, and she had been soaked to the skin. She hadn't told Cole, but her shoulder hurt from casting and the bruise on her knee throbbed. She also hadn't told Cole about the three blisters she had acquired from the booties on the waders. She didn't want him to feel bad, she decided as she applied blister bandages. They would be as good as new in a few days.

She and Maisie had snacks, then Alex got her sketch pad out and wandered onto the deck to work on the designs. She made a preliminary sketch of the waders she was thinking about and then started on the carrying case. She wanted to research the waders to make sure there was a need for them.

The light was waning by the time she finished and her stomach had already growled a couple of times. She closed the sketch pad and got up to stretch. Maisie did the same, apparently also ready for supper.

Alex was in the middle of grilling chicken breasts and a combination of sliced peppers, onions, and potatoes when Cole appeared around the corner of the cabin. Maisie greeted him with her usual excitement and Cole returned the favor, giving her a good scratch behind her ears.

Cole looked up at Alex, who looked young and sweet in her yoga pants and t-shirt, and pink fuzzy slippers. She shut the grill lid and walked over to him.

"I knocked at the front door, but you didn't answer," Cole explained. "I'm supposed to invite you to a picnic tomorrow."

Alex's eyebrows rose. "Supposed to?"

Cole nodded. "And I'm not supposed to take no for an answer." He spread his hands in front of him. "Orders from Mary Louise."

"Well, in that case, I guess I accept." It wasn't the most romantic proposal in the world, but she knew he wouldn't ask if he didn't want to go, even if he was being coerced.

"And why does Mary Louise think I deserve a picnic?" Alex put her hands on her hips.

Cole smiled. "I told her you fell in the river. She was very upset and thought you should have a treat. Anyway, I thought we could hike to Lost Lake and have our picnic there."

Alex remembered he had suggested that hike the other day. She had looked it up in her trail guide and thought it sounded like a great hike. At the very least, it wasn't straight up.

"Did you have other plans tomorrow?" Cole asked when she didn't answer.

Alex shook her head. "I don't have any plans for tomorrow, I thought I could decide in the morning. A picnic sounds amazing." She walked back to the grill, then turned back to him.

"Have you had dinner? I'm grilling chicken and veggies and have enough for you too, if you want to stay."

"I never turn down food, so you've got a dinner guest. Can I help?"

Alex transferred everything to a plate. "You could get the door, that would help," she said.

Cole stayed and helped with the dishes, drying them after she washed them. It was strangely intimate and made Alex wish it could be this way every night.

Afterwards, they sat on the deck with glasses of wine and watched the stars come out. They were so bright here, Alex decided, and wondered out loud if she could try to set up one of those pictures of the Milky Way everyone always posted online.

Cole laughed. "Only you would think of that."

"Could it be done?"

"Absolutely." Cole raised up out of his patio chair and set his glass on the table. He pulled Alex out of her chair and offered his hand.

"Where are we going?"

"You'll see." They walked down the steps and around the cabin, then across the drive and around to his cabin's front porch. Maisie followed them, off-leash for now.

It was very dark on this side of his cabin. Alex had no idea why they were standing in this particular place in the dark.

"Look." Cole pointed towards the southwest and there it was, just above the peaks of the mountains. The Milky Way. If Alex had ever seen it before in person, she didn't remember. She sighed. It was magnificent, a milky white color, filled with the glitter of thousands of distant stars.

"I don't know how good a picture you can get with your phone," Cole said, "but you should definitely try it."

Cole sat on the stop step of the porch and Maisie came to sit with him.

Alex took several pictures, turning this way and that, then sat next down next to Cole so they could look at them together.

"These are pretty good," Cole stated, "considering how dark the rest of the night is."

Alex turned her screen off and leaned into Cole. His arm went around her, and they sat that way for what seemed like hours to Alex, just watching the stars and the night.

At last, she raised her head to tell Cole they should probably head back to the cabin.

Apparently, he had the same thought, Alex decided, because he turned his head at the same time. Their lips met, tentatively at first, and then more insistingly, tongue meeting tongue, each tasting the other. Breathing became labored and Alex could think of nothing except the man in front of her.

Maisie let out a soft woof, pulling them back to the present. Cole immediately grasped her collar when he heard the soft scuffling in the trees to the right of them.

"Easy there," he cautioned Maisie. "It's probably just a deer or an elk."

Alex looked anxiously into the trees. "Not a bear? Or Bigfoot?"

Cole laughed and the scuffling sounds moved away into the night until it was silent again.

"I'm not ruling either of those out, but bears prefer to be farther away from people than this. And the last Bigfoot sighting around here was about fifteen years ago. Either way, let's not take any chances. I'll walk you back to your cabin."

"Come on, Maisie." Alex took Cole's hand and they started across the driveway. Maisie looked back at the trees like she wasn't convinced, but she followed the couple anyway.

CHAPTER SIX

Alex and Maisie met Cole at the office the next morning.

He was cheerful, Alex thought, as he greeted them with smiles. Maisie got a quick rub before they loaded their gear into the Jeep. It seemed like only a few minutes before they were at the trailhead parking lot. It was the same one they parked in to go to the mountain's peak. Were they hiking up there again? Alex wondered. Cole had made it clear she wasn't ready. He must have noticed her confusion because he spoke just as she started to ask the question.

"I thought maybe today we could hike up to Lost Lake. It's not a difficult hike, but there's enough challenge to make it fun and it's a great place for a picnic." He got out and went around to help her out of the Jeep.

Alex smiled and put Maisie on her leash after she jumped out of the back seat. "Lead on. I should warn you though, I'm taking lots of pictures, so there may be stops on the way."

"Stops are always encouraged. The altitude can kick your butt even if you're used to it." Cole indicated for her to go ahead of him on the trail and then wished he hadn't. He was distracted by the gentle curve of her hips.

They walked in comfortable silence for the first stretch of the trail, pausing now and then to allow Alex to take pictures of alpine flowers, little streams, or a bit of snow here and there. Cole managed to sneak in a few of his own shots, but they were of the woman and the dog as they interacted with each other and enjoyed the day.

They found a fairly flat rock at the edge of the lake to sit on to eat the lunch that Mary Louise packed for them. Alex pulled what looked like a sleeping pad out of her bag. With a couple of punches at a button on one side, it inflated into a smaller version of a sleeping pad, perfect for two people to sit on.

"Don't tell me...this is another of your designs," Cole said as they made themselves comfortable sitting side by side.

"It is," Alex replied. "They're designed for day hikes. I found out a long time ago that sitting on the ground in the shade of a pine tree left me with pine needles and resin stuck all over my pants. I eventually got them clean, but decided I could do better. So, I did."

Cole squirmed a bit. "I love it," he said, looking directly at Alex. "It makes the rock much more comfortable, and it didn't seem to take up much room in your pack."

"There's actually a collapsible chair that's an alternative, and it doesn't take up much room in a backpack either. I just thought this was the better choice for today."

Alex suddenly realized how close together they were sitting on the pad. She turned away and focused on retrieving her water bottle and Maisie's collapsible dish from her pack.

Cole felt her pull away and wondered what happened as he took three plastic containers and a small wooden tray out of his pack. He set out pretzel bites, a small dish of chili con queso, pepperoni and hard salami and a variety of cheeses, then added strawberries, grapes, small chunks of honeydew, and both black and green olives.

Alex watched, dumbfounded. She'd been to five-star restaurants that didn't serve food this fancy.

"Is this what you usually eat when you hike?" Alex took an olive and popped it in her mouth. "I feel completely inadequate. I would have brought a granola bar and an apple."

Cole laughed. "I would have brought a couple of tortillas with peanut butter and maybe some grapes and several cookies. For today though, Mary Louise thought lunch should be fancier, so here we are. She likes to cook and make fancy dishes. She made the pretzels from scratch."

"But...she's not German?"

"Absolutely not," he agreed, "but mostly Mary Louise is about food...all kinds of food. So, she made these pretzels and the queso we're dipping them in."

Alex dipped a pretzel in the queso and took a bite. She closed her eyes in bliss. "Umm, this is so good. I never thought you could eat like this out on a trail. All we need is a bottle of wine."

Cole pulled a stainless-steel bottle out of his pack.

"You didn't bring.....wine?"

He shook his head. "It's just water. Wine sounds good, but alcohol at this altitude can be lethal, so we'll have to save that for another time."

They munched happily, enjoying the moment and the food, and watched Maisie. She was sleeping in the sunlight, lying on her back with legs sticking up. Alex had let her off leash at Cole's suggestion, and Maisie had explored while they were getting lunch ready, staying close to them. The big dog was obviously ready for a rest. Alex knew how she felt.

It had been a long time since she just sat and enjoyed the moment, Alex thought, and loved that two people who had known each other such a short time could be this content to do just that. She suspected that Cole wasn't a huge conversationalist and that was okay, neither was she.

"Ready for dessert?"

"We have dessert? After all that, we have dessert?"

Cole dug in his bag and pulled out a little blue box. He opened it and presented four pretty little chocolates to Alex.

"Wow, these are beautiful. If you tell me Mary Louise made these too, I'm going to...well, I don't know what I'm going to do." She selected one. "They look too good to eat."

Cole took two and offered the box to Alex, which she accepted. She bit the first one in half and closed her eyes to savor the rich taste. "Oh my...I think I've found Heaven."

"Mary Louise didn't make these," Cole replied as he watched her enjoy the treat. "I did."

Alex opened her eyes and looked at him in disbelief. She swallowed her bite and tried to find words. "You made these?" she finally sputtered. "You really made these?"

He shrugged. "It's something I do, but you really think they're good?"

Alex put the other half in her mouth and nodded. "I really, really do, and these look professionally done, like the ones I've seen in fancy candy stores. I can't wait to hear this story."

Cole shrugged. "It's not much of a story, although I think Mary Louise may have rubbed off on me. The winters can be hard up here and despite having chores, there are days when cooking is the best activity. One year Mary Louise suggested I try making some candies for Christmas and I ended up with these."

"Now, you're the genius. Are they available in stores? They should be." Alex savored the second chocolate. The man was a surprise. He fought fires, rode horses and looked like he could be a model for the cover of a romance novel, and he made chocolates. Fancy chocolates that were very good.

"We provide a store in Laramie with them," Cole admitted, "but it's only a hobby. The ranch is my livelihood."

Alex brushed crumbs away and slid off the rock. Cole came up right beside her to steady her as she stumbled.

"Whoa, be careful. Are you okay?"

Alex laughed. "I would have thought with all of the grueling... and I mean really grueling...physical therapy I've had in the last year that my legs would be ready for anything. I guess not. I didn't think we hiked very far."

Cole looked at the trail and then at the lake, anything to keep him from thinking about her being in pain. He knew about pain, and he wished she didn't have any.

"Only a couple of miles, but we've been going up and down, so you're probably using some muscles you're not used to using. Can you walk?"

Alex made a couple of little circles around the rocks. "I think they're okay now. We might have sat too long."

They collected their things and started back down the trail.

"Tell me more about your accident, if you don't mind," Cole suggested, hoping he wasn't intruding. Still, he would like to know what happened. "I know you told me a bit about it earlier, but it was a car accident, right?"

Alex nodded. "Let's find a place to sit and I'll give you all the details."

They found a log that made a decent bench and Alex sat down. Cole sank to the ground next to Maisie, who rolled over onto her back. Cole obligingly gave her a gentle rub as Alex started to talk.

"It's been just over a year...a year last month. My fiancé James and I planned to be married, a year ago next week. I think I already told you that. Anyway, we were planning to take our delayed honeymoon out here somewhere." Alex sighed and stopped for a moment, looking off into the distance. "We were on our way to meet with the caterer when a drunk driver crossed the median on a four-lane highway and hit us head-on. James was driving and that side of the car took the bulk of the hit. It was over in a matter of seconds. I don't remember anything after the impact. I had broken ribs and my left lung collapsed. I had a mangled leg and was in a medically induced coma for about three weeks."

Alex wiped away a tear, took a deep breath and continued. "The other driver died too. I never got to say goodbye to James. I think that's what hurt the most. We had known each other for forever and were best friends. As I started to heal, I realized I didn't want to even live." She looked at Cole. "They were dark days, but one morning I woke up and told myself that James wouldn't have wanted that, he would have wanted me to continue to live.

"Technically, my leg has healed, but I don't think it will ever be as strong as it was before. It was broken in two places above my knee and each of the bones below my knee were broken. The screws mostly hold everything in place, but the tendons and ligaments in my knee don't always cooperate, especially when I'm tired or not watching how I walk." She pulled her pant leg up to show him the scars on her calf. "The scars aren't pretty, but I can live with them, and I guess I have to live without James. Anyway, that's my story."

Cole reached and took her hand, held it for a moment. "I'm sorry that happened to you, it's so hard when you lose someone you love. I would do something if I could, to help you heal."

Alex took another deep breath and stood up. She met Cole as he stood up and put her arms around his waist. His arms wrapped around her back and they stood that way for a long time with only the noise of the wind around them. They only broke apart when Maisie whined, apparently tired of sitting.

"Thank you," Alex said. "I don't talk about it much anymore. Those who know the story don't want to hear it again, and those who don't know about it don't see the scars."

They started on their way, and a few minutes later, Alex spotted a moose in a marshy area away from the trail. She slowed, then stopped. "Look," she whispered to Cole. "Can I take a picture?"

Cole nodded and took out his own phone to take a couple as well. "As long as we don't encroach on her area, she'll leave us alone," he whispered back and took Maisie's leash and the hiking pole from Alex so she could get her pictures. In just a few seconds, they were on their way again.

"It just keeps getting better," Alex said when they were out of hearing range of the moose. "I've never seen a moose before."

"And it never gets old," Cole added. "No matter how many moose or elk or even golden eagles I see, I'm always in awe."

They hiked in silence for a stretch and were almost back to the trailhead when Alex tripped on a rock. She clutched her hiking pole and automatically put one hand out to Maisie, and Cole, who was right behind her, righted her before she could fall.

"Steady there," he said softly. "Did your leg give out?"

Alex shook her head and looked at the ground. "Maybe I'm getting tired, but I was sure I lifted my foot over that rock." She looked down at the offending rock, sucked in her breath, and sank to one knee.

"What? What is it? Are you hurt?" Cole knelt beside her and focused his attention on Alex's leg. Maisie squeezed in next to them.

Alex shook her head and picked up an object that had been sitting under the rock. She held out her hand to Cole. "What's this?" she asked.

Cole took it from her and examined the small round container. He rubbed a bit of dirt off of it and noted the corrosion on the top. There were small dents in the cover, as if someone had used it for a very long time. "I think it's a compass. It's very old, and made out of brass. I think it's been here a long time."

"Look on the bottom, it's engraved with something," Alex pointed out as he turned the compass over.

Cole looked closer. "D. R. Interesting. And look, it opens." He worked it open and held it out to Alex.

"It is a compass," she said as she took it from his hand.

CHAPTER SEVEN

Alex turned it one way and then the other as Cole watched.

"Oh, it doesn't work. It's stuck in one place. That's too bad."

Cole took it from her and examined it, flicked a little latch on the side and then moved it around. "Here, I think it does work. It has a safety to keep the needle from moving when it's being carried. I think it's working now," he said as the little arrow moved with the movement of his hand.

"Do you suppose someone dropped it?" Alex asked, looking around to see if there was anything else nearby.

Cole examined the rock Alex had tripped over. The outline of the container was clearly imprinted in the dirt. It had obviously been under the rock for a while. It appeared that someone had intentionally put it under the rock. It was a good place too, Cole thought, because the rock kept it away from the elements and intact.

He shook his head. "I don't think so. I think someone put it there on purpose, a long, long time ago, although why anyone would do that is beyond me. If you have a compass out here and know how to use it, you would keep it with you. Anyone who was coming back for it is probably long gone. Anyway, it's a great souvenir for you." He handed it back.

She looked up at him and realized Cole was looking at her. Their faces were only inches apart and Alex had to look back down to keep from kissing him.

"It's okay if I keep it?"

Cole shrugged and focused on her voice to pull his attention away from her lips. He had almost kissed her and she had pulled away. "Sure, you found it." His voice was a little gruff.

Alex put the lid on the compass and stuck it in her jacket pocket. They replaced the rock and continued down the trail to the Jeep.

"Want to see a few more sights before we head back?" Cole asked when they were settled in the vehicle.

Alex nodded and looked around. They were parked in a trail parking lot at the edge of lake. "I would like that. I don't know how you get anything done living out here. I just want to sit and watch the mountains and the sky. I love how the blue of the sky shows off the gray of the rocks and the snow topping them. Look how the lake reflects it all."

Cole laughed. "I think it's different knowing you can see it every day and don't have to leave if you don't want to, but there are days when all I want to do is sit and watch the clouds go by and the shadows on the mountains change." He put the Jeep in gear, and they drove back to the main road.

They stopped several times for Alex to take photos, so by the time they got back to the ranch, it was getting late.

Mary Louise waved them down as they got to the office. "How was your picnic? You look like you had fun, but I'm glad you're back. Cole, Buck has a problem with one of the horses," she said. "It's probably not serious, but he wanted to talk to you as soon as you came back."

The older woman turned to Alex after Cole loped off in the direction of the stables. "It's just beautiful out here, isn't it? Of course, I don't hike, but I love the mountains, don't you? Are you going to go horseback riding? There's nothing like horseback riding in the mountains and Cole is a natural on a horse. He's so sweet, isn't he?" She only stopped for breath when the phone in the office rang. "Oh, I have to go, I'll see you later."

Alex stood silently for a moment and then called Maisie. "She's quite the character, isn't she?" she asked the dog. "Come on, let's go home."

It was dark by the time Cole and Buck got done working with the horses. He and Buck walked back to his cabin where Mary Louise was just finishing up making dinner. She had made enchiladas with her special Spanish rice. The men washed up and joined her at the table. Cole's cabin was attached to the office and was larger than the other cabins, two stories with a cathedral ceiling and a loft. The west wall was mostly huge glass windows that allowed a view of Medicine Bow Peak and Sugarloaf Mountain, when it wasn't dark. Mary Louise chatted about her day while the men concentrated on their food.

"Did you enjoy your hike and your picnic?"

Cole nodded. "It was nice. We hiked up to Lost Lake and had our picnic there. Your choice of dishes was a hit." He leaned over and gave her a peck on the cheek. "You know how much I like your pretzel bites."

"Well, that young woman seems nice. She seems a bit sad though," Mary Louise continued. "Did she tell you about her past at all? It's odd that she came here on her own, no family or friends, you know. Anyway, it's good that you got some time away, you work too hard."

Cole and Buck exchanged glances. Neither was surprised that Mary Louise wanted to know more about the woman in Cabin One, but they were both surprised she didn't already know Alex's life history.

Cole shook his head. "We've talked a little about her past. I've discovered she's a pretty private person. I do know that she's in between jobs. She had a car accident about a year ago and has had a rough time of it since then." He and Mary Louise didn't have many secrets between them, but he would let Alex share her story with Mary Louise if she chose to.

Mary Louise looked from her husband to Cole and nodded. "I wondered. I saw her limping. Did she hurt her leg hiking? Wouldn't that be awful? It's too bad that she had to take a vacation by herself, but you can keep her company." Her look brightened as she looked at Cole. "She likes you, I'm sure of it."

"Now, Mary Louise, let's not get ahead of ourselves here," Buck admonished his wife. "He's only known her a couple of days. We've always respected the privacy of our guests, let's keep it that way."

Mary Louise started to speak and decided against it. She and Buck had only known each other a couple of days before she knew he was the man she had been waiting for. They had gotten married less than three months later. But Mary Louise could be patient. After all, Alex Bennington was the one, Cole had told her so.

"I wanted to talk to you about something else," Cole said, turning to Buck. "We found an old compass out on the trail today. I mean, it was really old. It looked like it had been hidden."

Buck considered. "I don't know anything about a lost compass, but I do know there are some stories about a treasure being buried around here. I don't think there's much to them, but you know how people like to tell tales."

"A treasure?" Mary Louise's voice got quiet. She pushed her glasses up and looked at Buck. "You've never said anything about a treasure," she accused her husband. "Why haven't I heard anything about a treasure around here?" She couldn't believe there was something about this place she didn't know.

"It's just stories," Buck replied, rising from the table, and taking his plate to the sink. He would help Mary Louise clean up before they headed home for the evening. "Stories to tell around the campfire."

Alex didn't see Cole the rest of the day, but after dinner, she and Maisie took advantage of the evening and went for a short walk. The sun had set behind the mountains, but there was still plenty of light for a walk.

There was no car next door to indicate her neighbors were home and after a moment of wondering what the young couple was really up to, she put them out of her mind.

Alex approached the cabin where Jackie and Steve Cooper were staying and waved at them and John Campbell, who was seated at the table with them.

"Hello, have you come to visit?" John asked Alex.

"Oh, no." Alex was immediately flustered to think they thought she had come over uninvited just to visit. "We're just out for a little walk. It's beautiful out tonight."

"It is beautiful," Jackie replied, "and John was just trying to be funny. But seriously, come on up and visit for a bit."

"I don't want to interrupt." Alex was feeling even more uncomfortable.

"Nonsense," Steve said. "We're just telling old stories and we've all heard them a dozen times."

Alex and Maisie walked up the three steps to the deck, Steve and John stood and Steve pulled out a chair for Alex. "We can't stay too long, we want to get back before it gets completely dark."

"We understand that," John stood again. "Would you like something to drink? We're having wine." Alex nodded and John disappeared into the cabin. He was back a minute later, and Alex accepted the glass of wine he handed her.

"Thanks so much." Alex took a sip, wondering what to say. She was a little rusty on conversation skills, but then again, she had no problem talking to Cole. "Did you go hiking today?"

The three nodded. "We go out everyday, we have our favorite trails and then we like to explore new areas," Steve said.

"You've been out here before, right?" Alex asked.

Jackie nodded. "Every year for about ten years, even before Cole bought the place. It's a lot nicer now, and we love that we can rent UTV's and do things like going fly fishing."

"Cole took me yesterday," Alex said and then noticed Jackie's raised eyebrows. "I mean, he invited me on a fishing trip. Apparently, there was a cancellation, and they had an extra space available. We went with another couple. It was a lot of fun, but I didn't catch anything."

"That happens sometimes," John said, "and you can't go wrong with Cole and the young men working for him. They're all good guys."

They talked about the weather and exchanged stories about the wildlife they had seen so far. Alex settled in and soaked in the stories of their adventures. It wasn't until Maisie stood up to stretch, that

Alex realized she should have already walked back to her cabin. It was completely dark.

"That's no problem," John said, when she mentioned it. "I'm happy to walk you back. I could stand to stretch my legs a bit before I go back to my own cabin."

They said their goodnights, then Alex and John started down the path.

"It's a little creepy out here at night, isn't it?" Alex asked.

"It can be, I guess," John said. "It's easy to be intimidated by how big the area is and how few people are out here."

"I think you're right," Alex replied. "And it's so dark."

John laughed. "It is dark, that's for sure. It seems even more isolated when it storms."

That made Alex laugh too. "The other night when it stormed, I swear I was about to be murdered by some maniac stalking my cabin."

"Really?" John was suddenly serious.

"Really," Alex replied with a smile. "It was Cole, just checking to see if anyone in the cabins needed anything. I saw his shadow and by the time he knocked on the door, I was looking for something to bash him with."

"And did you?" John asked.

"No, but Maisie totally tackled him the minute I opened the door." She smiled at the memory. "I'm afraid we didn't make a very good impression."

"Well, he seems to have forgiven you." John stopped at her deck steps. "We're here. I'll wait until you get inside. Have a good night."

Alex went up the stairs and to the door. As she opened it, she waved back to John and watched him walk away. It was only a second or two before he disappeared into the dark.

"He's a nice guy," Alex told Maisie. "They all are. I never expected to get to know anyone while we were here and look at us, we have all kinds of new friends." She ruffled Maisie's fur on her neck. "Let's go to bed."

The air was fresh and crisp the next morning, and Alex and Maisie were ready for a new adventure. The hike and picnic with Cole had been great and it had been sweet of him to treat her to a picnic feast. Her legs only protested a little from yesterday's hike, but they loosened up with a walk around part of the lake.

Cole was waiting on her deck when she and Maisie returned. Maisie dashed up the steps and bounded over to Cole. He stopped her before she could knock both him and the chair over and scrubbed her fur with his hands.

"Well, hello there." Alex greeted him as she walked up the steps and sat in the chair next to Cole. "What are you doing today?"

"I was going to do paperwork and then help Buck service one of the UTV's," Cole replied, "but both Mary Louise and Buck shooed me away, told me to go and enjoy the day." He shook his head. "It makes me wonder who's the boss in this outfit."

Alex laughed. "So, what are you going to do with all this new-found freedom?"

"I absolutely don't know, that's why I came over here. What are your plans for today?"

Alex considered. "We went for a short walk, but we're a little lazy today, so we weren't planning on hiking. We don't have any plans set in stone, but I was thinking we could go for a drive."

Cole thought for a moment. "I have an idea. I'll be back in an hour." He turned to walk away.

"Do I need my pack and gear?" Alex called after him.

He turned back, but just for a moment. "Absolutely, and some sunscreen." He jogged off towards his cabin.

"Well then, Maisie, I guess we'll have a surprise day, but we'll still have an adventure, I'm thinking."

He was back with a UTV exactly an hour later to find Alex and Maisie waiting for him on the front porch.

Cole helped Alex with a helmet and goggles, Maisie got in the back, and they were off.

Cole drove a few miles on the highway, then turned off onto a dirt road that wound through a forest of pine trees. The wind rippled their shirts and Alex was glad for the helmet and goggles, even though she was sure her hair was going to be a mess when she took them off. She never imagined when she decided to come here that she would be flying down the road in a UTV with a handsome cowboy, the trees whizzing by, without a care in the world.

Cole slowed down from time to time and stopped completely when a waterfall came into view. Without a thought for her hair, Alex removed the helmet and goggles, then walked with Cole and Maisie to the rocky edge of the pool the waterfall made as it came off a cliff to flow into a small creek.

"Be careful, it's slick," Cole cautioned, and offered his arm. Alex accepted the help and they picked their way to a spot where the mist rose off of the water. Alex closed her eyes and lifted her face. It felt amazing, she thought, and just stood and basked in the feel of the water and the vibration the rushing water created under her feet.

When she finally opened her eyes, Cole had stepped away and was taking photos. She looked down and realized Maisie had struck the same pose and still stood, her face to the mist. Alex got out her phone and took some photos as well, pausing now and then to look at a shiny rock or a log that was caught in the rocks.

"Come on girls, you're getting all wet," Cole finally said, and helped Alex back across the rocks. He pulled towels out of a duffel behind his seat and offered one to Alex. She wiped her face, but Maisie just gave a good shake and let nature get rid of the water that had collected on her fur. They were on their way again minutes later, winding through the trees, going up and down hills and through valleys until the road opened up to a huge lake.

Alex gasped. It was beautiful and she felt like they were on the top of the world. The tops of the mountains off to the northwest were almost even with the horizon.

"Are we hiking here?" Alex asked as they removed their helmets. Cole replaced his with a ball cap that sported the CG Ranch logo and handed another one to Alex.

"We can walk a bit, but I'm feeling a little lazy, so I thought we would sit for awhile and enjoy the sunshine. And I brought us lunch."

"I like it."

Cole unpacked what appeared to be a big toolbox and handed Alex a water out of a small cooler.

Alex clapped her hands. "Another picnic? This is great. What did Mary Louise pack for us today?"

Cole laughed. "I'm afraid you have to rely on my cooking skills today."

"So, peanut butter roll ups?" Alex teased.

"Well, I didn't have a lot of time to plan something elaborate, but I managed to do better than peanut butter."

Cole spread a blanket on the ground and retrieved several plastic containers and a basket wrapped in a dish towel. "No wine today, just water and a jug of iced tea, if you want it. I don't really know your tastes, so I brought a few different things."

"I think you do know my tastes," Alex exclaimed as Cole opened containers and handed her a plastic plate. She took several ham chunks and some cheese, then hesitated as she started to select a tortilla-wrapped pinwheel.

"It's a salmon roll up." He shrugged. "I wasn't sure about those."

Alex selected one and took a bite. "Umm. I like it. I wouldn't have thought to use salmon in a roll up, but it's way better than peanut butter. I taste cream cheese and see the lettuce. Is that dill? Nice."

Cole unwrapped the basket and offered it to her.

"What's this?"

"Irish soda bread, my mom's recipe. Here's butter for it."

Alex took a slice. "It's still warm. How did you manage that?"

"That's why I needed an hour. I made it this morning," Cole explained. "Here, you need some butter."

"Every time I think it can't get better, you surprise me," Alex said as she buttered her bread. She took a bite. "It's so good," she said as soon as she had swallowed. "I love it. And raisins too. You're going to spoil me."

Cole smiled as he buttered his own bread. That was exactly what he wanted to do, everyday for the rest of his life. Earlier, when he saw her standing in the mist of the waterfall, he was so taken he couldn't move, could only stare. A moment later, though, he had moved, so he could take a picture and record the moment. He loved that she didn't care about her hair, or makeup, or that her clothes were wet. She was just enjoying the moment.

When they couldn't eat anymore, Cole packed up the leftovers and everything went back into the toolbox, which he locked with a padlock, and strapped it back onto the UTV.

"Don't want anyone stealing our bread, I see." Alex said.

"Bears. I don't want bears stealing our bread," Cole explained. "One's not likely to wander around here in the daylight, but I'm not taking chances."

They walked along the lake's shore, stopping to skip rocks or throw a stick for Maisie to fetch. Cole threw one into the lake and they watched as Maisie sprang after it.

"I had no idea she liked water... or would fetch, for that matter." Alex laughed as Maisie splashed back out of the water with the stick. She shook and water went flying. Alex turned to avoid the spray and bumped into Cole.

"Steady there," he said as he took her arm to steady her. They stood that way for a moment before Maisie nudged their legs. Cole mentally cursed as Alex moved away. He could have kissed her, would have kissed her, but the moment was gone. They turned and walked back to the UTV for the ride home.

He might not have gotten the kiss, but being able to spend the day with Alex was priceless, he decided as he put the UTV in gear and pointed it in the direction of the ranch.

CHAPTER EIGHT

"Care to share leftovers for dinner?" Cole asked when they were back at the ranch. They had stored the UTV and put the helmets in the UTV shed for Buck to put away before walking across the driveway.

"Yes, please," Alex replied, realizing it was really time for dinner. "I could have that bread for every meal. I'm not sure my hips would like it, but I might be willing to risk getting fat."

"It was an everyday staple for the Irish, still is, I believe, since it's faster and easier to make than regular bread. And it only takes a few ingredients."

"Could we eat at my cabin? I need to feed Maisie."

Cole was fine with that. They carried the food into Alex's cabin and put it out on the counter. Alex got plates and silverware for them.

"How did it get to be dinner time?" Alex asked as she set things on the table, then got Maisie's food for her. "Did we really go that far?"

"Farther than you might think," Cole replied. "We can eat on the deck if you want." He helped her carry everything outside.

"I love eating out on my deck," Alex said, "it's just so nice out here. Oh, do you want some wine? We're not hiking or driving tonight."

"You stay here, I'll get it," Cole said as he went back inside.

The food was just as good as it had been at lunch, Alex decided, as she and Cole enjoyed the last of their wine and the last of the daylight.

"You're enjoying yourself, aren't you?"

Alex nodded. "I truly am," she said. "This wasn't supposed to be a trip I took by myself, but you've helped turn it from something sad to something fun. I never really thought I would be riding in a UTV, even if James had come with me, I don't think that's something we would have done. But I loved it, and I can't wait to go again."

They talked about everyday things until the air turned chilly. Finally, Maisie stood and yawned, her signal that it was time for bed.

"I guess that's my cue," Cole said, standing up as well. "I've got to get up early in the morning, I have paperwork to do that seems to never end. I prefer to get it done while everything is quiet."

"Thank you for taking me today," Alex said as she gathered their empty glasses.

Cole stepped to her and kissed her on the forehead. "Thanks for agreeing to come. I enjoyed it too." He bounded down the stairs and with a quick wave, disappeared into the darkness.

Alex sighed. "Why am I disappointed?" she asked Maisie as she let the dog in the door. "Did I think he was going to kiss me madly and have his way with me?"

Maisie let out a soft woof. "Okay, maybe I did," Alex replied. "But he didn't, so let's go to bed."

Alex woke up the next morning with a plan. She didn't want to make Cole miss another day's work, so she loaded the SUV with a pack and a lunch and headed west toward the mountain peaks. She stopped at a flat place along with the highway that had an observation deck. The deck looked like a crumbling castle, made out of rock. The view was not disappointing and there were dozens of groundhog-looking creatures darting in and out of the rocks that were strewn on the ground below. Marmots, Alex decided, as she remembered reading in the brochure. She took pictures, and while Maisie definitely wanted to investigate, she settled for sniffing the air and watching the creatures from a distance.

They drove on to a lake along the highway and took a short walk to a waterfall. This was a popular place so there were families everywhere. They could see trout swimming in the little creek that created the waterfall. Maisie was especially interested in the fish moving under the surface of the water, but again, she didn't bother them.

Alex sat on a bench near the little lake and looked at the magnificent peaks holding court over the landscape. She and James had planned to take a delayed honeymoon and come out here. That had played a part in her decision to come here now. They were planning to hike to the top of the middle peak. Alex blinked back the tears that threatened. That wasn't going to happen now, she had tried it without James and had failed.

Alex and Maisie moved on, driving down the winding road to the west of the mountains. She had never been in this area of the country and knew she would have to come back another time. She found a small town that offered several hot springs, and Alex pulled off. There was a restroom, so she changed into shorts and waded into one of the natural pools along a river that ran through the town. Maisie sat on shore and waited to assist if Alex needed help, but the water was too hot for the big dog.

Alex sighed as her body absorbed the water's heat. Steam rose over her, and Alex relaxed, truly relaxed, glad she had stopped.

Alex had just parked at her cabin and let Maisie out when Cole walked up to her. She wasn't expecting to see him, was aware that her hair was a mess, both from the steam of the hot springs and the wind blowing off the mountains.

He didn't appear to notice.

"Hi there," he greeted them. Maisie rushed to him for a rub and nearly melted onto the ground when he obliged. "I missed you this morning, did you go hiking?"

Alex knew he disapproved of people hiking alone but didn't admit that had made a difference in her plans.

She shook her head. "We just went for a drive. It's beautiful out here. We found a hot springs so I tried that. It was wonderful." She sniffed her arm. "I may still smell like minerals, but it felt good."

Cole nodded. "I bet. I love hot springs and I wish I could have gone with you, but I had to lead a couple of trail rides." He followed her lead and sniffed his arm. "I may smell a little bit like horse, but I can live with it. I've smelled worse."

"You grew up with horses." It was a statement, not a question.

Cole nodded again. "On a ranch about three hours north of here. It's a good place to grow up. How about you, do you ride?"

"I have a few times, but not since the accident," Alex replied. "I don't really know how it would go, so it's something I would have to try again. The doctors didn't say I couldn't. Can you stay awhile? I think I have a beer in the refrigerator."

They walked into her cabin as she talked.

"That sounds great," he replied and accepted the beer. She got one for herself and led the way to the deck.

They sat in chairs as Alex talked about her day. This was vacation, she decided, sitting on a deck with a good-looking man and enjoying the afternoon.

Alex jumped. "What's that?"

Cole jumped out of his chair, beer in hand, and bounded down the stairs. "It sounds like gun shots. Stay here." Three more shots rang out.

Alex looked at Maisie, who had jumped up as well. "Yeah, right. We're not just sitting here. Get your leash and come on." Unlike Cole, Alex set down her beer before fastening Maisie's leash. They moved much slower than Cole had, walking down the steps and around the cabin.

There was no one in sight and it was quiet.

"Where did he go?" Alex asked. Maisie whined softly and pulled on her leash. "Do you think it's safe? Maybe we wait at the office?" They walked over to the office, sat down on the steps, Maisie still on full alert.

Cole skidded to a stop at the end of the driveway of the ranch.

A pale blue and very old, very small van was spewing white smoke from its underside. An older lady who looked like she just stepped out of the 1970s hippie movement was standing beside it. Cole stared, he couldn't help it.

She wore round black, thick-rimed glasses that took up much of her face and had blond hair with strands of gray in loose braids hanging over her shoulders. She wore a long, flowing skirt that had some sort of green pattern on it with a brown tank top, covered with a fringed leather jacket that he knew existed, but had never seen in person. She wore Birkenstock sandals and a battered straw cowboy hat. A chunky turquoise and silver necklace, turquoise bracelets and rings on nearly every finger added to the seventies' look.

"It just popped a couple of times and started smoking," she told Cole as he reached her.

"But you're okay?"

"Oh yes, but Alfie, what am I going to do about him?" she moaned.

"Alfie?"

The woman gestured to the van. It appeared to be a 1960s van, a Dodge van, Cole decided as he took a closer look. It looked as if it had seen better days.

"My Alfie. We've traveled together for years, in fact, I bought him new in 1969. It would be a shame to lose him now, when we have so much more traveling to do."

Cole continued to look at the vehicle. He didn't know where she had traveled, but it looked like Alfie had gotten the worst of the deal.

He didn't have time to respond as Alex, Maisie and Buck pulled up in the side-by-side. Alex had flagged Buck down as he drove by and asked him for a ride.

"What's all the commotion?" Buck asked. "Never mind, I can see it for myself. Whew, that is some van. Is that a '69?"

The woman nodded. "It is. I'm Sandy," the woman introduced herself to the three of them. "My life is in that van. And I just can't leave him here to die. I'm not quite sure I know what to do now." Her lip started to quiver.

"It's okay, we'll think of something," Cole replied. He didn't want to her to break down and cry. "Is there someone you can call?"

Sandy shook her head. "Not really. I can call my travel insurance company, but I know from experience it sometimes takes a day or two when I'm out somewhere remote."

"That's too bad," Alex said. "Is there a car mechanic around here?"

"In Laramie," Buck replied. "Unless we call a tow truck, it will never make it that far."

They were still discussing options when Danny and Noah pulled up, back from a fishing trip. The Coopers and John pulled in right behind Danny and Noah, and everyone had to get out of their vehicles to find out what was going on. There were introductions and many more discussions on what to do with the van. In the end, Cole and Buck decided to pull it into the ranch with the side-by-side and go from there.

"I can look at it if you want me to," John Campbell told Sandy. "I know my way around motors, especially those that are almost as old as me."

"You're sweet." Sandy cocked her head towards John. "I appreciate your help. I've had him forever. And I can pay you for the work."

"I don't think that's necessary," he replied with a smile. "I haven't had the fun of looking at an old engine for a long time. You can pay for parts if we need them, though."

Buck opened his mouth to say something and closed it again. Alex was sure he was going to offer to help until he saw the look that passed between John and Sandy. She saw it too, and decided John was already smitten with the older woman, after a whopping three minutes.

Sandy steered while Buck pulled the van into the drive. The others drove up to the office and Alex, Maisie and Cole walked the short distance back to the office. Cole picked up the beer bottle he had dropped while running toward the road.

"What are you going to do with Sandy while she's waiting for the repairs?"

Cole looked down at Alex. "What do you mean?"

"Is she going to stay here or is someone taking her to Centennial to the motel? I saw one there."

"Hmm. I hadn't thought that far ahead." Cole stopped and looked around. "I don't have any extra cabin space here, and I'm pretty sure the motel in town is booked as well."

"I figured that," Alex said. "I could offer to let her stay with me a day or two."

"I'm not sure I like that idea. We don't even know her."

Alex laughed. "A few days ago you didn't know me and yet, here we are."

Alex had just finished her sentence when Cole broke into a run, shouting at Buck to stop.

Alex caught up just in time to hear him tell Buck not to unhook the van yet.

"What's wrong?" Sandy got out of the van.

"If we put the van over by that grouping of trees, could John work on it there?" Cole turned to Sandy. "I was thinking if we could park it where you could still stay with it, you would have access to all of your things. Do you have a tent?"

"Sure," Sandy replied. "I always sleep in my tent unless the weather's bad. I use the van for a backup place to sleep, but I love being out in nature. I was actually headed down the road to a little campground I saw last time I was out here."

"We don't offer camping here, remember?" Buck asked Cole. "There's no bathroom facilities."

"True," Cole said, shrugging, "but she could use the bathroom in the Commons. It would only be for a few days."

Buck looked like he had doubts, but Cole was the boss.

"Are you sure?" Sandy asked. "I'm already causing a lot of trouble. I don't want to impose."

Alex looked at Cole. He didn't look sure, but she was pretty certain that helping ladies in distress might be one of his things.

"It's no trouble. Buck, let's set her up over there."

"I have a better idea." John stepped back over and into the conversation. "How about we park her over in my second parking space? There's shade there and she can use my facilities. Shoot, as far as that goes, she can use my extra bedroom." He smiled at Sandy, who nodded.

"I would be okay with that," she said, "and then we wouldn't have to worry about the tent."

Buck looked at Cole and shrugged.

"That's what we'll do then." They were both adults and could make their own decisions, Cole decided.

He and Alex, along with Maisie, walked back to her cabin. Alex found them each another beer.

Cole eventually stirred. "It looks like it could rain. I had better get back and help Mary Louise finish getting ready for the potluck tonight. In case you didn't know, we all get together one night a week to socialize. It's Mary Louise's favorite time."

Alex laughed. "She does like people, doesn't she?"

Cole's potluck was popular with guests, Alex decided, as she walked into the Commons with a fruit salad. It looked like everyone from every cabin was here. She didn't have much to contribute, so this would have to do. Alex set her bowl on the table with the rest of the food and found a place to sit. She didn't see Cole or Mary Louise anywhere. They were probably outside. It had rained, but the sun was out now, setting over the mountains. She saw several people out on the patio visiting, including the Coopers and John Campbell. Her next-door neighbors were sitting on a sofa near the fireplace having a whispered conversation. Alex really wanted to know what they were talking about.

Cole came in a few minutes later with a platter of grilled hamburgers and hot dogs. Mary Louise and Buck followed him, each carrying a covered dish.

Alex hurried over to them. "Can I help?"

"We just need to set them on the serving table," Mary Louise replied, "if you can make us a little room."

"It smells delicious." Alex moved a few of the dishes out of the way and Mary Louise set her dish on the table. Cole and Buck did the same.

Alex realized she hadn't really talked to Buck since she'd been here. He reminded her of the grizzled cowboy in all the westerns she'd ever seen, tall and lean with slightly bowed legs. His hair was gray, what she could see of it, since he was wearing a weathered cowboy hat, and he had a gray handlebar mustache. Very handsome, Alex thought.

He wore crisply ironed blue jeans with a western plaid shirt that even had the pearl buttons. His brown cowboy boots were scuffed and worn. His smile was warm and inviting, and his eyes were a friendly brown. He didn't seem to have much to say, Alex thought as she watched him with Mary Louise, but then again, maybe he did more listening than talking with Mary Louise around.

"Food's ready, everyone," Cole announced, and people gathered to make a line at the serving table. When it was her turn, Alex looked at all the available choices and wondered how she was going to decide. A few minutes later, her plate held a hamburger, Mary Louise's baked beans, potato salad and a piece of chocolate cake topped with chocolate frosting and sprinkles. She couldn't go wrong with that. It was probably more than she could eat, but she wasn't going to worry about that now. She found a place to sit at the end of the long table in the middle of the room, put there for just this event, and took her first bite of the sandwich.

"You look like you just found Heaven," Cole observed as he sat down next to her.

Alex opened her eyes, raised her hand to cover her mouth, and swallowed.

"So good, just so good."

"Thanks," Cole said. "We aim to please."

"It's nice that you do this," Alex said as she put her fork down after a bite of potato salad. "It makes it feel like summer camp."

Cole looked at her with raised eyebrows. "You went to summer camp?"

"Well, no, but this is what I imagine it would be like, everyone gathering and eating together."

They were interrupted when Sandy and John sat down across from them. "Hello, is it okay if we sit here?" Sandy greeted them.

"You remember Cole," John said to Sandy, "and this is Alex. Alex, this is Sandy Bradson."

"It's nice to meet you," Alex replied, and they shook hands across the table.

"Have you settled in?" Cole asked.

Sandy nodded. "It's nice of you to let me stay while Alfie gets repaired."

"Let me know how much extra I owe for Sandy," John said, "since she's using my spare bedroom."

"Nothing," Cole replied. "She's your guest, so she's our guest too. All you need to do is let Mary Louise know if you need extra towels."

"We appreciate it." John offered his hand and Cole shook it. There would be no more discussion.

"Sandy," Alex said a moment later. "Do you live in Alfie all the time? I don't mean to be nosy, but I always thought it would be fun to drive around the country and live in a van."

"I have a house in Bloomington, Indiana, but if the weather is nice, I'm usually out and about."

"She's an artist, you know," John explained. "She paints the most beautiful watercolors. They're in galleries all over the country."

Sandy nodded. "I used to be a college art professor, but after my husband died about ten years ago, I decided to retire. Now I drive Alfie around and choose my subjects, you know, flowers, landscapes, people, wildlife, whatever I feel like at the moment, then I sketch and paint. When I get home, I mat and frame them and send them to different galleries, depending on who needs restocked."

"So, how many galleries are we talking about?" Cole asked, interested.

Sandy shrugged. "I'm not exactly sure, maybe seventy-five or eighty, I suppose. I lose track."

Cole whistled, and Alex was sure her surprise showed. "Wow, that's impressive. I don't even know what to say. You're probably famous, aren't you, and here we are having supper with you."

Sandy shrugged again. "Some of my paintings might be, but I'm not really. I'm just me."

"Do you have any paintings with you?" she asked. "I would love to see them."

"Sure I do, honey, you just stop over sometime, and I'll show you what I've been doing."

Alex made a mental note to do just that, after she looked her up on the internet. Alex drew sketches, mostly of clothes and back-packs and things like that, but she used pencil colors or markers when coloring them. Maybe she should try watercolor. She might not be any good at it, but it sounded like fun.

Alex tried to help clean up, but Mary Louise wouldn't hear of it. "You go sit and visit. Enjoy yourself. This will only take a few minutes." She smiled. "We're pros at it by now."

Alex and Maisie found a cozy chair that was empty, Alex curled up in it with Maisie at her feet. She smiled as two little girls ap-proached them. Alex had seen them at the playground but hadn't talked to them. She knew exactly what was coming.

"Can we pet her?" one asked. She was about eight, wearing bright pink leggings and a princess t-shirt, long, blonde hair was caught up in a ponytail.

The other nodded. Alex figured she was about six and was also wearing leggings in a bright green, with a tie-dyed t-shirt and the same blonde hair, but instead of a ponytail, it swirled around her shoulders. Both of them had bright blue eyes and were cute as but-tons.

"Sure you can." Alex reached over and rubbed Maisie's head. The girls followed suit, barely touching the fur.

Normally, service dogs weren't supposed to be handled by other people, but Maisie refused to adhere to that rule. She loved people, and Alex was sure she could be a comfort dog, if that's what was needed. Alex knew that as she grew stronger, she would need Maisie less for physical help, but the comfort and companionship she pro-vided was always going to be needed.

She and the staff that provided Maisie as a service dog, had discussed options for that, and it was decided that Maisie would stay with Alex. Alex had been relieved. They had become family now, and Alex honestly didn't know what she would do without the big dog. She was glad she didn't have to find out.

She stayed for a few minutes longer after the girls wandered away. Cole was nowhere to be seen, so Alex decided to call it a night.

CHAPTER NINE

Alex protested when Maisie woke her up by tugging on the sleeve of her t-shirt.

"It's not even light out," Alex groaned as she pushed her hair out of her face and sat up on the side of the bed. She put on her slippers and sweatshirt, then shuffled to the patio door. It wasn't exactly dark, she decided, the sky had a grayish dawn look to it. She opened the door and was met with a light mist. It gave the landscape a surreal look. The trees were drooping with the weight of the water, and except for one or two that were close to the cabin, they were blurred. It was foggy, but not exactly foggy. The whole scene was a little eerie. Maisie, standing next to her, must have felt it too because she didn't move.

"Oh, no, out you go," Alex told her. "If I have to go out, so do you. You're the one who woke me up. I was happy snuggled in bed, and asleep, I might add, so come on."

They were both a little wet when they came back inside a few minutes later. Alex dried them both off with towels, then checked her phone. It was already after eight, which surprised her. No wonder Maisie needed to go out.

They shared scrambled eggs, although Maisie also had oatmeal and some pureed pumpkin with hers. Alex added sausage to make a breakfast burrito.

She was surprised at how hungry she was. Maybe it was the hiking, or the fresh air, but either way, it was okay. It had been a long time since food was anything more than something she needed to stay alive. The food at the rehab center was okay, but it was nothing special.

Alex decided she may as well do laundry and straighten the cabin since she was confined to indoors. Okay, she admitted to herself, she wasn't confined, but she wasn't hiking in this weather either. She shivered at the thought. She doubted the trails were visible for any distance, and seeing the mountains would be impossible. Alex imagined if she took several steps off the trail, she wouldn't be able to find her way back. She wasn't even sure she could find her way around the lake right here. Another shiver ran down her spine. A day in would be great.

After lunch, she revised that decision. She was ready to get out, so with raincoat on, she tucked her computer inside and she and Maisie headed to the Commons.

Apparently, every else had the same idea. Merri and Anthony were hunched over a laptop and Jackie and Steve Cooper were playing cards with John Campbell and the lady with the broken-down van. Sandy. Alex finally remembered her first name but couldn't come up with a last name.

The two little girls from the night before were putting together a puzzle with their parents, and another couple was watching a movie on the television. The scent of buttered popcorn filled the air. It felt a little like a party and Alex wasn't sure she felt like a party.

She almost turned around and left, but Jackie was already waving her over.

"How are you doing?" she asked Alex. "And you, Maisie?"

"We're good, we just decided we needed a change of scenery," Alex replied. "You all look like you're having fun." She turned to Sandy. "I'm so sorry about your van. Have you had any luck getting it fixed?"

"Oh no, John says it needs a part. We had to order it, so we're just waiting on that." Sandy smiled at John, who grinned back. Jackie and Steve shared their own smile.

Was there a romance budding here? Alex wondered. It certainly looked like it even though Sandy had only been here, what, less than a day? Well, good for them, she decided.

She excused herself and found a cozy, padded chair. She opened her laptop to look at emails. There was nothing that was important, so she switched her attention to researching her compass.

Alex was engrossed in the story about compasses in the Civil War when Cole walked in a little later.

He stopped to chat with the Coopers, John and Sandy, and the couple with the kids before stepping over to Alex and Maisie. He crouched to ruffle Maisie's fur, causing Alex to look up. She didn't even realize he had come in. She looked at Maisie in amazement because she hadn't alerted her.

"Look at you, two beautiful girls socializing," he said in a low voice that made Alex's stomach flutter. She smiled and blushed just a little.

"Not exactly socializing. How did you get in here without Maisie knowing?" She also spoke softly, so as not to be overheard.

"Oh, she knew, but she let me shush her so we wouldn't bother you. She is a pretty smart cookie." He ruffled Maisie's fur again. "What are you working on so intently?"

"I was just doing some research on my find." Alex whispered this time. She wasn't sure why she didn't want anyone to know about the compass, but she didn't.

Cole slightly cocked his head at the young couple at the desk. "What do you suppose they're up to, planning a murder maybe?"

Alex laughed out loud, drawing the attention of the card players, then put her hand over her mouth. "I have no idea, and yikes if they are. I don't suppose we'll ever know, will we?" She answered just as softly.

"So, what are you doing later?" Cole asked, changing the subject. "Would you like to go out to dinner with me this evening? I know a place that has a great atmosphere and some pretty good food."

Alex looked down at Maisie. "What do you think, should we accept?"

Maisie woofed softly.

"I guess we would," Alex answered.

"I'll pick you up in a couple of hours, but for now, I have paperwork to finish. Oh, and it's casual, if that's okay."

He was gone a moment later and Alex turned back to her computer, but she couldn't concentrate. She immediately started to second-guess herself. Was this a date? Was she ready to date? She twisted her ring on her finger. Was it not a date, were they just going out as friends? She realized he never spoke about his relationships, for all she knew, he had a girlfriend.

She gathered up her things and walked back to her cabin, then spent the time she had left getting ready. Should she wear a dress? She had tone or two, but she preferred wearing pants. Dresses meant her legs were visible and questions inevitably followed that she didn't want to answer. She considered a pair of white jeans and decided against those as well. He said it was casual. So maybe jeans. She didn't have many choices for clothes, but finally decided on skinny jeans and a pair of black ankle boots with a short heel. After changing several times, she chose a silky blue pullover blouse. She didn't have a blazer or sweater, but she had a blue jean jacket that would work.

She applied makeup for the first time since she'd been in Wyoming and curled her hair into waves that framed her face. She looked in the mirror and decided it was as good as it was going to get.

When she opened her door to Cole, Alex could only stare. Somewhere inside her head shouted date. Gone was her hiking buddy. In his place stood an honest-to-goodness Wyoming cowboy. He was still wearing the familiar t-shirt, but the flannel shirt was buttoned and tucked into a pair of crisp dark blue jeans and topped with a leather belt with a big, shiny belt buckle. He was wearing a pair of black cowboy boots and a black cowboy hat. She could have swooned, if women did that anymore.

"Like what you see?' he asked with raised eyebrows.

IIis voice made her shiver a little. She cleared her throat. "Umm, yes, thanks, I do. You clean up nice. Nice hat." She was aware she was babbling, but couldn't stop herself.

He just smiled and reached down to rub Maisie's head. "So do you. So do you."

The bar was crowded, and country music played from somewhere, creating a festive air. People were having dinner, some were having drinks and several couples were dancing on a small dance floor. There wasn't a live band and Alex was happy about that. It was so difficult to hear when the music was loud.

A young woman came to ask for their drink orders and left menus. Alex took some time deciding since it all looked good but was ready to order when the waitress came back.

Alex couldn't help but notice the flirty looks she gave Cole, how she touched his arm and her smile and friendly laugh when he handed back his menu. The young woman might have a crush on him, Alex decided, as she handed back her own menu. She didn't get a friendly laugh and even the smile dimmed as she noticed the diamond on Alex's left hand.

"Oh Cole, congratulations. I had no idea you were engaged." She tried to make her voice light. "I didn't even think you were seeing anyone, but how exciting for you."

Several other patrons turned in their chairs and looked at them, clearly able to hear every word the server said.

"No, no, wait, Becca," Cole started, but she was gone. "We're not engaged." He trailed off.

Alex and Cole were left looking at each other in an awkward silence. Alex was mortified and couldn't seem to make her mouth work.

"Well," he finally said.

"I'm so sorry Cole, I didn't even think about my ring and the message it might send." Alex met his eyes.

Cole just smiled. "I think you just broke her heart."

"Did you date her?" Alex asked softly.

Cole shook his head. "Everyone here knows everyone else and we're friends, but no, I didn't date her. I don't date much." He shrugged, dismissing the incident.

"Aren't you worried she'll tell everyone?" Alex asked, still concerned. "Maybe I should take it off." She tugged at the ring and Cole immediately covered her hands with his.

"No, don't. When you're ready to take it off, then do it. But don't ever take it off for someone else, especially because you're worried about what people might think." He stroked her fingers with his thumb.

"Are you sure?" she asked, close to tears. "I mean, nobody at the ranch has said anything about it, so I didn't think about us being together in public and people getting the wrong idea."

"I'm sure. Look, here come our salads." He let go of her hands.

Becca set their salads down, and she wasn't rude, but she wasn't quite as friendly as she had been.

After she left, Cole picked up his fork and started on his salad. Alex hesitated. "Don't you think we should tell her the truth?"

"I don't," he replied. "She jumped to a conclusion. For all she knows, you could be a relative, you know, a widowed aunt or something."

Alex actually giggled. "Really? A widowed aunt? Wouldn't I be like, eighty or something?"

"Not necessarily. Maybe I have very young parents."

"Do you?" Alex cocked her head. "You know, you've never talked about your family. Do you have one?"

"I do, but that's a conversation for another time. Look, here's our dinner." He turned to Becca who carried two large plates.

"How's your steak?" Cole asked later, as Alex stabbed the last bite.

"I don't know why I don't eat more steak, it's so good." Alex had ordered a rib eye steak with vegetables. She couldn't believe how good it tasted and how much she had missed it. She looked at her plate that was nearly empty. She couldn't believe she had eaten it all.

Cole had removed his jacket and hat and the hat sat upside down on the large table of the booth they were sitting in. Alex had never seen a hat sitting that way, so she asked him about it.

"It's just to protect the brim," he said. "I could have left it on like some of the guys here, and if I was out on the dance floor, I'd be wearing it. I generally don't leave it sitting around."

Alex nodded. She totally understood. "I really don't know much about cowboys." she admitted.

Cole smiled. "I can teach you," he said in a low voice that sent her stomach into somersaults.

"That was really nice," Alex said as she opened the door to her cabin a while later. "I feel like it's been forever since I ate somewhere other than a fast-food place. Do you want to come in?"

Cole was holding the door so she and Maisie could go in. He shook his head, and Alex was disappointed. She would examine that emotion later, because Cole was speaking again.

"I've got to be up early in the morning. I have bookkeeping to catch up on, then Buck and I have a full day of work."

"I know you've taken off a lot of time, probably too much, to show me the area and hike with me." Alex paused. "I think I'll use the time to go into Laramie to get groceries."

"I've loved every minute of the time I've spent with you," Cole replied. He reached for her and gave her a long, sensuous kiss, then patted Maisie's head and walked back to the Jeep so he could park back by the barn.

All Alex could do was stand there and watch him go. Finally, she forced herself to move and closed the door. "Whew," she told Maisie. "That was intense. If I were a swooner, I would definitely do it now." And he made her want more, she realized. Much, much more.

Cole was just finishing the last of his paperwork, sipping on a cup of coffee and enjoying the quiet, when Mary Louise burst into his office, skirt flying behind her.

"You're engaged?" she almost shrieked. "Engaged, and I have to hear about it at the post office. How could you do that? Of course, I'm happy for you and Alex, ecstatic in fact, since I love you both, but why didn't you tell me?" Mary Louise paused to take a breath.

Cole stood up and engulfed her in a hug. "Shh, shh, we're not engaged."

Mary Louise pushed out of the hug and held him at arms length. "What do you mean you're not engaged? Everyone said they saw you and Alex at the bar last night, and she was wearing this great big diamond on her finger."

Cole cupped Mary Louise's face and kissed her gently on the forehead. "She was wearing a ring."

"But you just said," Mary Louise interrupted. "What is going on here?"

"Alex was wearing her engagement ring, the same engagement ring she's worn since we met her."

"Ohh," Mary Louise breathed.

"Becca Green saw it and immediately jumped to the conclusion that we must be engaged." Cole shrugged. "We tried to explain, but she was already across the room before I could get out of my chair, so we just left it. I didn't realize she was going to tell the whole town." He kissed her forehead again.

"You'll be the first to know if it happens, but you know Alex. She's carrying around the past, and she has to be free of that before we can build a relationship. We have to be patient."

"That's okay, then." Mary Louise was placated, at least for the moment. "But what about Alex? If she hears this, she could back away completely. What if she leaves?"

"Mary Louise, you have to trust it will all work out," Cole soothed, "because it will."

Alex and Maisie did a quick tour of Laramie, then took an hour to tour the Territorial Prison Museum. In the back of her mind, Alex thought she might find a compass similar to hers. No such luck, she decided, but it was full of history and interesting displays. She found books on area history in the gift shop and purchased it to read later.

After lunch at a little sandwich shop downtown, Alex and Maisie found a geological museum, which was just as interesting as the prison museum, but different. She enjoyed learning more about the state and had never given much thought as to how the past sculpted the landscape. She made a mental note of some of the sites around the rest of the state she would like to visit if she ever had the chance.

She walked through the aisles of the grocery store, restocking her food supply, picked up more beer and a bottle of wine in case Cole stopped by. Not that she intended to get him drunk and have her way with him, she thought. Her hand stopped in midair, still holding the wine bottle. Where had that come from? She shook the mental image away and finished her shopping.

By the time she got back to her cabin, Alex was ready to sit. Her leg ached, which surprised her, since she didn't think she had walked that much. Even so, hiking in the mountains was different than walking in stores. She supposed it was a different kind of stress on her leg. Grocery shopping was almost as hard as hiking up a mountain, she decided, as she carried a glass of iced tea out to the deck. The weather was spectacular, warm and sunny with just a light breeze.

After a short and unexpected nap in her chair, with Maisie dozing on the deck next to her, Alex decided she should do something constructive.

She went in the bathroom and splashed her face with water, grabbed her laptop and the two of them walked over to the Commons.

The building was empty when Alex wandered in with her laptop, Maisie following beside her. She found a desk that offered a computer and a printer, which might come in handy later, if she needed to print anything. After logging in, she skimmed through her emails and answered a few from coworkers, then sent a letter-type email to her parents to let them know all was good.

Once that was done, Alex switched to exploring when her compass might have been made. An hour later, she really only concluded that it was old, but she couldn't tell if it was from the 1850s or the 1920s.

She supposed it didn't matter, but the fact that it had initials engraved on it intrigued her. If, as Cole said, the compass was likely left there on purpose, then it begged the question, why? People just didn't leave their compasses behind, especially when they were out in the mountains. Having a compass could mean the difference between life and death out here, so a person wouldn't just ditch it. She could see losing it, but that didn't explain why it was under a rock.

It was a mystery, she decided. And she liked a good mystery. Maybe she would talk to Cole about the history of the area. She had looked it up but found very little information that was useful.

She had just closed her laptop when the door opened and the young couple from the cabin next door walked in.

"Hello, you two," she said, turning in her chair. "You're back early today."

The couple looked surprised and if she used her imagination, a little guilty. Alex still felt like they were up to something, but had no idea what that could be. She had only noticed yesterday that they had left their cabin before she woke up and didn't come back until after dark. She didn't think they were the hard-core hiking type, but if Alex were doing it, she would have just camped overnight.

"Oh, hi," Anthony said, and Merri waved. "We were just going to use the Wi-Fi for a little bit." Anthony held out a laptop to show her.

Alex stood. "You can sit here, I just finished." She and Maisie started toward the door.

As she moved across the room, Alex could hear the whispering. Was she limping? Alex straightened and made sure she wasn't. The whispering continued.

As she opened the door, Merri spoke to her.

"Um, do you know this area very well?"

Alex turned around. "Not really. This is my first trip out here. I've got the normal brochures and a trail map, but I'm not an avid hiker, so I'm pretty much sticking to the more popular trails. How about you guys?"

Anthony and Merri looked at each other, then back at Alex. "We don't know much about the area either, but we're trying to explore the whole area."

"I see you've put in some long days." Alex walked back towards them. "Have you thought about camping out overnight?"

They nodded in unison. "We're going to do that for sure. We just haven't really decided where or when."

"There are lots of beautiful places out here, so you have lots of options." Alex wasn't sure where this conversation was going.

Anthony answered that question. "We're wondering if you ever heard of any legends from around here? We've heard of a couple, but we haven't come up with anything concrete."

Alex considered it. Did her compass count as a legend? She didn't think so. Could it be attached to a local legend? Maybe, but she hadn't found anything like that. She would have to ask Cole, or better yet, Mary Louise. Mary Louise seemed to know everyone and everything about everyone. She didn't know if Mary Louise was interested in history, but she might be the one to ask about the compass. Maybe she would seek her out after she took her laptop back to the cabin.

Realizing the couple was waiting for an answer, Alex shifted back to the present and shook her head. "I haven't really looked at the history here and I haven't heard of any legends. Sorry, but you know, I've only been here a few days. Are there any you're particularly interested in?"

Anthony and Merri looked at each other and back to Alex. Anthony took a big breath and released it before answering.

"We heard there was a treasure buried out here somewhere. We were wondering if it's ever been found."

CHAPTER TEN

Alex raised her eyebrows. "A treasure. Well, that's interesting and exciting. Have you been looking for it?" That would explain the long days and air of mystery around them.

"We actually found a map. We think it's old and it's from right here, but we're not having any luck trying to read it. We only have a few clues to go by, and we finally decided we need help."

"Have you talked to Cole about it?" Alex asked. Maisie's ears perked at the name. "I think he's pretty familiar with the area and might be able to help."

Anthony and Merri shook their heads. It seemed a little eerie to Alex that they did everything as one.

"The thing is, we don't really know him. We've heard you guys have spent some time together, maybe you could ask him for us?"

Alex supposed she could, but she didn't understand why they didn't go straight to Cole. He was friendly and pretty approachable. Since she was curious, Alex made a decision.

"Sure, I can ask him. Maybe you would like to come over for dinner tonight. I'll ask Cole, and maybe he will know something that will help you."

Anthony's face widened into a grin. "We would love that." Merri nodded. "We weren't going to share our information, you know, like with anyone, since we don't want anyone to know we have a treasure map. But like we said, we're stuck, and now we admit we need help."

Alex smiled too. Maybe it would be fun. And they would learn a little bit more about the couple. But a treasure map, if it was even close to real, would be reason enough for them to be mysterious. It made sense now.

"I'll go talk to Cole and we'll see you about six?"

The couple nodded as one.

"Good," Alex said. "Come on Maisie, let's go find Cole." At the command, Maisie bolted out the door. Alex shook her head. She was fairly sure her dog was in love. It seemed like Maisie was becoming Cole's dog instead of Alex's.

Maisie was waiting impatiently for Alex to catch up, standing and wagging her tail excitedly.

Alex wondered where she would find Cole. She hadn't seen him since yesterday, but having said that, she had been gone all morning herself.

The office was empty when they entered. She called out for Cole, but didn't hear anyone reply, so they went out and around to the stables. Several horses were gone, so Alex decided Buck, and maybe Cole too, were out on a trail ride. She was about to give up when Maisie started prancing in front of her. She turned to the right and there was Cole, looking so good in jeans and a t-shirt. No flannel shirt today, Alex thought, and admired the muscles in his arms that were finally visible.

"We were looking for you, do you have a minute?" Alex asked. Maisie made a beeline to the man, just stopping short of running him over. Cole responded by rubbing her ears and neck.

"Sure, I was just walking back to my cabin. I've been out on an UTV run and could use a break."

He fell into step beside Alex as they veered towards the cabin attached to the office, and up onto the large deck that connected his living quarters with the Commons.

"Come on in," he offered.

Alex and Maisie stepped inside to a massive kitchen.

"Wow. This is huge." She turned in a circle. The kitchen was big, with commercial appliances. A counter extended from the end, giving a place to set out a buffet if he wanted.

Off to the right was a dining area and a huge great room occupied the rest of the area. Alex wandered over into the area and stopped to take in the view of the mountains. The whole west side of the cabin was windows, even the triangular area just under the cathedral ceiling. She turned around and looked back. A loft was built against the back part of the cabin with stairs leading from one side. There was a huge fireplace, and she could see a couple of doors that likely led to bedrooms. A door to the ranch office and reception was located towards the west side of the room.

"This is amazing." Alex didn't know what else to say. When she thought of cabins in the mountains, she thought they would all be one-room cabins, and without much for amenities. She had been pleasantly surprised by her cabin, but it was nothing compared to this.

"The cabins here weren't too bad, so I pretty much left them, but there wasn't any place for me to stay unless I took one of the cabins. There wasn't an office, so I was working out of my cabin. I decided to build this and added the Commons to allow guests to have a shared area."

"You accomplished that, this is beautiful." She walked back to the kitchen where he was waiting.

"It also means Mary Louise and I have enough room to cook and bake. Many days I come in and find fresh bread or cookies waiting for me."

"So, where is Mary Louise? I haven't seen her all day."

"She had some errands to run, so she wasn't in today. If nobody is moving in or out of cabins and there isn't much housekeeping to do, I like to give her a break. She'll be in tomorrow."

"Good. I was thinking about asking her about the compass."

"I mentioned it to her and Buck, but Mary Louise didn't have much to say about it and Buck decided it was probably just lost."

"What do you think?"

Cole shrugged. "I don't know. It's interesting, but there've been a lot of people out here over the years and anyone could lose something. Over the years, I've picked up all sorts of things, from a tent and sleeping bag to water bottles, hats and occasionally, a shoe." He grinned. "Those are always interesting."

Alex laughed. "A shoe? Not a pair of shoes?

Cole shook his head. "Just one random shoe."

"Don't you ever wonder what happened to the other one? I know I've occasionally seen a shoe on the side of the road as I was driving and wondered what the story there was. I mean, how does one shoe just end up on the side of the road?"

"Or on the trail. I don't carry an extra pair of shoes with me when I hike, I mean, who does that? So, if I were to lose a shoe, does that mean I'm hiking with one on and one off?" Cole indicated his feet. "How uncomfortable would that be?"

"And what about the rocks?" Alex added. "It sounds painful. So, who would do that?"

Cole shook his head again. "It never fails to amaze me. So, you were looking for me? Did you need something for the cabin?"

"Oh, no, everything's fine there. I was at the Commons checking on my emails and trying to research the compass...."

"Did you find anything?" he interrupted.

Alex shook her head. "Nothing unusual, but when I was leaving, Anthony and Merri came in and started talking to me. Actually, they asked me questions."

Cole tipped his head, immediately suspicious. "What about?"

Alex relayed the conversation to him and told him about dinner. "So, would you come over for dinner?"

Cole nodded. "Sure, that could be fun. They really have a treasure map?"

"I didn't see it, but it's likely something someone drew up as a prank," Alex replied. "They said they would bring it. They're hoping you can tell them all about it."

"I doubt that I can tell them anything they don't already know, but I wouldn't miss it. At least that explains some of their reasons for acting strange. Should I bring something?"

"Oh, I hadn't thought about the food situation. I wasn't really planning on having a dinner party. I have no idea what we're even going to eat."

"I have the ingredients for lasagna, I could make that if I start now," Cole looked at his watch.

"I have salad ingredients," Alex offered.

"Maybe we add some garlic bread?" Cole walked over to the refrigerator and looked into the large freezer section. "Yep, I have a loaf of French bread. We could make that up."

"I have a couple of bottles of wine that I picked up."

Cole nodded. "That should do it then. It will be interesting to find out what they're up to."

Cole brought the lasagna and bread over early and popped the pan of lasagna into Alex's oven to keep it warm. They would add the bread just before they ate to toast it.

Alex opened a bottle of the wine and offered Cole a glass. They walked out to the deck to wait for the younger couple, who came out of their cabin a few minutes later. They bounded down their steps and over to Alex's deck in a burst of energy. Anthony was holding a plastic shopping bag and Merri had a backpack slung over her shoulder.

"We brought dessert," Anthony announced as he handed Alex the shopping bag. "It's just store-bought carrot cake, I hope that's okay."

Alex set her glass down to take the cake. "It's wonderful," she said, taking it inside and coming back to the glass door. "Do you want some wine?"

The young couple did that look with each other that Alex was actually becoming familiar with.

"You're old enough to drink, aren't you?" Alex asked belatedly.

"Sure, I'm twenty-three, Merri is twenty-two," Anthony replied. "We usually just drink beer though. We don't know much about wine."

"We'd love to try some though," Merri added. "We didn't bring any fancy drinks with us on this trip."

Alex wasn't sure she believed they were actually old enough to drink, but she didn't want to be rude and question their honesty. She would watch how much they drank and offer water with dinner.

Dinner was an affair of getting to know each other and the lasagna was delicious, Alex decided. There had been an awkward moment when Merri asked if there was meat in it. It never occurred to Alex that they might be vegetarians.

Cole's look indicated he was thinking the same thing. "It does, but I used ground turkey instead of beef. Is that okay?"

Merri and Anthony conferred for a moment. "We don't eat much red meat," Merri said, "but we're willing to try it." In the end, they devoured their portions and asked for more.

After they cleared the table, Anthony pulled a rolled-up piece of brown paper out of the bag and spread it on the table.

It was a treasure map and it looked old, Alex thought and decided Cole agreed because he gingerly touched the ragged edges.

"Where did you find it?" Cole asked as he picked up the map to inspect it.

It looked like the real deal, Alex thought, peering at the drawings on the paper, but she didn't know much about treasure maps.

"In a thrift store," Anthony replied.

"A thrift store?" Alex repeated.

"Yeah, we found a cool old picture of a guy in this neat frame in a thrift store in Austin...Texas, where we're from, and stuck to the back of it was this map. We thought it was just the covering for the back of the picture."

"We could see some printing on it where one corner was loose," Merri added.

"So, we pried it off and found this." Anthony indicated the map.

Cole carefully examined it. It was hand-drawn in ink that was faded and showed wear, like it was many years old. There were mountains and lakes and even a trail that apparently came from the south that led to a big 'X'. North was marked with an arrow and off to the right of the map was another arrow that was marked 'Laram'. He touched it gently with his finger.

"That's what led us here," Merri said as she watched his finger move. "We did some research but couldn't find anything else."

"This looks like it could be Laramie," Cole said, "and I know where Hell's Canyon is, I've been there. This mine? Crazy Jack's Mine. I think I've seen it. And here's a cemetery, I think I know where that is, too."

"Do you really think we're in the right place?" Anthony asked.

Cole nodded. "As strange as all this is, I do think the map is of this area. Look at the location of the mountains." He traced the mountains to the west. "Do you have anything else?"

Merri and Anthony shook their heads at the same time.

"Were you able to identify the man in the picture?" Alex asked. "That may be a clue."

Anthony shook his head. "There isn't anything written on the back of it." He took out his phone and flipped through some photos until he found one of a picture of a young man. He showed Alex and Cole, then showed them the one that showed the back of the photo.

Cole silently whistled. The picture was old. He wasn't a historian, but it was clear the picture was taken sometime in the 1800s.

So, they had a map that looked like it could be very old and a picture that was clearly very old, but did any of it mean anything? Cole wasn't sure. He took out his phone and turned on its flashlight.

"Can you three hold the map up so I can look at it more closely?" They did and Cole ran his flashlight along it. There was more writing on it, very faint and very difficult to read.

"I see something," he said. "It looks like 'wher I hid the gold. D. Rans, 1882'."

Anthony gasped. "You see writing? We looked and looked and never found anything."

"This looks like it's real," Cole said, showing the others the writing. He turned off his flashlight and put his phone in camera mode. He took a picture of the writing and looked at it, blowing the image up to be able to see what it said.

"Why didn't we notice that?" Anthony asked. "I swear we went over it an inch at a time."

Merri nodded. "We looked at it very closely."

"It's hard to see," Alex said, "so you can't blame yourselves for that. The bigger question is, what can we do with it?" She turned to Merri. "Did you guys try looking up lost treasures?"

Merri nodded again. "We searched all over on the internet and didn't come up with much for Wyoming except for a couple of bank robbers...." She trailed off. "Wait, I did see something like that, why didn't I think of it earlier? We found a story about three guys who robbed a bank in Laramie City. They hightailed it to the Mummy Range in Colorado where they caught two of them and got back about half of the money. I think they hung them."

"How much money are we talking about?" Alex asked.

Merri got up and started pacing. "It was, like, $40,000 in gold and silver, and they found the silver, which amounted to $20,000. That means they didn't find the other $20,000 in gold."

Cole couldn't believe what he was hearing. Even Buck said there was likely no treasures around here. "What happened to the third guy? Did he get away?"

Merri stopped pacing and shook her head. "No, eventually they caught him and hung him, but the legend is that he never said what happened to the gold."

"Do you know his name?" Alex asked. "That might be helpful."

"It was David Ranscomb or Ransome or something like that," Anthony interjected. "I remember thinking it was a weird name. Wait, I can run back to our cabin and grab our research. We printed it all out and brought all of it with us. I'll go get it." He was out the door before anyone could say anything.

Alex got up and refilled everyone's wine glasses, then cut the cake into slices, putting each slice on plates she brought back to the table.

Cole and Merri had just taken their first bites when Anthony knocked on the door and stepped back into the room. He was carrying a small box that he set on the table.

Merri sat her cake aside to pull papers out of the box. "Here it is. David Ranscombe, one of three bank robbers, caught in 1882 and hung in Laramie City." She read silently for a moment. "It says there are several theories about the treasure that have been floating around. The most popular is that he buried it along the road or in the mountains in Colorado. Based on the map, we think it's here somewhere." She passed the papers to Cole.

Cole looked at the papers and back at the image. "D. R-A-N," he read. "This could be the guy. If it's true, this may be an actual picture of him, and could very well show where he hid the gold. On the other hand, it looks like one theory is that the lost money was buried along the Fort Laramie Road. Fort Laramie is in the eastern part of the state. That doesn't match any of the rest of this."

He was silent for a moment, until he noticed Alex's raised eyebrows. Their eyes met. The compass. The compass they found had the initials 'D.R.' engraved on it. David Ranscombe. Cole raised his eyebrows in question. Alex sat there for a moment, then nodded. She abruptly got up and left the room.

CHAPTER ELEVEN

"What's that about?" Merri asked as she watched the older woman leave. "Is she mad about something?"

Alex was back before Cole could answer. She sat down and held out her hand. Merri leaned closer.

"What is that?" she asked as she gently touched the cover.

"It's a compass. Cole and I found it the other day when we were hiking." Alex worked the lid off to show the compass to everyone.

"It's very cool, dude." Anthony looked closely at it. "And it works, but what does that have to do with the treasure map?"

Alex turned the case over to reveal the engraved initials on the back. There was quiet for several minutes.

Anthony finally spoke. "Wait. Dude. Are you saying this belonged to....? The bank robber? That David Ransom or whatever?" He looked up at Cole.

"It seems like it could be," Cole replied. "We don't think someone lost it, we found it under a rock."

"Under a rock?" Merri asked as she glanced at Anthony, who suddenly looked uneasy. Merri turned her attention back to Cole. "Were you hunting for it?"

Alex cleared her throat. "Well, about that. I may have tripped on the rock and upended it. We think someone must have hidden it there.”

“Like this David guy?” Merri asked.

“Maybe. I don’t know why someone would get rid of their compass on purpose, but it’s possible,” Cole said.

“So, what do you think, Cole?” Anthony asked. “Could his treasure be here?”

Cole looked at the pages of research again and considered. If the robbers had made it all the way to the Mummy Range, it would make more sense to leave it there. According to the research, Ranscombe wasn’t found until later, but nothing was mentioned as to where he was found. Cole didn’t believe in coincidences, so with everything they had, maybe Ranscombe had come back here.

“Did you try looking at the Mummy Range to compare your map to the area there?”

Anthony shook his head. “Once we saw the name that we think is Laramie on the map, we decided this was the place.”

“Why don’t you take a look at that in the morning and see if it could be in Colorado instead of Wyoming. Did you say you’ve been out looking since you’ve been here?”

Merri nodded. “We’ve been out on just about every trail. We have this map that we’ve been using, but it seems like we’re just walking in circles.”

“We actually found the old mine marked on the map and Hell’s Canyon, so we tried to work our way north from there, but we got lost about here.” Anthony pointed to a spot on the map.

“I think we need a topographical map,” Cole said as he looked at his phone. “I have one, but since it’s getting late, maybe we meet again tomorrow and put a plan together for you.”

“Oh, thank you,” Merri said. “Do you guys want to help us

look?"

Cole looked at Alex, who shrugged. "I'm game if Cole is. What do you think, Cole?"

Cole wasn't sure what to think. He sincerely thought any treasure had been found years ago, but then again, Alex was here for the hiking, which he enjoyed as much as spending time with her. It seemed like a win-win situation. There was also the matter of his brother Cash. He didn't talk much about him, but Cash had gone missing just a few miles from the ranch last spring. The search for him...or his body...was something he wasn't willing to drop. He hadn't searched for some time so maybe this would be a good time to revisit that.

"It sounds like fun. I'll have to check my schedule for the next few days, and maybe get Buck to help with the UTV's, but sure, let's go look for treasure."

If Cole expected Merri and Anthony to be excited, he was mistaken. They were huddled together and urgently whispering to each other.

"What's wrong?" he asked. "Have you changed your minds about having us help?"

"No, not at all," Merri answered. "We were just thinking we don't really want anyone else to know, I mean, we'll have to share the money with you guys already, and like, well, we don't want anyone else to help."

Cole looked at Alex, who shrugged. "Sure, we can keep it quiet, right, Alex?"

Alex smiled and nodded. "We're just here to help you. It'll be a great adventure for us."

They chose Alex's cabin for the meeting the next morning so others wouldn't see them congregating at Anthony and Merri's cabin. Anthony had suggested that before they left last night, and Alex was okay with it. She considered it unnecessary since all the ranch guests seemed to keep to themselves and likely wouldn't notice anyway, but here she was, rushing to get dressed and have breakfast before they all got here. She privately thought the hunt for the treasure was a wild-goose chase, but hey, she had already found an old compass, so who knew?

Cole showed up first, knocking and making Maisie run to the door. After Alex let him in, he handed her the maps and squatted down to give Maisie some attention. He spent several minutes playing with the big dog before she would let him do anything else.

He was good with dogs, Alex thought as she put the maps on the table, patient and gentle. She suspected he was equally adored and loved by children and would be just as good with them. A pang struck somewhere in her chest and her hand automatically went to her heart.

"Are you okay? Is your leg hurting?" Cole asked, noticing her distress. He stood up to face her.

Alex smiled weakly. "I'm fine, really. It was just a wayward memory that snuck up on me."

"Good. I wanted to talk to you for a minute before the others get here. I know you had other plans for your vacation, so if you don't want to do this, you don't have to."

Alex shook her head, cutting him off. "I think this could be fun and why can't I do both? I say we incorporate treasure hunting with any of my other plans, not that I really know what those are. But, how confident are you that there's a treasure out there?"

"Not very. There's no way it's buried out here. Digging in this area is a chore, especially for someone I would figure wouldn't be carrying around a shovel since he's trying to escape the law. And if it's not buried, where would it be?"

"Under a rock?"

Cole cocked his head and laughed. "I know you're joking, but that would be exactly right. Under a rock, stuck in between two rocks or, if it is buried, it's buried somewhere where the ground isn't so rocky."

"All good places to stash a treasure. I didn't think about how hard it would be to dig a hole out here. I thought I saw Merri and Anthony load a shovel into their car. I think carrying a big shovel would be hard when you're hiking."

"Definitely." Cole paused before he spoke again. "There's something I need to tell you before we go out."

He suddenly looked very serious, a stark contrast to a moment ago, and Alex was immediately alert.

"Okay?"

"It's about my brother Cash."

"Your brother?" They hadn't talked much about either of their families, Alex realized. She didn't even know he had a brother, didn't know where he had grown up.

"Yeah..."

A knock at the double doors to the deck interrupted him. They turned to see Merri and Anthony waving at them. Alex went to open the door and the moment was gone.

Cole laid the map out on the table so everyone could see. He had marked places he could identify off of the old map. He asked the younger couple to mark the places they had already been.

Merri marked the areas around the 'X' from the old map and an area to the south by an old abandoned mine.

"We just figured it was up here." She pointed to the 'X'. "But since the mine and this canyon were marked, we checked around there too. We've been working on this for the two weeks we've already been here, but our time is running out. We only have, like, only a few days left."

Cole suggested they widen their search area and drew an area in pencil on the topo map. "We're going to start down by Hell's Canyon and check out the mine. Why don't we meet at the Commons after dinner this evening, and see how we did?"

"Sure," Anthony said. "Are you ready Merri? We'll see you later."

After they left, Alex and Cole walked over to the UTV building, Maisie trotting along beside them. Several people who weren't staying at the ranch were trying on helmets and goggles getting ready to go out for a ride, asking Buck for advice and filling out the forms he had attached to clipboards. One wall held the UTV supplies, another held fishing gear. Danny and Noah were helping the Coopers and John Campbell get ready for another fishing trip. Alex spoke briefly with them, exchanging pleasantries, while Cole picked out a helmet for Alex. He had his own helmet and grabbed each of them a pair of goggles as they went out to get their UTV.

"Are you sure you have time to do this?" Alex asked as the three of them settled into the two-seated UTV. Maisie took the back and sat with her tongue out, already anticipating a ride. "It looks like you're really busy."

"It's really okay." Cole put the UTV in gear and pulled out of the parking lot. "We stagger days for UTV adventures and horseback riding, so if Buck needs to cover for me, he can. Danny and Noah almost always handle the fly fishing. They're college students who love to fish, so it's a great fit for summer work. The guests love them."

"Okay then, you've convinced me." Alex laughed. "Let's go hunt for treasure."

They drove down a winding road, over hills and down into valleys and when Cole stopped the UTV, Alex looked around, a little confused.

"Is this it?" she asked. "There's nothing here."

"Yeah, we're going to have to hike a little way." He passed her backpack to her and shrugged on his own. They didn't have to hike far, and finally stopped at an old, abandoned mine. Alex thought it looked like every old mine she had seen on television, built into the side of a hill and shored up with old wooden beams. It definitely didn't look safe. The area was beautiful though, rugged hills littered with rocks and tall pine trees that creaked in the breeze.

Goggles and helmets off, they looked around the area as Maisie explored on her own. She was off leash, but with Cole around, Alex was pretty sure she wouldn't go very far since she was clearly in love with the man. She watched Cole crouch next to the dog, both examining something on the ground. That little pang hit again. Alex was sure that if she didn't watch herself, she could easily be in the same boat. She turned away as Cole rose and strode back to her.

"I think this is Crazy Jack's Mine, the one marked on the map. There wasn't a ton of mining done up here, but there was a gold mine near Centennial that was pretty successful. Maybe this was a gold mine too. Do you have the map that we marked up this morning?"

Alex retrieved it from her backpack and unfolded it. They hadn't needed it up until now since Cole was familiar with the area. She wondered briefly about that. Of course, he was a Forest Service employee so it made sense, but she had the feeling he didn't grow up here. She started to ask, but he spoke instead.

"Yeah, here we are." He pointed to a small circle on the map. "And it was marked as a place Merri and Anthony had searched."

"Why did we come here if they already checked this area?" Alex cocked her head.

"About that. I wanted to talk to you about something. It's about my brother. Cash. My brother Cash."

"You know, we've never talked about your family." Alex smiled. "So, you have a brother?"

"Actually, I have three brothers, and two sisters. But Cash is three years younger than me and has been missing since April."

"Your brother is missing?" Alex watched those piercing blue eyes darken. She wasn't sure she wanted to hear any more. She had a feeling this story wasn't going to end well.

Cole nodded. "We haven't found his body or any sign of him since April. It's like he just vanished into thin air."

"Do you think he went missing in this area? Or somewhere else?"

"In this area," Cole said. "He stopped by the ranch one evening and we had supper, then he said he was going to go meet a woman. I didn't ask him who the woman was, or where they were meeting, or even why they were meeting. I figured he was going back to Laramie for a date. He had been seeing a woman off and on for a couple of months. I regret that now.

"A forest service worker found his pickup the next morning at the trailhead west of the ranch. His phone was gone, but his wallet and all of his things were still in the pickup, including the keys. His dog, Piper, was still in the truck. Cash never went anywhere without that dog."

Alex remembered the night they met. Cole had been surprised to see Maisie, had started to say a name. Piper.

"You thought Maisie was Piper, when we first met."

Cole nodded. "Just for a second....she's a Bernese Mountain Dog too...but Piper's with my parents now. I kept her for a while, but she only moped around and wouldn't eat. Every noise made her jump."

A thought occurred to Alex. "Did you think I was the woman Cash was meeting?" She wondered if that's why he was spending so much time with her, to find out if she knew anything.

"Oh no, never. That never crossed my mind. I think her name was Darla or Brianna or something like that. I never met her and I don't know where she was from, but there was no reason to connect any of this to you, just because you have a dog that's a spitting image of Piper. The authorities think he met her and they left together, went to California or someplace. I disagree. He wouldn't have left and never contacted me, and he sure wouldn't have left Piper behind."

Alex didn't know much about missing persons, but the fact that his wallet was in the pickup meant he didn't just walk away.

"Did you try pinging his phone?" Cole nodded. "Of course, you did and I'm sorry I even asked. That's the first thing cops do on television shows."

"The battery's either dead or Cash turned it off. We know his last call was from Laramie, but the number he called was a burner phone, so the police couldn't trace it back to anyone."

"You've searched out here for him?" Alex looked around.

Cole nodded. "I feel like he didn't leave, that he's here somewhere. The authorities investigated the area and found what might have been a place where there was a scuffle, but nothing else. There was no blood, no clues left sitting around. We figured the scuffled area could have been caused by some animal scratching its back. So they decided he's not here."

"Do you think he's ..." Alex couldn't say the word.

Cole shook his head. "I don't. I tried to scout the area with Piper, but she wouldn't even get out of the truck until we got back to the ranch, then she refused to go more than thirty yards away from the house. We put up flyers, we've had search teams out, and I feel like I've walked every mile of this range, but I've never come up with anything. No body, no nothing. I keep looking. There's a lot of land out here and I'm not giving up. I took Piper back to Bishop Hills to my parents because all she did was sit on the front porch and whine."

Alex stepped the two feet between them to surround him in a hug. A wash of emotion swept through her. She couldn't imagine what he was going through and although there wasn't anything concrete she could do, she could offer comfort. She felt affection and something else that made her heart beat faster. The moment was broken when Maisie wedged herself between them. Alex took a step back and looked up at his face.

"Thanks for telling me," she said with sincerity in her voice. She looked around the clearing with a new purpose. "So, are we looking for gold, or looking for Cash?"

Cole couldn't stop his smile. He felt lighter for having told her about Cash. "Both. That's one of the reasons I agreed to help the kids. We look for gold and maybe we'll find a clue that tells us where to find Cash."

Alex moved to the mine's entrance.

"Can we go in?" Alex hoped not. She decided it looked downright dangerous. Rotten timbers sagged on one side.

Cole shook his head. "It's too dangerous. I snooped around here a couple of years ago and the mine is actually caved in a few feet back. If anything is hidden in there, it would take an excavating crew to dig it out." He looked around. "You know, we probably should have brought a metal detector with us."

"I didn't even think of that, not that I have one." Alex smiled. "Should we take a few minutes to check under some rocks?"

Cole grinned and nodded. "Let's find some gold."

Alex refolded the map and tucked it away. They searched in comfortable silence, checking for places something could easily be hidden. Maisie continued to follow Cole, which didn't surprise Alex at all.

"Find anything?" Cole finally asked.

Alex held up three plastic bottles and a rusty tin can.

Cole held up two more bottles and a sleeping bag.

"A sleeping bag?" Alex exclaimed as she examined it. She looked up at Cole. "Who leaves their sleeping bag behind?"

"You'd be surprised what people leave out here. I don't know if they actually forget things or get tired of carrying them."

"Amazing. But I suppose it's always been that way or we wouldn't have found a compass, and if there's gold out here, well, I wouldn't have left it out here."

Cole nodded. "But if you were hiding it to come back and get it later, I could see that."

"Do you think someone is coming back for the sleeping bag?" Alex asked.

"Nope, and supposedly no one came back for the gold. I personally don't think it's here. Should we move on?" Cole stashed their finds in the back of the UTV and set out, traveling down dirt Forest Service roads. Alex loved every minute of it, the sun shining down, the wind blowing, the smell of the trees and the fresh air. It all combined to put a smile on her face, despite the sad story Cole had told her about his brother. She glanced at Cole and realized this was what she had missed the last year, someone to share a day with, someone she could talk to, or not talk to, if they didn't feel like it. She loved it and wanted to kiss him.

Before she could put that thought into something more, Cole pulled off to the side of the narrow track they were on and turned off the motor.

"How about it? You want to try it?"

Alex sucked in her breath and looked at him in alarm. What? Had she just said that out loud? She...

He saw her confusion and rephrased his question. "Do you want to take a turn at driving?"

Alex breathed out. "Me? Can I really? I would love that."

They traded places and Alex discovered she absolutely loved it. They bounced along through the rocky areas and Alex careened around curves, making Cole hang on. By the time they got back to the ranch, she was breathless.

Alex pulled off her helmet and goggles and turned to Cole. "That was the most fun I've ever had...." She trailed off as he took off his own helmet. He wasn't smiling. In fact, he looked a little sick. "What's wrong?"

He could only shake his head and was saved from answering by Mary Louise's appearance on the porch of the office.

"Did you have fun?" She smiled broadly, then caught Cole's expression. "What happened? Did something happen? Oh, no, you found...?"

Cole shook his head at her. "Nothing happened, except I let Alex drive."

Alex, still smiling widely, nodded. "He said I could, and it was soooo much fun.”

"It looks like you had fun, but Cole maybe not so much?” Mary Louise asked. She cocked her head to one side.

"I just found out that this woman, who to all appearances is shy and kind and gentle, has a bit of a wild side.” He shook his head again. "She was a demon out there.”

"Thanks, I think,” Alex said. "I just drove the way you did.”

Cole opened his mouth to say something and closed it again.

Mary Louise erupted into laughter. "Ah, Cole, this one. You will get used to it, I think. Now, lunch.”

Alex started to speak, then realized she had no idea what they were talking about.

CHAPTER TWELVE

As they walked back to Alex's cabin, Buck called out from the corral.

"Duty calls," Cole said. "I'll see you later this afternoon so we can touch base with Merri and Anthony."

Alex decided this would be a good time to visit with Sandy and look at her artwork, so she and Maisie wandered over to John Campbell's cabin. He and Sandy were sitting on the deck finishing their lunch.

"Oh, I can come back later," Alex replied as they invited her to sit. "I had a few minutes, and I was hoping to look at Sandy's art."

"You just sit and I'll get rid of these dishes," John said. "Then you can have a nice visit."

"I really came to see your paintings," Alex told Sandy. "I don't want to take up too much of your time."

"Nonsense, it's a beautiful day out and we have plenty of time," Sandy replied. "We went out for a drive this morning and now we're just enjoying the sun. I'll be right back."

Sandy disappeared around the side of the cabin and returned with a large black artist's portfolio and a big red tote bag. She opened the portfolio so Alex could look at the watercolors she had completed recently. They were just slid in, not mounted so they could be easily taken out.

"Sandy, these are beautiful." Alex carefully held up one painting and then another. "No wonder your work is in galleries around the country. And you should be famous."

"Thanks honey, I do enjoy it." Sandy picked up one of the thick pieces of paper with a painting of a waterfall. It was done in soft natural colors, leaving the scene muted, but so subtly done that all one noticed was the beauty of the waterfall.

"It keeps me busy and adds a little bit to my retirement fund. I hear you design outdoor gear."

Alex laughed. "Well, I did. I'm currently unemployed. I thought I would use these weeks out here to look for a job, and I have, but I haven't found anything that suits me yet."

"Have you thought about changing direction?"

Alex looked up from the painting in her hand. "Like what? I'm not really qualified to do a lot of things. I have some graphic design background, but my degree is in textile design."

"You sketch your designs, don't you?"

Alex nodded. "I color them in with colored pencils or markers and outline with a pen, but they're not really artsy."

Sandy sorted through some of the papers until she found what she was looking for. "Look at this." She held it out.

Alex took the picture of a moose standing in a marsh and just stared for several minutes, absorbing the brilliant colors, the specific light source that made her feel like she was standing on the other side of the marsh.

"I'm starting to get nervous that you aren't saying anything because you hate it," Sandy finally said as the silence lengthened.

Alex looked away from the moose. "I'm so sorry, I just... well,

I'm speechless. It's stunning. Is this really colored pencil?"

Sandy nodded. "It's not the medium you use, it's what you do with it that makes the difference."

"Do you actually think I could do something like this?"

"I do," the older woman replied. "I haven't seen your work yet, I should have told you to bring a couple sketches along, but I'm told you're pretty good with designing. You might have to practice, but you already have the talent and the training. It all starts with a good sketch."

Alex laughed. "You've inspired me. I have paper and colored pencils, even markers, maybe. I'll give it a try."

"Here, take this." Sandy pulled a small box out of the red tote and handed it to Alex.

Alex opened it to find a set of watercolors and several brushes.

"But... I can't take this," Alex sputtered.

"You can and will," Sandy replied as Alex closed the box and tried to hand it back. "And I've got some other things here too." She pulled out a pad of watercolor paper, some painter's tape, and a sketch pad board. "You have to tape the paper to the board to keep it from warping, so you're going to need these."

"But why?" Alex asked. "You hardly know me."

"I'm selfish. I want to see what you can do," Sandy said. "I have extra, so don't think you're taking all my supplies." She put the sup-plies back in the tote and handed it to Alex.

"I don't know what to say, this is so generous of you." Tears glistened in Alex's eyes.

Sandy enveloped her in a hug. "Just come show me a couple of pieces when you get them done."

"I will." It was Alex's turn to hug Sandy.

"Now, how about we get a soda and visit about something else?"

Sandy disappeared into the cabin and came back a minute later with a couple of cans of soda. She sat back down and smoothed her colorful skirt. "So, tell me about Alex," Sandy invited.

Alex hadn't realized how much she needed to talk to another woman about James, her crushed dreams and her uncertainty about the future until she was done with her story.

"Oh, wow, I'm so sorry. That was a lot." Alex wiped tears from her face.

Sandy took her hand. "I know, and I'm so sorry you're going through all this. I remember how lost I was after my husband Don died. I depended on him for everything, and I thought we were invincible, that we would be together until we were old and gray. Then, one day, he opened the front door to go to the grocery store for a gallon of milk. In the blink of an eye, he was gone."

Alex pressed her hands to her face. "How long did it take you to get past it?"

"Oh, honey, I wish I could tell you that you will get past it, but when you love someone, they're always a part of you. But you can and will love again and have your chance to be happy. You deserve that."

Alex twisted her ring on her finger.

"You still wear your engagement ring."

Alex's fingers stilled. "Yes, I haven't had the courage to take it off. I feel like I'd be betraying James."

Sandy patted her hand. "Don't worry about it, you'll know when you're ready, but remember, it's still just a piece of jewelry. Wearing it or not wearing it doesn't change your feelings. Your love won't be diminished, and you won't forget James, even if you're not wearing the ring."

John came out of the cabin a few minutes later and Alex gathered up her gifts from Sandy.

"Don't leave on my account," John said. "I just came to see if you girls need a snack." He offered a plate of cookies.

Alex paused. "I appreciate the offer, but I've taken up enough of your time, and now I want to go home and try my hand at creating some art."

She hugged Sandy. "Thank you so much for the supplies and the talk. I'll be back soon with something to show you."

Alex's heart felt lighter than it had in over a year. Maybe she could move on after all.

She spent the rest of the afternoon playing with the watercolors, seeing what she could do and experimenting with techniques. When Maisie finally nudged her leg, Alex was surprised to find that it was time for dinner.

The sun had set behind the mountains and Cole was just happy to sit and drink a beer on Alex's deck while waiting for Anthony and Merri to arrive. He hadn't seen their vehicle when he came over, so he figured they were still out. After he had gotten over the shock of Alex's driving and wild abandon, he decided he could appreciate her sense of adventure. In fact, it was endearing.

"I had hoped to go back out today," Cole said. "I thought we should hike back to Lost Lake and take another look around where we found the compass. It occurred to me that since the compass was there, the gold could be in that area."

Alex nodded. "We weren't really looking at the time so we could have missed something. Do you think we should pool our resources and go out with Anthony and Merri?"

It was as if saying their names conjured them up, because just then, the younger couple stepped out of their cabin. They waved and practically ran down the steps and over to Alex's deck.

"We found something!" Anthony fished around in his pocket and pulled out a coin. He held out it out Cole, who took it to examine it. Alex moved closer and for a moment, Cole lost his focus on the coin and just breathed in her scent. She smelled like sunshine and woman. All woman. His body tightened.

"Cole?" Alex's voice brought him back to the present.

"Yeah. Sorry about that, I got lost in another thought." His voice was husky. He shook his head to clear it.

"It's nothing, isn't it?" Anthony asked.

"It's not nothing, it's a pretty well-worn coin. And it looks like it's gold, the real thing." He turned it over. There was a lady on one side, an eagle on the other side. "Could you read what's on it?"

Merri shook her head. "We tried, but it's pretty faded."

Cole pulled out his phone and took a picture of both sides of the coin, then handed the coin back to Anthony. He enlarged the picture of the front. It worked as a magnifying glass. He had one at his house, but this would work for now.

"It says 1894." He enlarged the picture of the back side of the coin. "United States of America Ten Dollars."

"Really? Is that good?"

Cole laughed. "It depends on how you look at it, but yes, it's good. It's not from the treasure because it's from 1894 and that's too new, but it's a ten-dollar gold coin from 1894. I'm not a coin expert, but I expect it's worth something."

Anthony turned the coin over in his hand. Cole could see the disappointment on his face. Apparently, Merri saw it too.

"We could look it up on the internet to see how much it's worth," Merri suggested. "And, hey, we found something."

"You did," Cole agreed. "It's a start. We drove to the south just to rule that area out and were thinking we should hike back to where we found the compass and have a closer look. How much ground were you able to cover?"

Anthony pulled the map from his back pocket and unfolded it on the table. He traced a line from the ranch north and west. "This is where we found the coin, for sure."

"I think we're going to have to go farther north, around Sheep Lake, but I definitely think we should have another look where Alex found the compass." Cole ran his finger up to a small blue spot on the map. "Maybe tomorrow?" He looked at the sky. There were clouds building in the west, and he didn't think it would amount to anything, but it was nearly dark.

Anthony and Merri nodded eagerly. "We'll head back to our cabin now," Anthony said. "We still haven't had dinner, and we want showers."

The younger couple was ready and on time the next morning. They likely wouldn't spend all day out, Cole decided, since he had a horseback ride to guide late in the afternoon.

Alex packed her bag with snacks and water, and on a whim, grabbed a couple of the prototype jackets. Merri and Anthony always wore sweatshirts, and it looked like it might rain. Anyway, she thought, they were hers to give away.

"You can ride with us if you want," Cole offered.

Merri and Anthony exchanged that glance they did so well.

"We'll take our own vehicle," Anthony said, "that way there will be more room for Maisie, for sure."

Merri nodded in agreement. "And we have all our gear in our

vehicle already."

Cole didn't argue, and he and Alex followed them out of the driveway. It wasn't very long before they were parked next to the younger couple's vehicle in the trailhead parking lot.

Alex sat down on a rock and Maisie sat down on the ground next to her. Her leg hurt. They had traipsed around this area for several hours and had found nothing of interest.

"Ready to give up?" Cole crouched on the ground next to her and ruffled Maisie's fur.

His hair was ruffled by the breeze and his jeans had dirty spots on the knees from kneeling down. He looked good. Really good. Alex licked her lips.

"Ah, yeah, and I hate to admit it, but my leg hurts a bit."

Immediately, Cole reached to rub it, his fingers massaging the exact place that hurt. How could he know that? She closed her eyes and moaned, and the fingers stopped.

"Did that hurt? I'm sorry."

Alex shook her head. "Not at all, it just felt so good, I couldn't stop myself."

The fingers resumed. "We can go back to the ranch." He wiggled his eyebrows above those striking blue eyes. "I bet you didn't know this, but we have a hot tub."

"You do? How did I not know that? Sign me up."

He smiled and rose, then walked over to where Anthony and Merri were searching around an outcrop of rock.

"We're going to head back to the ranch, are you guys ready to go?"

The young couple looked at each other and then back at Cole.

"We're going to keep looking," Anthony answered, "maybe hike a little ways to the northeast."

"Okay, just don't stay out here too late, it looks like rain is moving this way."

Merri grinned. "We won't, and look, we have these great rain jackets that Alex gave us." She spun in a circle to show off the bright pink jacket. "Who knew she could design something like this? We love them."

Anthony nodded in agreement. He was wearing his as well, bright green over his sweatshirt, and rubbed the sleeve. "Dude, we'll be safe from the rain with these, but we plan on being back before dark, for sure."

Alex and Cole turned to wave as they walked back to the vehicles, but the couple was already out of sight.

"That didn't take long," Alex mused. "Do you think we were hampering their progress?"

Cole laughed. "Maybe, but I'm convinced there's nothing around here." He held up the camping stove he had found in a clump of bushes. "Except this."

"And who would leave something like that out here?" Alex asked.

Cole shook his head. "I have no idea. It's expensive, but maybe they decided it didn't work."

"Or they didn't know how to use it."

Alex woke up early the next morning. They had never made it to the hot tub, since it had started to storm just after they got back to the ranch, so Alex had to settle for a hot shower to loosen up her muscles. It was still dark when she let Maisie out, chilly and had rained again sometime in the night. Maisie, who never went more than ten feet off the deck, ran straight to Anthony and Merri's deck.

"Come back here," Alex scolded. "You know better."

The big dog came back but put her paws on the deck railing and whined. Alex looked at the cabin. It was dark.

"They're probably still sleeping. Oh crap." Their vehicle was gone. A feeling of dread formed in the pit of her stomach. "No, no. They just left early. It's okay Maisie, they're fine."

Maisie looked like she wasn't convinced but allowed Alex to coax her back into the cabin. Alex started coffee and dressed in dark pants and a tank top, then added a tan button-down shirt that she left open, and hiking boots that were starting to look well used. It was pretty much the same outfit that Cole wore everyday, but it worked when hiking.

As she munched on a granola bar, Alex walked to the front door and looked out. The sky was beginning to lighten and there was still no vehicle at Merri and Anthony's cabin. She convinced herself they had left early and was going to leave it at that. Maisie had other ideas and paced the floor.

"You really think they're in trouble?" she asked the dog. "If we go out hunting for them and they didn't want our company, we're going to look pretty stupid." Maisie sat in front of her and gave a soft woof. "It really isn't any of our business, you know, they may not appreciate it if they think we're checking up on them."

Alex looked at Maisie again, sitting there looking at her with her big brown eyes. "Okay, you win. Let's go." She grabbed her jacket and her backpack and Maisie's leash.

CHAPTER THIRTEEN

Cole had just stepped out of the shower when he heard the banging on the front door, it was incessant.

"What the hell?" He wrapped a towel around him and went to the door, still swearing under his breath. It was probably one of the cabin's residents needing towels or something, but that could have waited. Cole opened the door, stopping in his tracks when he realized it was Alex and Maisie.

"What's wrong?" He opened the door wider to let them in. The concern was evident on Alex's face. Maisie sat down and let out a whine.

Alex was immediately flustered by the sight of Cole in just a towel, wet hair curling over his forehead, muscled chest and arms bared, but she didn't forget why she came over in the first place.

"We don't think Anthony and Merri came home last night, and we're worried." She sputtered to a stop, then drew a breath. "I thought maybe they just left extra early, but it was still dark when we got up, and they don't usually leave before it gets light. Anyway, Maisie won't leave it alone, so here we are."

"Maybe they changed their minds and decided to camp overnight." Cole turned to walk back to his bedroom to get dressed.

Alex followed behind him and almost ran into him when he turned around. She put up her hands to prevent falling into him and met wet, warm man. She hastily dropped her hands and stepped back. This was no time for raging hormones.

"They were supposed to hike out first thing this morning with us, remember?"

Cole nodded. "Just let me get dressed, and we can go have a look."

Alex paced in the living area until he came out, fully dressed.

"Do we need to call the sheriff or someone?" she asked, then paused. "Maybe I'm overreacting."

"Maybe, but maybe not, and I don't think we need to call the authorities yet. They may have car trouble and just bunked down in their vehicle. I've done that before, but it won't hurt us to go check on them. Let me get some coffee and my pack and we'll go."

Less than ten minutes later, they were driving towards the trail-head they had parked at yesterday. Neither said much, each worrying about what might have prevented the younger couple from coming back to the ranch. Cole slowed as they pulled into the parking lot. The small SUV the couple drove was sitting right where it was yesterday afternoon. They checked to see if the couple was inside, but no one was in the vehicle.

Cole looked around for a tent nearby and saw nothing. Maisie, on her leash, strained to move down the trail.

"This makes you nervous, doesn't it?" Alex asked. "I know it does me."

Cole nodded. "It hasn't been that long since Cash went missing. We searched and searched and found nothing. I don't want it to be the same with Merri and Anthony."

"I feel like we shouldn't have left them out here, we should have stayed with them."

Cole turned to her and gently grasped her arms. "We have to remember they're adults and they've been traipsing out here for the better part of two weeks now. There was no reason for us to think anything would happen to them. It's still most likely that they decided to camp overnight. They would have had no way to let us know."

"Did they even have a tent?" Alex asked.

"I don't know." Cole dropped her arms and turned around, put on his pack. They started down the trail, Maisie in the lead and straining on her leash. She appeared to be a search dog now, more than a service dog. Alex gave her leash to Cole and relied on her hiking pole to steady her.

"You said you tried to search with Piper?"

"We tried, but she refused to get out of the pickup until we got back to the ranch. We brought her back a couple of times with the same result. Whatever happened scared her enough that she didn't want to come back." He shrugged. "Maybe Cash told her to stay in the pickup and wait. She wouldn't disobey."

Alex glanced at the rocks and trees around them. "Why would Anthony and Merri change their minds and stay out here?"

"I don't know that either. We are way farther on the trail than we were yesterday. I wonder if they went the wrong way. I really hope they're okay."

They continued to walk, and Cole stopped a couple times to check his watch to gauge long they had been out.

The path curved around a rock and Maisie started to bark. Alex followed Maisie's gaze and saw what looked to be one of her survival tents off in the distance.

"Look! I think that's them."

"I think you're right, but they are way off the trail. Let's go." They walked as fast as Alex was able, but it still took a good ten minutes to cross the rocky terrain. They had to skirt a lake as well, but they got there at last.

Anthony crawled out of the little shelter as they approached. There was no sign of Merri.

"We thought we heard a dog bark. Oh man, are we glad to see you guys. We thought we were going to be lost out here forever, for sure," Anthony said.

"Are you okay? Where's Merri?" Cole asked.

Merri poked her head out of the shelter. "I'm here."

"Yeah, sure, we're okay." Anthony answered.

"What happened?" Alex asked. "I was sure you said you were coming back to the ranch last night. When I saw your vehicle was gone this morning, I started to worry."

"We stayed out too long and all of a sudden, it was dark, really dark and then it started to storm." Anthony sighed. "We had lights, but they didn't help much. We had veered off the trail and couldn't find it again. We tried walking in the direction of the trailhead, but I think we went the wrong way. We finally just stopped and decided to try again this morning, but when we got up, we didn't even know which way to go."

"You know, it's really scary out here at night." Merri shivered inside her jacket. "There were noises, lots of noises. We didn't have any way to make a fire and it got really cold."

"But we had your jackets, Alex," Anthony continued, "and set one up. We used the other as a tarp for the bottom and shared. Dude, you should mass market these." He ran his hand down the sleeve. "They're genius."

Cole laughed out loud for the first time today. "That's what I said when she first showed it to me." A little of the tension he and Alex had been feeling dissolved.

"We're just glad you're safe. We were so worried." Alex added.

"We're sorry we worried you, for sure," Anthony said, "but we're glad you came looking for us. Who knows how long we would have been stuck out here?"

"Did you have enough food?" Cole asked. "We have some extra granola bars and some water." He wanted to lecture them about leaving the trail, staying out in the dark and most importantly, the need to have a compass and know how to use it. They didn't know how lucky they were not to have fallen into a ravine or off a cliff and broken an arm or leg. Or worse.

"Thanks, dude," Anthony said as Cole handed him a water and a granola bar. "We tried to ration, but we were afraid we were going to have to start looking for berries if no one found us."

"I imagine other hikers will be out and about soon enough and would have found you." Alex said. "But then again, you were pretty far off the trail."

"Yeah, and we're glad you came looking for us. Do you know how spooky it is out here at night?"

They could see Merri's shudder. "We heard things," she said, shuddering again. "Like, big things. Like someone stalking us..."

"Yeah, just like that. How do people camp out here? It's frightening. Dude, no one's ever sighted a Bigfoot out here, have they?"

Cole laughed. "Some actually have. Of course, they'd been drinking so I'm not sure they're reliable witnesses. It was probably a curious deer or elk."

"A bear maybe?" Alex asked.

"Maybe, but they usually stay away from the more traveled areas."

"It doesn't matter now, we're just ready to get back to civilization," Anthony said. Alex and Cole helped gathered up Anthony's and Merri's gear and they all hiked back to the trailhead.

"Do you think you're up to another hike tomorrow?" Cole asked.

Merri's usually happy expression dimmed. "By ourselves? I don't think I want to do that. I don't want to get lost again."

Anthony nodded in agreement.

"Not at all," Cole replied. "We'll go with you. I think you've been on at least part of the trail, but I've been thinking about it and I have an idea about where that mark is on the map."

Anthony looked questionably at Merri. She nodded.

"We're in, then," he replied. "Maybe we'll have more luck than we did yesterday."

"But for now, we want showers and food," Merri said. "And maybe a nap. I swear I didn't sleep at all last night."

"That was nerve-wracking," Alex said as they unloaded the Jeep back at the ranch. "You really could be out here and not be found. I understand now what you mean about hiking alone. Even two people could get into trouble, and it's easy to get lost."

"When it's light out, you should be able to use the mountain peaks for reference," Cole explained. "Go towards them and you'll find the main trail eventually. But once it gets dark, you need to stay put."

"Good to know." Alex boosted her pack onto one shoulder. "So, now what?"

Maisie looked up at them and woofed softly.

Cole reached down to rub Maisie's head and considered the question. They were supposed to go back out today, but it was past lunch.

"I don't know," he answered. "I guess we have the rest of the day to do what we want. Buck isn't expecting me."

"More hiking?" Alex asked.

"I don't think we want to do that, we had a pretty good hike this morning. Why don't we get some lunch and talk about it?"

"Am I cooking?" Alex asked. "You're getting peanut butter if I am."

"I think I can find something for us that is better than peanut butter." Cole said. "Let's go raid my refrigerator. I'm starving and I think I missed breakfast this morning."

They were just finishing their lunch of leftover chicken breasts and scalloped potatoes when Mary Louise came in from the office.

"Well, hello, you two, I thought you were hiking today," the older woman said by way of greeting. "Did you decide not to go?'

Cole bit into a piece of chocolate cake Mary Louise had made yesterday. "We went out early. Merri and Anthony didn't come back last night, and Alex was a little worried, so we went and found them. They stayed out a little too long yesterday and when it got dark, they couldn't find trailhead again."

"Really? Those poor things, got lost, did they? I bet they were scared, but they're okay now, right?"

Cole nodded. "Terrified was the word they used, but yes, they're fine. Just tired. We'll go back out tomorrow with them."

"You've been spending a lot of time with that young couple, haven't you?" Mary Louise asked as she pushed her glasses up. "Is there something going on I don't know about?"

She caught the look Cole and Alex exchanged. "There is something going on, I knew it."

Cole didn't usually keep secrets from Mary Louise and Buck,

but the treasure map was something Merri and Anthony had shared in confidence.

"They're just investigating some old legends from the area," Cole explained, "but they needed some help finding landmarks in the area, so I've been helping them." It wasn't the whole truth, but close enough for now.

"You mean like that treasure you asked Buck about the other night?" Mary Louise lowered her eyebrows. "Buck said it was just a campfire story."

"I'm sure that's all it is," Cole replied in a soothing voice, "but Alex wants to explore the area too, so it works for everyone."

Mary Louise considered that. She certainly wanted the two of them to spend time together, so Alex could get to know Cole better.

Alex pushed her empty cake plate away and wiped her mouth with a napkin. "It's been really fun so far, I mean, we've only hiked with them once, but they're okay once you get to know them. We're becoming friends."

"That's good then," Mary Louise said, nodding. "What's your favorite thing to do here so far?"

"UTV rides," Alex answered immediately, "but fishing was fun. Hard, but fun. And I loved the picnic. I don't think I ever thanked you for making that picnic lunch for us. It was wonderful."

Mary Louise waved off the compliment, but her smile was genuine. "Oh, go on, it was nothing. Now, you two get out of here and go enjoy the sunshine. I have work to do and you're in my way."

After Cole and Alex cleaned up their lunch mess, they let themselves and Maisie out.

"Speaking of UTV rides," Cole said. "Are you up for another one? I've got a fence to look at, but we could go for a ride and do that at the same time."

Alex laughed. "I'm always up for a ride, I love going places we can't usually drive to. Lead on."

They picked up helmets and goggles, and waited for Maisie to jump up and find her seat, then took their own seats. "Are we going far?" Alex asked as she adjusted her goggles. "I didn't bring a jacket or anything."

Cole shrugged. "We can go as far as we want, but it's pretty warm right now, so it should be okay and we'll be back before dinnertime."

Cole drove to a fenced pasture and once he determined all the fencing was okay, they wound around the wilderness, up and down roads, slowly if they saw a deer or elk, faster when he could. Alex loved every minute of it, and when they finally got back to the ranch, she was ready to go again. She didn't say anything though, since her stomach was starting to growl.

Cole grilled hamburgers and they sat on his deck and watched the shadows grow. Finally, Alex couldn't suppress her yawns. "You're tired," Cole said. "Let me walk you back to your cabin."

"It's a good tired, though," Alex said. "It's been a long day."

Cole gave her a kiss on the cheek before he left her at her door, and Alex walked inside, disappointed. She decided she had been hoping for more.

She was too tired to dwell on it though, Alex realized, but it was in the back of her mind as she got ready for bed and crawled under the blankets. She fell asleep almost as soon as her head hit the pillow and slept soundly all night, not waking until Maisie put a paw on the bed to wake her up the next morning.

"Everybody ready?" Cole hefted his pack onto his back. The

others followed suit. They had ridden together today. Merri and Anthony said nothing about wanting to drive themselves. Instead, they seemed happy to have Alex and Cole's company.

"Lead on, dude," Anthony replied. "We're as ready as we'll ever be."

The first part of the trail was easy enough to hike, Alex decided, and familiar since it also led to Lost Lake. Merri and Anthony chatted in the front of their single line, but Alex, who was next in line with Maisie walking just in front of her, preferred to watch the scenery and look for wildlife. This was a well-used trail with a couple of popular trout lakes within an easy hiking distance, according to Alex's trail guide.

She was pretty sure Cole wouldn't let any of them out of his sight. She wondered if he felt a little bit like a babysitter at this point, watching over the younger couple so nothing happened to them.

They had hiked more than an hour, past the first of the two lakes, when Cole stopped them. "We'll take a break here," he said as he set his pack on the ground.

Before them, covering a huge portion of the valley, was a jumble of huge, white boulders. Alex looked at them with trepidation. Some were enormous. She looked for a way around.

"Do we really have to cross this?" she asked Cole in a soft voice. "I'm not sure I can do it."

Cole smiled back at her. "You can do it, but I'll help. I have a plan."

His plan was to take her pack across and come back for her. She watched as he hopped from one to another, dropping the pack on the other side. He came back the same way, making it look easy, but Alex mentally shook her head. She did not hop well.

Cole motioned for Merri and Anthony to start across, then took Maisie's leash from Alex.

"Use my arm and your hiking pole and we'll take it one rock at a time. You can do it," Cole encouraged.

Alex wanted to jump up and down when Cole helped her down from the last rock. She made it. Merri high-fived her and congratulated her like Alex had just won a marathon.

They continued on, mostly uphill, Alex decided, as her legs started to protest.

"Let's stop here and catch our breath," Cole announced a moment later. It was like he read her mind, Alex thought, but she wasn't going to question it. She found a rock to sit on and got her water bottle out of her pack.

Cole pulled his water bottle out as well and walked over to where Alex was getting Maisie a drink. He never questioned that she shared her water with Maisie, he knew most dogs drank from streams, but some streams contained bacteria that could make a dog sick.

"How are you holding up?" Cole asked.

"I'm okay, but happy for the rest. How much farther do we have to go?" They had been watching for anything that looked like a mine or cave as they went, but with no luck.

"If I've figured this correctly, the mark on the map is just over that rise." He pointed to a ridge off to their right.

"Do you really think we're going to find a mine, dude?" Anthony asked as he walked over to them. Merri trailed behind him.

"I think we have a pretty good chance of finding a mine, but remember, there may not be any treasure, even if there was in the beginning. Someone could have found it years ago." Cole picked up Maisie's dish and handed it to Alex, then adjusted his pack.

"Ready to go?"

As they came over the ridge Cole had pointed out, Merri, Anthony and Alex all stopped abruptly. Cole nearly ran into Alex. "What's wrong?"

"This never gets old," Merri breathed. "Even if we don't find the treasure, we'll never regret coming here."

Anthony nodded in agreement. "Dude, it's just so beautiful." The couple continued on up the trail.

Alex couldn't argue with that statement and after she snapped a few pictures, she caught up with the younger couple.

Cole veered off the trail and the others stopped. He checked his watch and the map, then gestured for them to follow him.

"Check over there," Cole directed Merri and Anthony, "but don't stray too far. We should stick together."

Again, Alex was sure Cole felt like he was babysitting the three of them. She was also surprised he had agreed to come along after yesterday's incident. He acted more like he was conducting a guided hiking trip than going out with friends, all business and not so many smiles.

An hour later, Alex was done looking. She was tired, hot and hungry. There was nothing here. She found a rock and scooted up onto it, basking in the warm sunshine. She could seriously take a nap right here, she decided, as she took out her phone and took more pictures, mostly of Cole still poking around with his hiking stick. Maisie came and sat with her.

Cole turned from what he was doing and watched them for a moment, then took his own picture to remember the two of them sitting relaxed on a worn rock. He put his phone away and walked over to them.

"Tired?" he asked when he reached the rock.

"Tired of looking for something I wouldn't know if I saw it," Alex replied. "But for now, we're just taking a break." There were no mines in this entire area, Alex was sure. All she had found was a tube of lip balm, several plastic wrappers and a small flashlight, now temporarily residing in her pack. Cole showed her his finds, including a wool sock, an expensive water bottle and a cigarette lighter. He also tucked his finds in his pack.

Cole checked the time on his watch and looked at the sky. "We'll have to be packing it up soon to make the hike back. I wanted to give them as much time as we can to look."

They sat on the rock and watched Merri use the metal detector while Anthony scoured the area, looking in rock formations and bushes to see if he could find a mine.

They finally wandered back over to the rock. "I think we're done here, for sure."

Anthony and Merri, using the metal detector, had more luck finding things than Alex and Cole had. They found a quarter, several old pennies and a very old, very rusty belt buckle.

"But it's really nothing," Merri said, holding it up to show everyone.

"This belt buckle is pretty cool," Cole said as he took the buckle to examine it. "It could be something. You should take it to an antique dealer when you get home, to check it out."

"Dude, sweet." Anthony stashed the buckle in his pack. "I guess the trip hasn't been a total wash."

Merri nodded. "And we're glad you guys came along. We're really glad we asked for your help."

"Well, we have one more place to hunt before you have to go home," Cole said, "so don't lose hope. We still have a chance to find something really big."

"Are you thinking about going out tomorrow?" Merri asked. "We could use a day to ourselves. We want to do some real sightseeing."

"Let's take tomorrow off," Cole replied, nodding. "This was a pretty big hike and I need to help Buck tomorrow, at least part of the day. Are you okay with that, Alex?"

Alex nodded. "Maisie and I need to check emails and such, so that will be fine with us."

They headed back down the trail and this time she was determined to cross the boulder field by herself, carrying her own pack.

They met a group of hikers as they crossed, two older ladies and four younger men. Their packs were set up for camping overnight. Alex thought it was an odd group, but they were all laughing and talking like family, so they probably were.

One of the ladies stumbled and nearly went down on her knees, but one of the boys, a great big kid with curly red hair, probably in his late teens, immediately caught her and offered his arm. He didn't offer to carry her pack, Alex noticed, but it was heart-warming to watch him help her off the boulder. He guided the older women across the rocks, one at a time. Alex spoke briefly to the other lady as they passed by. She said they were having a great vacation with grandsons, and then they were off on their own adventures.

Alex looked back once as they made their way down the trail, then smiled and continued on with her own group.

CHAPTER FOURTEEN

When they got back to the ranch, Cole helped Alex, Merri and Anthony unload their gear, then went off to help Buck. Alex's legs had protested as she showered and put on clean clothes, but she supposed that was to be expected, since they had hiked quite a ways and over rough terrain. She ignored the pain. She wanted to go into town to check her phone messages, and she needed to pick up a few things from the store, but she decided to wait until tomorrow.

Alex got out her painting supplies instead and set up out on the deck. She sketched a new scene, a marmot peaking out from behind a rock and painted to the breeze in the trees until Maisie stood and stretched.

"Oh my, it's getting late," Alex said to Maisie as she looked around and realized the sun had already set behind the mountains. "I suppose you're ready for some dinner."

Maisie walked over to the patio door and Alex laughed. "Okay, okay, I'm coming." She gathered her paints and took everything inside, but instead of putting it away, she spread it out on the dining table.

"I'm on a roll here, so dinner's going to be quick," she told Maisie. She fed the big dog and rummaged around for something that would be easy. "I wish I had some of that Irish soda bread,"

Alex muttered. She settled for leftover chicken and veggies, heated and wrapped in a tortilla, and a bowl of honeydew melon. She topped it off with a couple of chocolate chip cookies she had picked up on her last grocery run. Alex hadn't realized how hungry she was until she started eating.

She went back to her painting and spent the evening engrossed in her project. There was no noise at all in the cabin except for the refrigerator when it kicked on, and Maisie's even breathing from her place on the floor.

When she was finally done with the painting, Alex stood up and just about sat down again. Her legs were nearly asleep from sitting on the hard chair and she had to limp to get to the bathroom. Maisie followed her and offered assistance as she changed into her pajama pants and t-shirt. "Yeah, I know," she told Maisie, "sitting all that time was a bad idea, but painting is like designing, once I start, I don't want to stop."

Alex let Maisie out one more time and as she stood on the deck in the darkness, she looked up at the sky and wondered what Cole was doing. She thought he might stop by, but decided he must have been busy.

Alex woke with a sense of purpose. She even surprised Maisie when she jumped out of bed, ready to go. Maisie looked up at her, clearly puzzled, and gave a soft woof.

"I know, I know, you're usually the first one up, but we have things to do today." Her legs weren't sore and when she opened the door to the deck to let Maisie out, she knew it was going to be another gorgeous day. She wanted to finish up a couple more paintings so she could get Sandy's input. They probably weren't going to be up to Sandy's standards, but Alex thought she had made good progress with the watercolors.

After a breakfast of scrambled eggs and toast, she and Maisie walked around the lake. Alex was surprised how much easier this walk was compared to when she first tried to do it. Not only did her legs not hurt, even after yesterday's hike, but she no longer had to stop and catch her breath. Maisie, who still stayed close to Alex when they walked, wasn't panting, and Alex decided this part of her trip was a win. She still had no job and no place to live, but her body was healed.

Once back at the cabin, Alex poured her a cup of coffee and spent an hour or so working on a watercolor. She let it dry and placed it inside her sketch pad.

"Come on, Maisie, let's go for another walk." Alex hoped Sandy was still around, she hadn't seen her for several days, she realized as they walked towards John's cabin. A thought occurred to her. Had Sandy gotten Alfie fixed and left already? She hadn't considered that, but it was a possibility. She walked a little faster.

Alex breathed a sigh of relief when she reached John's cabin and Alfie was still sitting in the driveway. She breathed another sigh of relief when she saw John and Sandy sitting at the table on the deck. She had come uninvited and had been worried about disturbing them.

"Hello Alex, and you too, Maisie," John called out. He waved and stood up. "Come join us."

Sandy added her own greeting and ruffled Maisie's fur as the big dog reached her, clearly wanting some attention.

"How are you two this morning?" Alex asked as she sat down in the chair John offered her. "Any luck getting Alfie fixed?"

"We're good and so is Alfie," Sandy replied. "John said it was my float, whatever that is, that went bad. He was able to replace it and now Alfie's as good as new."

"Your float?" She had no idea what that was, but from the sound the van made when it stopped on the road, Alex was sure it was going to need a new engine.

"It's part of the carburetor," John explained, "but easy enough to fix."

"Are you leaving soon, then?" Alex asked Sandy. "I'll be sad to see you go."

The older couple shared a look. "Well, as for that," Sandy said, "John said I didn't need to hurry off, so, well, I'm staying a bit longer."

"That's great," Alex replied, not quite knowing what else to say. She decided to change the subject. "Anyway, I brought a couple of paintings to show you." She handed the sketch pad to Sandy and there was only the sound of the breeze in the trees while Sandy, with John looking over her shoulder, flipped through the paintings, considering them one by one. Alex held her breath.

"I knew it," Sandy finally said, looking up at John. She handed him the painting Alex had done of Maisie sitting on a rock, and he nodded.

"You did say she had talent," John replied, "and you were right. These are very nice."

Sandy held up another, this one a softly colored painting of Alex's cabin.

"If you ever want to change careers, I think you could be an artist." She looked directly at Alex. "I think I could get these placed with mine in a couple of different galleries."

Alex pressed her hands to her suddenly hot cheeks. "You don't mean that. These are the first paintings I've done since high school.

James was the artist, that's why he taught elementary school art. James was good, really good, but he never thought he could make money with his art. And now you're saying I could?" Alex heard the squeak in her voice.

"Oh, honey, you could, and you can. We'll have to get them matted and framed but that's no problem. Can I keep them? I want to make a few inquiries."

Alex nodded. "Are you sure? I was just doing this to practice and play around with the colors, I mean, I like them, but I don't think they're good enough to be in a gallery with yours."

"I've taught thousands of art students over the years, and I could usually feel the talent in them. Some have it, some don't." Sandy smiled. "You do."

Alex went over that conversation again and again, still amazed that someone thought she was good. She had stayed to have lunch with Sandy and John and the Coopers, who came over from their cabin next door. They were so much fun, Alex thought, recalling the many conversations they had, laughing and telling stories of past vacations. Alex didn't think she had ever been as full of life and as happy to be alive as these four appeared to be.

Alex smiled as she sat in her deck chair a while later, just absorbing the afternoon and marveling that someone she had just met would be so nice to her, when Maisie suddenly raised her head. Her tail thumped on the decking. Maisie jumped up as Cole came around the corner of the cabin.

"Well, hi there, you two." He stopped to give Maisie some love before he sank into the chair next to Alex. "I just wanted to make sure you remembered the potluck tonight."

"I made a pan of brownies that just came out of the oven a few minutes ago, so I'm all set." She stopped for a moment and then made a decision and stood up. "Don't go anywhere, I want to show you something."

She disappeared into the cabin and came back out a minute later with a sketch pad.

"Did you get the fly rod case designed?" he asked, intrigued.

"I'm still working on that, as I told you Sandy gave me some watercolors, so I've been experimenting. I have some done." Alex smiled. "I left some with Sandy, but I have some here too. Sandy said I might be able to sell them. In a gallery, like she does. I don't know though, I don't think they're good enough for a gallery."

Cole had never seen her so animated. He liked this Alex, and hoped he would see more of her. He also didn't doubt that she could paint well, she designed textiles for a living, and frankly, he was sure she could succeed at whatever she tried if she was willing to try.

"Some of these I didn't show to Sandy, they weren't the best, so I didn't take them."

Cole took the paintings, done on heavy paper, and looked through them, then looked at Alex.

"You thought these weren't good enough? I'm not an art expert, but these are amazing."

He went back to one of a lake with the mountains in the background and could see the familiar scene in the soft colors and strokes. He picked up another one, this one of Crazy Jack's mine. She had captured it perfectly, the weathered and worn timbers, the color of the dirt around it and the shading.

"It's like I'm right there," Cole finally said. "Did you do these from memory?"

"Some yes, but you know I took lots of pictures, so I used those to help me get the spacing right."

"They're amazing."

"You're just saying that to be nice."

Cole shook his head. "I wouldn't do that, but I don't need to, either. They're really good. I didn't know you were working on anything like this."

"Sandy convinced me to try, but I've just been working on them here and there, in between hiking. I didn't know how much fun it would be."

"You've done a great job, and the paintings reflect how much you enjoy it." Cole looked at his watch. "Look, I've got to get back to help Buck, but I'll see you later at the potluck."

Alex nodded as he kissed her on the forehead and turned to leave. "You will. I want to run to town to check my messages and stock up on snacks, but I'll be back."

Alex stopped with a brownie halfway to her mouth.

With a quick intake of breath, she realized that today was her anniversary, or what should have been her anniversary. Alex carefully set the brownie back on her plate and sat unmoving. How could she have forgotten such an important date?

Alex looked down at the ring on her finger, the diamond glistening in the light. She was a horrible person, she decided. She had known the day was coming and had already decided to spend the day quietly, reflecting on memories, maybe driving into Laramie for dinner at a nice restaurant. But she had forgotten. She had gone hiking, spent time with friends and bought groceries, and enjoyed it all. The day was nearly over and couldn't be gotten back. Had she moved on? It felt like it, whether she had intended to or not, but that didn't make her happy.

"You're very quiet tonight."

Alex looked up at Cole. The light in his eyes was dimmed a bit as if they reflected her own mood. She couldn't summon a smile.

"I know I'm not very good company, it's been a long day. I wasn't ready for all these people, and they're having so much fun."

Cole handed her a glass of wine and sat down beside her. He looked around at the gathering. Ranch guests were talking and laughing, comparing stores of hiking and spotting wildlife. They were eating hamburgers and chips and had chosen side dishes from the variety they had each provided. Several small children were running around, evidently playing some game they had invented for the occasion.

Alex followed his gaze. Everyone was happy, that was obvious. Except for her, and she was just...just numb.

Alex knew it was time to put her past life behind her, but it was so hard. She missed James and the life they were to have together. She missed her job. She missed her friends, and she wasn't sure that coming to Wyoming had been the answer. All she was doing was putting off the inevitable. She had no home, no job and while she had the money from the insurance claim after the accident, it wasn't going to be enough to live on forever. Then there was the man sitting beside her, waiting patiently for her to say something. There had been that immediate attraction, and it had only grown since. They had become friends, and would become more if she would allow it, she was sure of that.

"Maybe I'll head back to my cabin, have an early night." She rose and Cole followed. Maisie raised her head but didn't move from her place on the floor.

"I'll walk you. Just let me tell Mary Louise I'm leaving."

"That's not necessary," Alex replied, turning away. "It's just across the way, you know." Maisie stood and followed her.

Cole caught up with them just outside the door.

"Hey, hold up. Tell me what's going on. Have I done something wrong?"

Alex shook her head and hugged her arms to her stomach. "I just got lost in a memory for a moment. I'll be fine."

Cole let her go but stood at the door and watched her until she and Maisie went into their cabin. He turned around and nearly ran into Mary Louise.

"Something's wrong, I can feel it, what did you say to her?" Mary Louise planted her body in front of Cole.

He shrugged. "I don't know. She was fine, in fact, she was more than fine, and then she wasn't. She was talking and happy, and suddenly, she went quiet and looked like she had seen a ghost. I'm going to give her some space and I'll talk to her in the morning."

"Are you sure you shouldn't go now?"

"No, I'm not, but I'm not even sure it has anything to do with me." Cole kissed the older woman on the forehead. "We're going hiking tomorrow, so maybe she will talk about what's bothering her then."

Alex kept the tears at bay until she was safely alone in her cabin, but barely made it to the sofa before the wrenching sobs came. Maisie sat on the floor next to her, offering the little comfort she could.

As she tried to stop the tears, Alex wondered why she was crying. Was it because her dreams had been crushed in an instant, her one love gone in that same instant, or was it because she was angry at herself for forgetting and moving on with this new life? She didn't know.

Eventually, Alex sat up and stared at the fireplace, empty and dark, exactly the way she felt. Maisie whined and brought her back to the present, the dog needed to go outside. Alex walked out with her and when they came back inside, Alex straightened her shoulders and wiped her face with her sleeve, then sniffled and fought back more tears.

Okay, enough crying, Alex told herself. She went to the bathroom and washed her face. Looking in the mirror, she only saw a sad woman with blotchy skin, red eyes and a red nose. Her eyes were dull.

Alex sighed. She was supposed to have loved James forever, but while the promise had been made, the vows had not been taken. He was gone and she couldn't change it. What would he say to her now?

Almost eerily, she heard his voice in her head, in that gentle tone he used with those he loved, telling her to let him go, to go and live her life and be happy. And most of all, find someone to share her life with. Alex thought she already had found someone to share her life with, she just wasn't sure it was the right time. The voice in her head said, yes, it is. Let yourself love again.

With another, heavier sigh, Alex brushed her teeth, changed into her pajama pants and t-shirt, then crawled into bed. They were supposed to have one more hike with Merri and Anthony tomorrow, their last chance to look for a fortune in treasure with them. Maybe tomorrow would be the day. With that thought, she fell asleep.

CHAPTER FIFTEEN

"Hi ladies, are you ready to hike some more?" Cole asked the next morning. Maisie wagged her tail and trotted over to Cole for a rub. Alex followed her and set her pack on the ground.

Cole immediately noticed that Alex didn't reply.

"Are you okay?" He looked with concern at her white face and red eyes. "You look like you have a hangover."

That got a small smile out of Alex, but she just shook her head.

"I've got a headache, that's all."

"Do you want to skip the hike?" Cole asked. "We can get Merri and Anthony started and they can go out alone." He let her walk away last evening, so he still didn't know what had happened. She was back to the sad woman he had met that first night. He was pretty certain she didn't have a hangover, Alex wasn't the type to drink by herself. Of course, he amended, he didn't know if she had been alone or not. Doubts crept in and he mentally swore. He was sure she was alone and likely hadn't been drinking, but what had happened? Maybe he should have gone after her like Mary Louise suggested.

"Do you think that would be wise?" Alex asked, bringing him back to the present. "The last time they went out alone, they got lost. I'm not sure I'm up to that kind of stress today."

"You're right." Cole picked up her pack and put it in the back of the Jeep just as Merri and Anthony came out of their cabin with their gear. They were chatting happily and both gave Maisie a scratch behind her ears before they loaded their gear.

Alex didn't have much to say on the way to the trailhead, but Cole could be patient. They would talk when they got back to the ranch.

When they stopped at the trailhead parking lot, Anthony frowned from his seat. "I think we already went this way, Cole. Why would we go back?"

Cole glanced at Alex in the rear-view mirror. She shrugged.

Cole pulled his map out of his shirt pocket and showed it to Anthony. "I want to head off in that direction and circle around here. Cole pointed toward the east. "I've got it kind of in a grid and I think you went here, right?" He pointed at the map and Anthony nodded. "So, I think if we go a little farther east, over here, we might find something. I feel like this might be a possibility. Worth checking out, I think."

"What's this over here?" Anthony pointed to an area on the map. Cole had marked grids on the map and color coded them.

"These are all the places we've already looked, and this area is one we haven't been to."

"Why don't we go there then?"

"It's way farther away and pretty much off the map that you had," Cole replied. "We can't take the Jeep up this road, so Alex and I may tackle it another day. This seems like the better choice for today."

Anthony didn't answer and finally turned to Merri who was sitting in the back seat with Alex. "Are you okay with this?" he asked her.

"I don't know. I didn't really like this trail, remember? It was eerie."

Cole's eyebrows raised. He looked at Alex again in the mirror before he responded. Merri sounded sincere, but...there was something else. "Eerie? How so?"

"It was, oh, I don't know, like someone was watching us," Merri said.

Anthony nodded in agreement. "Maybe we could look somewhere else."

Cole was instantly suspicious. Why wouldn't they want to hike this trail? It was a popular place to hike, and the parking lot had several vehicles parked in it. Saying it was eerie sounded like an excuse to him.

"If it helps, I've been on this trail many, many times, and I've never felt like that," Cole said. He really wanted to know the real reason they didn't want to go. "And we'll be with you." He was losing his patience and was close to canceling the whole hike. He and Alex had other things they could do.

Merri nodded. "That's true. It'll be okay, Anthony. Maybe with two more sets of eyes, we'll find something we didn't see when we came out here."

"Only part of the trail is the same, so once we get here, we'll be searching new territory," Cole explained as he showed Anthony the map.

Anthony looked at the map, then looked out of the window as he considered it. He finally nodded. "Okay, let's do it, but if I see Bigfoot, I'm not waiting for y'all, I'm hightailing it out of there."

Cole was sure they weren't going to see Bigfoot, but he still wanted to know why they were so reluctant to go this way.

"What do you think? They aren't happy to be hiking this trail," he whispered to Alex as they followed Merri and Anthony down the trail. "Mass murderers disguised as treasure hunters?"

That got a weak smile out of Alex. "Maybe we've been reading too many murder mysteries, but they are definitely acting suspicious. I'll watch your back," she whispered back.

Cole laughed, and Merri and Anthony stopped, turned around.

"We're fine," Cole assured them and the young couple turned back, then continued down the trail. He noticed they were having a whispered conversation as well.

"This is a bad idea," Anthony whispered to Merri. "We should never have come back out here. We know there's no treasure here, we looked already. And there's, you know..."

"Shh. I know, but maybe if we just stay close to the trail and act like we're looking, no one will be the wiser." Merri said. "We just can't act suspicious."

They fell silent and behind them, Cole and Alex exchanged a look, then Cole smiled.

"This might get interesting," he whispered. "I can't wait to see what they're up to."

They continued down the trail and around a large protrusion of rock, then hiked uphill for about ten minutes before walking through a grove of pine trees. As they came out of the trees, the landscape opened up to reveal a lake, with snow still hugging one shore.

"Look at this lake," Merri exclaimed. "It looks like one of those infinity pools, look how it just drops off into nothing. There's just sky behind it."

It was the first thing anyone had said since Cole and Alex's whispered conversation, and they had been hiking for some time.

"Let's just keep moving, for sure," Anthony told Merri. "We want to get to the area Cole was talking about."

"Oh. Okay," Merri said, sounding subdued.

Alex agreed the lake was pretty awesome. It was lined with brush and a few trees, and the sun glinted off the clear water. One shore was covered in snow, but a person could walk around the south side.

"Could we just stop for a minute?" Alex asked. "I need a rest break and I'd like to take a picture or two."

"'We'd like to keep going, if it's okay," Anthony said, pausing for only a minute. "I recognize this lake, for sure." He looked around. "We've already looked here and didn't find anything." Merri tagged along behind him.

Cole made the decision for all of them by dropping his backpack. "Let's rest for a few minutes and then we'll continue on. Alex said she needs to rest." He pulled out his water bottle and took a drink while Alex set her backpack next to his.

Anthony acted like he was going to continue on, only to be stopped by Merri. "Come on, Anthony, we can stop for a minute."

Anthony, not convinced, stopped when she tugged on his arm. "But it was...."

"Shh," Merri whispered. "Let's just have a snack and we can move on." She took cookies and some fruit out of her pack. "Let's sit over here." She walked over to several rocks under a tree.

Alex started around the south side of the lake. It looked like a little used trail went that way. "Where does this trail go?" she asked Cole.

He looked where she was walking and shrugged. "Probably nowhere. There's a deep drop-off there by the far edge of the lake, so be careful."

Alex and Maisie walked a few yards to take several pictures with her phone. She nearly dropped the phone when Maisie pulled on her leash.

She woofed several times, not the soft woof she usually used, but a louder, more forceful bark.

"What is it, Maisie?" Alex looked back at Cole. "I swear, she's acted stranger on this trip than I've ever seen her." Back home, Maisie was the perfect companion. She didn't tackle people and she didn't try to run away. She certainly never pulled on her leash like she was doing now. She wanted to go down the little trail.

Cole walked over to them and crouched to Maisie's level. She whined.

"What's wrong, Maisie?" He took the leash from Alex. "What do you hear?" He listened, but only heard the wind in the trees. Maisie put her nose to the ground and sniffed. "Ah, you don't hear anything, you smell something. Well, it's probably not a good idea to chase after it." Cole let Maisie lead him down the trail to the drop-off he had just told Alex about.

"You shouldn't go that way," Anthony called to Cole. "It's really dangerous." Cole looked back at Anthony with a puzzled look on his face, then looked in the direction Maisie was pulling.

"Whoa, stop Maisie, now," Cole and the dog stopped at the top of the drop-off. Maisie immediately stopped and sat, then looked lovingly up at Cole.

Alex put her phone back in her pocket and hurried over to Cole and Maisie. "What is it?"

Cole put his arm out to prevent Alex from going past him. "There's a body at the bottom. You don't want to see it."

Alex immediately looked down. There was definitely a body down there.

"Dude, we swear, we didn't kill it," Anthony called out.

Cole turned around. "What did you say?"

"We had nothing to do with it," Anthony said. He and Merri stayed where they were, still sitting on the rock about thirty yards away.

"What do you mean, you had nothing to do with it?" Cole glanced back at Alex.

"Dude, we didn't kill it," Anthony repeated. "I mean, like, we saw it the other day when we were up here, but it was already dead. Or maybe hurt. Or asleep. We didn't know and we didn't stick around to find out. I mean, we didn't do anything illegal."

Cole took a deep breath. Had he heard correctly? "Illegal? Hell, yes, it's illegal, and 'it' is a human body. Are you saying you saw a person, maybe hurt, or dead, and you just ran away?"

Anthony's face went white. "A human? There's a human body down there?" He looked at Merri, who was just as white, and shaking, and then back at Cole. "No way."

Cole tried to control his temper. He really wanted to go over and shake the younger man, started to take a step towards him to do just that. Alex must have realized his intent because she put a hand on his arm. He took another deep breath.

"Okay, you say you saw this body the other day, but you didn't know it was a human?"

"Dude, it was a bear," Anthony stuttered. "We started down that path and when we got to the ledge, we saw a bear down at the bottom. But it was just there, lying on the ground. We didn't know if he was dead. Maybe he was just sleeping, or injured. We just hightailed it out of here."

Merri was nodding. "Not a person," she said quietly, so quietly that Cole had a hard time hearing her. "We never saw a person. I've never even seen a dead person." Tears were welling up in her eyes.

"Me either," Anthony said. "Dude, I've never even been to a funeral."

Cole turned to Alex. "They say they saw a bear. Possibly a dead bear. But that's definitely a person down there."

Alex's eyes filled with tears. "Is it...?"

Cole pulled her into his arms. "Shh, it's not. It's only been there a day or two, I would guess."

"What are we going to do now?" Alex asked.

Cole thought for a moment, then fished the keys to the Jeep out of his pocket. "You three are going to go back to the ranch," he told Alex. He spoke quietly. "Find Buck and tell him what we found, have him call the sheriff."

"Do you think they'll be able to find you?" Alex asked. "I don't think I can give directions."

Cole marked the GPS coordinates with his watch, then took it off and gave it to her. "This will tell them where I am. Tell them I don't know who it is. Oh, and we'll probably need ropes. Do you think you can do that?"

Alex nodded. "I can."

He kissed her on the forehead, then whispered. "Don't let them out of your sight. Take them with you to tell Buck, then stick with them." He motioned to the couple still sitting on the rock. Both looked like they wanted to be sick.

Alex nodded again. Cole turned to Anthony and Merri. "I need you guys to go back to the ranch and find Buck so he can get the sheriff out here. I'm going to stay here."

Anthony and Merri moved fast, he had to give them that. They had their backpacks on and were ready to go before Alex stepped away from him, taking Maisie with her.

"Will you be okay?" Alex asked Cole with concern as she picked up her pack. "It might not be safe out here." She didn't elaborate, but he knew what she meant. If there had been foul play, a killer could be out there somewhere.

"Yeah, I know. I'll be fine, but hurry." He bent as she straightened and gave her a quick kiss.

The younger couple pummeled Alex with questions as they hurried back down the trail.

"Did you see the body? What did it look like?"

"Was it a man or a woman? How long do you think it had been there?"

"Was it decayed and gross?"

Alex didn't want to talk about it and waited until they ran out of questions before she answered. "Yes, I saw the body, it was a man, it didn't look decayed, but I'm not an expert. I haven't dealt with any dead bodies." She was also sure she would never forget the sight. She wished she could right now.

"Do you think Cole really should have stayed there?" Merri asked a few minutes later.

Alex paused, and Merri turned around to see why. "Why wouldn't he? He would want to keep animals and such away from the body, so the site won't be messed with."

"What if whoever murdered that guy comes back?"

Great. "Who said he was murdered?" she asked. "Maybe he fell."

"It's never an accident when someone dies out in the wild," Anthony explained. "That's the way it is in all the murder mysteries we watch."

Alex thought back to her own experience reading murder mysteries. They weren't wrong. She shivered, even though she had worked up a sweat walking as fast as she could.

"Well, he probably was murdered," Anthony ventured, then

caught Alex's glare. "Maybe he was attacked by that bear we saw, for sure."

That wasn't any better, Alex decided. What if the bear came back and attacked Cole? How would he defend himself? They fell quiet after that and no one said anything until they were back at the trailhead and the Jeep.

As they placed their gear in the back of the vehicle, a thought occurred to Alex. She straightened and paused. If the man had been murdered, who was to say Anthony and Merri hadn't done it? They had been acting suspicious all day. She wasn't sure it was actually safe to get in a vehicle with them, and in a brief moment of panic, asked herself how well did she think she really knew them? Alex tamped that thought down, they had fallen apart when Cole said it was a body. And she had Maisie. Another thought came right behind the first one.

"Why didn't you tell Cole about the bear after you saw it?" she asked as they fastened their seatbelts.

"We didn't know what to do," Anthony replied. "Are you supposed to report it when you see a bear?"

"I don't think you have to if it's alive, but I'm sure I read something about reporting injured or dead wildlife, especially a bear." Alex started the Jeep and backed out of the parking lot, then headed in the direction of the ranch.

"We didn't actually get close enough to see if it was dead or not," Merri said.

"Did you take a picture of it?" Alex asked. She was skeptical that they had seen a bear at all, maybe a movement out of the corner of their eyes that they thought was a bear.

Merri, sitting in the front seat, shook her head.

"We just turned around and ran as fast as we could back to our vehicle," Anthony added. "You know, just in case he wasn't dead."

Alex drove straight to the horse corral where Buck was brushing down a horse. As much as she would have liked to linger, maybe help with the horse, she had no time for that.

She left Anthony and Merri in the Jeep with instructions to stay put and gave Buck Cole's message and watch. "Oh, and he said to bring ropes, the body is at the bottom of a steep ravine. We'll be at my cabin, if you need us for anything," Alex added as she turned to get back in the Jeep. Buck nodded and strode into the house, she assumed, to call the sheriff.

All three gathered, along with Maisie, on Alex's deck. "We're going to stay here and wait for Cole," she told them. "I've got sodas and stuff for sandwiches we can eat out here while we wait." She wasn't hungry and she really did have a headache now, but eating would give them something to do while they waited.

"Why do we have to wait?" Anthony asked as Alex brought a tray out with the food and drinks.

"I expect the sheriff will want to talk to all of us, so it's best if we're all available when he gets here."

Alex picked at her food, but Anthony and Merri ate like they didn't have a care in the world. Of course, they didn't see the body, only had her and Cole's word that there was a body at the bottom of the ravine.

"I have a question for you," Alex said as she cleared the table. She had taken a couple of ibuprofen and her headache was better, but man, she was tired. She could use a nap.

"Alex," Merri said when Alex didn't say anything more. "You had a question."

"Yes, I did." Alex collected her thoughts. "If you thought the bear was dead, why didn't you want to go back on that trail today?"

She watched as they exchanged that look she had come to recognize.

"Well, you know, we didn't really know if it was dead, remember?" Anthony finally replied. "We said that. We just didn't want to run into it in case it wasn't really dead, and it wasn't there, was it?"

Alex shook her head.

"You can call us cowards if you want, you know, we're okay with that," Anthony continued, "but we were scared, really scared that the bear wasn't dead. And we were right, it wasn't dead."

Merri nodded. "We really didn't want to go back out at all after that, anywhere, and we thought it would be safer with you guys with us. We just didn't want to admit we were scared."

Anthony took Merri's hand. "And we were right to be scared, cuz, dude, today we didn't see the bear, but there was a body, no bear, like we thought there should be, so what does that mean? So did the bear come back and kill the guy? That could have been us." His voice rose to a high pitch. He stopped talking and took a deep breath.

Alex considered it. "And you didn't mistake the man for the bear?" They shook their heads. "Maybe you saw the man and ran."

Both pairs of eyes widened, and they looked at each other, then back at Alex.

"It was definitely a bear," Anthony finally replied. "Or Bigfoot. Do you think Bigfoot killed that man?"

"I don't think I've heard of Bigfoot actually killing anyone, so I'm going to say no." Alex decided they were telling the truth. She was sure they didn't see Bigfoot, and she was sure he didn't kill the man. Her headache was coming back. She rubbed her forehead.

"Anyway, we're going home tomorrow," Merri said, "so we can't even look for treasure anymore." She paused and looked at

Anthony. "We've decided we don't care about the treasure, we just want to go home. If you and Cole find it after we leave, you can have it."

Anthony nodded.

"You know you won't be able to leave until the sheriff clears us all?"

Both pairs of eyes widened again. "They'll think we killed him?" Anthony asked. "Dude, that's crazy."

"We wouldn't even kill a spider," Merri added. "No way we would, well, you know..." She trailed off, then whispered, "murder anyone."

Alex's headache was back full force. She rubbed her forehead again and decided to try to placate them so they didn't bolt.

"I'm sure it's just a matter of telling our story of what happened today. It will all be taken care of and you'll be able to go home as planned," she said. "Anyway, I've really glad you're waiting with me until Cole comes back."

"Weren't you scared too?" Merri asked.

Alex thought about it for a moment, then nodded, and chose her words carefully. "I was more concerned for Cole, that it might be someone he knew." She didn't think they knew anything about Cash Gilchrist's disappearance.

Merri shuddered. "I didn't think of that. It could have been someone from around here."

"Did he know him?" Anthony asked.

Alex shook her head. "I don't think so. Anyway, why don't we talk about something else? Do you have to go back to work as soon as you get home?"

CHAPTER SIXTEEN

Cole paced while he waited. There was no question that the man was dead, there was dried blood where his head had hit a rock, and his legs were at unnatural angles. Cole could see he had been dead for a while, and his mouth was open, glassy eyes stared at the sky. Animals hadn't gotten to him yet, but it would only be a matter of time. Cole didn't go any closer, didn't want to disturb any evidence of what might have happened. It looked like the man had fallen into the ravine, but did he slip, or was he pushed? Where was the rest of his hiking group? This trail was well enough traveled that there were footprints everywhere, so that was no help. Was he hiking alone? Cole was torn between the thought of him hiking alone and falling or being pushed by a member of his group and left behind.

Cole also had a moment of doubt, now that he was alone, of the wisdom of sending Alex back with Anthony and Merri. Upon reflection, he was sure the younger couple had nothing to do with the man's death. They didn't have time to come out here and kill anyone in the last couple of days, but he had to consider the fact that they had not wanted to come out here today, had adamantly been against it. Then again, they had freaked out at the thought of a dead bear, and when he announced the body was that of a person, he thought they were going to faint. Both of them.

Cole was still considering how the man could have gotten to the bottom of the ravine when he heard footsteps. He looked up and was relieved to see the sheriff striding towards him.

"There you are Ben," Cole greeted him. "I hated to bring you all the way out here, but we appear to have a situation."

Cole shook the big man's hand, and Sheriff Ben Graham was a big man. Standing over Cole, the sheriff was also larger, with broad shoulders and arms the size of a substantial log. His hair, cut short, was hidden by the Sheriff's department ball cap, but Cole knew his neatly trimmed beard and mustache was the same red color as his hair. His bright blue eyes were friendly, and he was older than Cole, but young for a sheriff. Ben had done a stint in the army before serving as a deputy sheriff, and when Sheriff Tom Jennings retired last year, Ben ran and won the position. He was a good sheriff, a good man, Cole knew, with a wife and two young children.

"Buck didn't give us many details, just that you found a deceased man out here." Ben looked around the clearing but didn't see anything unusual.

"Down there," Cole said, walking to the edge of the ravine and dipping his head.

"Damn. Now I see why you said to bring ropes, that's pretty steep." He looked around for a better way down and then back at Cole.

Cole shook his head. "Wanted to, but I didn't want to disturb anything, and I'm not sure you would have known where to look if I met the same fate."

Ben nodded as the rest of his law enforcement crew appeared in the clearing. "Do you recognize him?"

Cole shook his head. "And I haven't heard of anyone local gone missing."

"Nothing here either," Ben replied. "I guess we'll find out." He looked down into the ravine and back at Cole. "You can go back to the ranch, Buck's waiting for you at the trailhead. I'll be along later to get your statement. The others' too. Buck said there were four of you?"

"I sent them back to get help, but they're staying right there at the ranch."

The two shook hands and Cole loped off down the trail. He was glad to hand over the responsibility for the body to someone else.

It was nearly dark when Maisie, who was asleep on the deck, gave a soft woof and stood. Alex looked up from her cards as Cole came around the corner of the cabin. She had resorted to a game... or twenty or so...of rummy with Anthony and Merri, trying to keep them occupied.

All three of them had lapsed into silence at some point during the afternoon, out of things to talk about, the events of the day catching up with them.

Cole bounded up the stairs and ruffled Maisie's fur before speaking. "How's everyone doing? Oh, cards, I see."

"We're okay," Alex replied, setting her cards on the table. "It's starting to get chilly."

"And dark," Anthony added. "When can we go to our own cabin? I mean, like, are we being held prisoners? It kind of feels like it."

Cole laughed. "Not at all. I just thought it might be easier for the sheriff to get his work done if we're all together and he doesn't have to round us up."

"Dude, I guess that makes sense, but we're tired," Anthony said, "and we're getting hungry again, for sure."

"Just a little while longer, I promise," Cole said, taking Alex's hand and helping her stand. "Why don't we take this party over to the Commons? Mary Louise has been cooking and is bringing us some supper."

Anthony and Merri stood as well. "We're down for that," they said in unison. They moved quickly, heading straight for the Commons, which showed welcoming lights from the windows.

"Did you get everything squared away?" Alex asked as they followed the couple across the driveway, Maisie staying close to Cole.

"I left the sheriff to do his job, and I'm sure he'll be along soon, hopefully bringing some information. We all need to give a formal statement." Cole took Alex's hand as they walked, and Alex welcomed the warmth. What she really wanted was a hug, but maybe later, she told herself.

"I thought it might be easier if we were all together at the Commons, and Mary Louise does have dinner ready for us."

Alex wasn't very hungry, the emotions of the last twenty-four hours were catching up with her, but she placed a couple of scoops of Mary Louise's stew, that she referred to as her famous campfire stew, on her plate. It looked like it had hamburger and bacon, potatoes, and several kinds of beans in it, and smelled wonderful. Maybe she could eat after all. She buttered a homemade biscuit before joining Cole and the others at the table.

"It must have been terrifying for you to be out there alone with a dead body," Mary Louise said to Cole as Alex sat down.

"I wouldn't say terrifying," Cole replied, "but certainly stressful."

"Dude, I would," Anthony said around a bit of biscuit. "It was definitely terrifying, and we weren't even alone out there."

"Of course it was." Mary Louise patted Anthony's hand while

she frowned at Cole. "Maybe not to Cole, he's used to that kind of thing, but the rest of you..."

"What do you mean, not Cole?" Alex stopped with her spoon in the air and looked at Cole. "You make a habit of finding dead bodies?"

"Well, you know, working for the forest service, he has to deal with all sorts of things, not just bodies," Mary Louise backtracked.

"Now, Mary Louise," Buck interrupted. "You're scaring these young 'uns."

"Oh, I'm sure I'm sorry." Mary Louise apologized. "We'll just talk about something else. We're sure going to miss you two," she told Anthony and Merri. "We've enjoyed having you here. Now, everyone, I made us an apple pie for dessert, I'll just go serve it up."

Alex sat in silence as Buck asked Merri and Anthony about their home in Texas. She was hungrier than she thought and the stew was delicious. She felt better than she had all day. Now, though, she looked at Cole in surprise. "Is that true?" she whispered. "You've found more than the body today?"

"Mostly true," he whispered back, "but Mary Louise has been known to exaggerate. How about if I tell you about it later? For now, let's just get through dessert and our statements for the sheriff."

Alex nodded. "I'll hold you to it."

Sheriff Graham came in just as they were finishing their pie. He talked to each of them alone and when it was Alex's turn, she found him to be straight forward with his questions, and he kept her at ease while she answered.

He gave Anthony and Merri permission to go home to Texas. Cole told Alex that was probably more due to his own statement than theirs, which included the story of a dead, or not-so-dead, bear. No bear tracks were found in the vicinity, according to the sheriff, when Anthony asked about that, but Cole shrugged and blamed it on the rain they'd had since Anthony and Merri had been up that way.

The young couple gave everyone high-fives before they left to go to their cabin, clearly happy to be leaving in the morning. Mary Louise and Buck had gone home just after the sheriff had arrived, so when he left, Alex and Cole were the only ones left.

They walked back across the driveway and stopped at the bottom of the steps.

"What now?" Alex asked.

"Ben will find out who the man was, and forensics will find out what happened."

"That's it?" She looked up at him. "We could do some research and ..."

"You sound like Mary Louise," he laughed. "That's exactly what she wanted to do, but this isn't a murder mystery novel where amateurs try to solve a murder. For all we know, the poor guy slipped and fell."

"Oh, well, I suppose," Alex said, sounding a little disappointed, "and we do have our own mystery of the treasure."

"True," Cole replied. "Are we going to keep looking even after Anthony and Merri leave?"

"I think we should. They don't want to have anything more to do with it," Alex said. "They're leaving the map and their research with me."

"Really? Okay then, we will." He paused. "We didn't really sell them on the great outdoors, did we?"

He opened the door for Alex, and she started in, then stopped and turned. "Come in? I don't really want to be alone. I didn't want to admit it in front of the others, but I was a little freaked out too."

Cole was about to protest that Maisie would keep her safe but didn't. The truth was, he wanted to know what had upset her at the potluck. It seemed like an eternity ago, but he couldn't get it out of his mind.

"I'd love to," he answered. "Do you have any wine? I think we could both do with a glass."

She turned on the lamp next to the sofa while Cole took off his hiking boots and set them by the door. He went to the kitchen and brought back two glasses of wine. Alex took her shoes off and wiggling her toes inside her socks, took the glass he offered.

"This has been a very long day."

Cole nodded and sat down next to her.

"So, have you found many bodies?" Alex asked. The question had been on her mind.

"More than I would have liked, but I've found more people alive than dead," he answered as he took a sip of wine. "I've been out on a lot of search and rescues, not just here, but other areas. There are a lot of people missing out there, it's not just Cash, and if I can help find them, I will. I go out as part of the forest service, but if the sheriff needs help, I'll go help him too. I've been as far away as Utah and Montana."

"Good for you," Alex said. "I always wondered who helps with searches. Obviously, I've never done that before."

"Do I get a question too?" Cole asked as Alex took a sip from her glass.

"Sure, fire away."

"What happened last night?" The question was asked quietly. "And don't say it was nothing, it was obviously something."

Alex lowered her eyes. "You'll think it's stupid."

He took her free hand and held it. "I'm positive it's not stupid."

"It was just, well, yesterday should have been my first wedding anniversary," she finally admitted after a long pause.

"I'm sorry." Cole didn't know what else to say.

"That wasn't the worst of it," Alex continued. "I went out and had fun and laughed, and I totally forgot about the date, even though I knew it was coming up. I was sitting there eating a brownie when it hit me."

"And you were angry with yourself for forgetting," Cole said.

Alex nodded and raised her face to him, tears glittering in her eyes. "I absolutely forgot. I'm a terrible person."

"You're not terrible, and you know it." Cole moved his thumb soothingly on the back of her hand. "You're entitled to be happy and have fun. You've been through a lot in the last year or so, and you can't blame yourself for healing and beginning to move on to something that is real and now."

Alex pulled her hand away and looked at it.

"I guess I need to take my ring off." Alex twisted the engagement ring on her finger.

"You don't have to," Cole replied. He took her hand in his, kissed the knuckle with the ring. "It's a beautiful ring and reminds you of the beauty of your love with James. I don't want you to ever forget the time that you had with James. He had your yesterdays and that's okay. I just want you to save tomorrow for me, and all your other tomorrows."

Alex drew in a deep breath and tried not to cry. His comments were unexpected. Was he declaring his love for her? It felt like it, the words hinted at a future with him, even though she couldn't see it. She didn't even know what she was going to do when her time at the ranch was done. But Cole's words touched her heart.

"I can do it." She pulled the ring off and held it for a moment before Cole took it from her fingers, held it in his hand. She looked down at her finger, feeling naked without the ring that she'd worn for so long.

Cole studied it, then gently took her right hand. She looked back up at him, puzzled, and he put the ring on her third finger. "Would you wear it here?"

Tears fell from her eyes as she looked up at him. "Do you mean it?"

"Absolutely. I meant what I just said."

Alex threw her arms around his neck and kissed him. It was meant to be a happy, thank you kind of kiss, but Cole's arms went around her waist and it deepened into more. Alex ran her fingers through his hair and breathed in his scent, pure man and pine trees.

He pressed her into the sofa, and when she felt the weight of him on top of her, Alex lost herself to the sensation. Soon, it wasn't enough, she tugged his t-shirt out of his jeans, allowing Alex to run her hands along the warm skin of his back and sides.

Cole broke the kiss long enough to remove his flannel shirt. His t-shirt followed, giving Alex full access to his chest.

"Bedroom," Alex breathed.

Cole picked her up and carried her to the bedroom, depositing Alex carefully on her bed. He leaned down to kiss her and his hand moved up under her blouse, fingers exploring the soft skin of her breasts. It wasn't enough for Alex as she tried to wriggle out of the suddenly confining clothing. Cole raised up on one hand to help her, then with a flick of his fingers, unfastened her jeans. His fingers dived under them and knew just where she wanted touched.

It still wasn't enough, so Cole stood and removed both her jeans and underclothes, and his, coming back down to meet her now na-ked body. Hands moved and touched, lips moved from her breasts to her stomach.

"Do you have protection?" Cole's soft voice interrupted the wonderful sensations Alex was feeling.

"Protection?" She couldn't think and a second later, she was left holding onto nothing when Cole suddenly rolled off of her. She rolled to her side and looked at him, naked, muscled, and very aroused, lying flat on his back, eyes closed and breathing hard.

"What just happened?"

Cole sighed. "Two things."

"Oh?" Alex's eyebrows went up.

"We don't have any protection," he said, turning only his head to look at her. "We're responsible adults and here we are, without protection, unless you have something."

"Oh, well, I don't have anything. I haven't needed any for more than a year."

"Same here," Cole said. When her eyebrows rose again, he continued. "Mary Louise says I'm too picky."

"About protection?"

Cole chuckled. "About women."

"You don't have anything in your wallet?"

He grinned at her. "I don't even have my wallet."

"Oh." She was silent for a moment. "And the second thing?"

"I don't sleep with ranch guests."

The eyebrows went up again. "I see. Has that been an issue?" Alex bit her bottom lip to keep from laughing.

He levered himself up on one elbow. "You would be surprised."

"Would I really?"

"Women proposition me all the time. Young women, older women, it doesn't matter. They think I'm one of the amenities, and they can be relentless. There was one lady who was about seventy, she was amazing, and I almost took her up on it."

Alex couldn't suppress the giggle. "I can see where that could be a problem."

"It is," Cole replied in a serious voice, "so I had to make a policy. No sleeping with ranch guests."

Alex's giggles became a full-fledged laugh.

"It's true," he protested, sounding hurt.

Alex laughed harder. Finally, Cole had to give in, and laughed with her.

When Alex could finally control herself, she wiped tears from her eyes and kissed him on the lips.

He sighed. "I guess I'd better go home." He rolled off the bed and pulled his jeans back on, found the rest of his clothes. "To be continued?"

He heard giggling from the bedroom as he put the rest of his clothes on, and picked up his boots, pulled them on. Cole had to smile. Any sexual frustration he was feeling faded as he listened to her. He turned off the lamp and Maisie followed him to the door, waiting while he locked it from the inside and let himself out. He ruffled the big dog's fur before shutting the door and walking back across the driveway.

CHAPTER SEVENTEEN

Alex was just finishing a cup of coffee on the deck when Anthony and Merri came around the corner of her cabin. Maisie wagged her tail in greeting.

"We're off," Merri announced cheerfully as she stepped onto the deck, "and as promised, here's our map and all of our research."

Anthony set a small tote on the table.

Alex looked at the tote and then at the couple. "Are you sure you want to do this?"

They both nodded. "We've had a blast looking for this treasure, especially after you and Cole agreed to help us, but we're done now, for sure," Anthony said.

"And we actually did find some treasure, so it wasn't a total loss," Merri added. "We wouldn't have found that coin if you and Cole hadn't helped us."

Alex smiled and rose from her chair. "You truly did find treasure, and a body too, and a bear."

Anthony and Merri both shuddered. "Dude, don't remind us," Anthony said, "and technically, we didn't find a body, and we're okay with that."

"We had a great adventure," Merri said. "And who knows, maybe we'll come back here someday." She looked around and down at the lake. "Anyway, we need to get on the road."

"We didn't see Cole anywhere," Anthony said. "Will you tell him goodbye for us?"

Alex assured them she would and gave them both hugs before they turned to leave. They waved one last time as they walked back around the cabin.

It suddenly seemed very quiet, Alex decided, as she looked over at the empty cabin. Merri and Anthony had shared a secret with her and through that secret they had become friends. They certainly had shared some adventures and Alex was sad to see them go, she realized. She didn't think she would get to know anyone on this trip. She had this idea that she would come out here, take solitary hikes, read and relax, and she and Maisie would leave when it was time, and that would be it. But even if she left today, she would be taking memories made with new friends with her. The good news was, she wasn't leaving today.

She still had a week or so and was likely going to have to go back to Kansas City and find a job and somewhere to live, but Alex now knew she had the strength, both physically and emotionally, to do that.

She looked at the ring she still wore, now on her right hand where Cole had put it. Cole had given her that gift last night and it was one she wouldn't forget.

She did need to go into town, Alex told herself, and she had better get going. She changed into jeans and a stretchy, blue t-shirt. She added her blue jean jacket since it was a little chilly out yet, but she could always take it off if she got warm.

"Come on, Maisie," Alex said as she grabbed her purse and keys. "We have shopping to do." Groceries, more painting supplies, including an artist's board so she could return Sandy's to her, and a stop at the pharmacy. If she had the chance to get Cole back in bed with her, Alex was going to be prepared. She wasn't sure how to get past his policy of not sleeping with ranch guests, but she would work on that.

Alex stopped in the middle of starting the SUV. When did she decide she was okay with having sex with someone she had known for two weeks? That just wasn't something she did. Okay, she told herself, you almost did it last night and were okay with it. True, but that had been spontaneous. Now, here she was, planning for it. She argued with herself over right and wrong for several minutes, then decided it was a mute point. She was friends with Cole, she liked him and liked being with him, and they had grown closer in two weeks than she had ever been with James.

Where did that come from? Alex wondered, then to her chagrin, realized it was true. She could talk about anything with Cole and he didn't judge. He was okay if she didn't want to talk and didn't get angry when she cried. He was fun and kind and had helped her through a tough time. He was also one sexy man, Alex admitted, so that was that.

Cole walked out of the sheriff's office, assured he had done all he could. Ben said they had identified the body as Mark Rutherford, a social media influencer in his thirties. He had come out here from Chicago, determined to show his followers how easy hiking in the mountains could be. According to Ben, Rutherford had arrived the morning he died, put on a full pack and started out on the trail. He had a full bottle of water still in his pack and the conclusion was that he got altitude sickness and became disoriented. He apparently stumbled and fell down the steep embankment, leading to his death.

Cole shook his head. It was sad, but sadder was the fact that this Mark Rutherford apparently ignored all of the rules for hiking in the mountains, as so many did, and it led to his death. Cole was still thinking about it when he got to the parking lot and unlocked his Jeep. He had a couple of more stops to make, he decided as he put the Jeep in gear and pulled out onto the street, including a drug store. He wasn't going to get caught empty-handed the next time he had a chance to get Alex in bed. He grinned. There would be a next time, he was sure of it.

Alex and Maisie wandered from one store to another in downtown Laramie. She had found a little bookstore and although she didn't find anything on legends in the area, she did purchase a bird-watching book. She really liked the atmosphere here, she decided. Little antique shops, western wear stores, and for those who liked the outdoors, gear shops. She stepped into one, not a big, flashy store like some of the chain stores, but well stocked with all kinds of outdoor gear. A young man was helping another customer, and a woman was straightening a display. Alex stopped to look at a jacket, a hat. She thought about the gear she had designed. It seemed so long ago. The survival jacket had been her last, and it was just going into production a year later.

She fingered a brightly colored vest and was surprised when she realized it was her design. A surge of satisfaction when through her. This vest. Her backpack and the jacket. She had so many ideas and what was she going to do now? She had studied design and loved it. Design was a huge part of who she was.

"Can I help you?"

Alex jumped and turned. The clerk who had been straightening the display was studying her.

"Oh, I'm sorry. I was just looking around. This is a great store. I could spend hours here."

"Do you like the vest? I absolutely love it." She was an older woman with bright blue eyes and burnished red hair pulled back in a dignified knot at the back of her neck. Tall and thin, she was wearing jeans and a white blouse, the very vest they were looking at covering the blouse. A pair of brown cowboy boots competed her outfit.

"I do love the vest too, and it looks great on you." Alex's eyes lit up. "In fact, I designed it."

The clerk's eyes widened. "You designed it? Really? You're a designer?"

Alex nodded and smoothed the vest on its hanger.

"I used to work for Outdoor Gear, and this is one of my designs."

There was silence. The clerk looked like she didn't know what to say. Alex squirmed inside as the woman looked from Alex to the vest and back. Alex started toward the door, with Maisie following her.

"No, don't go. I'm just in awe," the clerk said. "I love the colors and the texture of the fabric. And I like the way it fits. Let me introduce myself. I'm Marta Graham and I own this store. Actually, we have three stores, but that's another story. We produce some of our own products and we're currently looking for a designer."

It was Alex's turn to stand and stare. A designing job? Here in Laramie? How could that be possible? She had researched textile designing positions across the country and hadn't seen anything about a position anywhere in Wyoming.

"I'm sorry, that was pretty abrupt. Come sit down, and I'll explain." She gestured to a bar table with two stools. They sat and Marta glanced at Maisie, who was sitting on the floor next to Alex.

"You have a service dog."

Alex looked down at Maisie and smiled. "Yes, I had a car accident that affected my legs and she's helped me recover."

The young man who had been at the counter brought them each a cup of coffee, then went to assist another customer who had just come in.

According to Marta, she and her staff not only sold gear to local outdoor enthusiasts, they designed and sewed their own product. Her designer had recently abruptly quit and moved to Florida with her boyfriend, so they were without a designer and someone to manage the production part of the business.

"We're not huge, but we manage to supply our stores here and in Salt Lake City and Cheyenne," Marta said. "We also have an online store, and a couple of stores in Montana and Colorado carry our designs. We sew everything right here in a studio in the back of the store."

They walked to the studio and Alex was impressed. State-of-the-art commercial sewing machines and cutting tables sat in several areas, and bolts of fabric lined the walls. Several women worked at the sewing machines, making them hum. No one stopped their work when Alex and Marta came in, but they looked up and smiled at the two of them and the great big dog walking with them. They clearly were happy and appeared to love Marta.

"We sew four days a week," Marta explained, as Alex fingered a bolt of green canvas. "The other days, when we're pretty busy in the store, the sewing staff helps out."

"I love this." Alex glanced at the ladies sewing. "It looks like they are enjoying themselves."

Marta laughed and turned to the seamstresses. Sewing machines went silent. "Everyone, this is Alex. I'm trying to convince her to be our new designer."

A cheer went up and the four women left their machines to come over to introduce themselves. They welcomed her like she was already part of the crew.

Alex was pleased and a little embarrassed by the attention. It never occurred to her that she could find her dream job right here in Laramie. Near Cole. She shoved that thought to the back of her mind.

Marta led her to a large and very neat office that had its own cutting table. Rulers and squares hung on one wall and a window revealed a little garden with paths and a patio set. A desk with a computer and a shelf of books and fabric samples took up the rest of the room.

Alex noticed the old limestone on the exterior wall. The old two-story building shared one wall with the adjacent building, a twelve-foot gap on the other side created the space for the garden.

Marta discussed pay, including profit sharing, benefits, possible start dates and the design program the previous designer had used.

"We can change that out if you prefer another program," Marta said, "and we can make Maisie a bed in here to get cozy on while you're working."

Alex was touched that Marta included room for Maisie in the deal. Although she could get through a day without Maisie, she preferred not to. She had come to rely on Maisie's company and didn't like the thought of leaving her alone all day, every day.

Marta led Alex back to the main store and they shook hands. Alex would start next week.

Alex could have danced all the way down the street to her vehicle. She was employed. She was staying.

Alex thought about the encounter on the drive back to the ranch.

It was crazy, but she had just accepted what appeared to be the job of her dreams right here in Laramie. She was so excited she could have started right then and there, but Marta had insisted she finish her vacation. Alex caught her bottom lip with her teeth.

She had a job now, but where was she going to live? She only had a short time to find someplace. She had stopped at a realtor's office before she left town, but the older man there wasn't optimistic. Housing was scarce and apartments that had been for rent had already been snagged by college kids coming back to school in August.

Maybe she could talk to Mary Louise about it. The older woman likely knew of places to live that weren't listed with the realtor. Alex made a mental note to do that as she pulled in the driveway of the ranch.

Alex couldn't find Cole anywhere. His truck was missing, so Alex assumed he and Buck were still off doing ranch stuff. Mary Louise had already gone, so there was no one to share her news with.

Alex and Maisie walked over to the Commons. It was quiet and empty. Alex sat and opened her laptop. She answered several emails, including an invitation to have a phone interview for a job from a company in California. She politely declined, then removed her resume from the search sites. She sent her parents a note and resumed her search for a place to live. The realtor hadn't lied and an hour later she admitted defeat. Her excitement at having a new job was starting to wane. It didn't do any good to have a job if she couldn't find anywhere to live.

Even if she could afford it, she couldn't stay at the ranch indefinitely. In fact, she only had a few more days before some other family moved into her cabin. It was perfect for her, Alex decided, and she only needed to find one like it somewhere between here and Laramie. At the rate she was going, Alex thought, she was going to have to get a motel room. She frowned. That didn't appeal to her.

Self-doubt crept in as she closed her computer and walked back to her cabin. Alex changed into a pair of shorts and a t-shirt, then curled up on the sofa with a book. She tried to read, but she couldn't concentrate.

She needed a place to live, and where was Cole? They had spent so much time together in the past couple of weeks, it was like she had known him forever. She had to admit she was lonely without him.

CHAPTER EIGHTEEN

Alex and Maisie caught up with Mary Louise the next morning as the older woman was trying to open the patio door to Cole's cabin, the folds of her colorful skirt rustling with the breeze. The older woman was carrying an armful of towels that needed to be washed.

"Let me help you," Alex offered.

"Oh, thanks sweetie, I should have made two trips, but I was in a hurry, I wanted to get this laundry started," Mary Louise replied. "So, what are you up to today? I thought maybe you would be out on the trail. You've done a lot of hiking since you got here." They stepped into Cole's kitchen. "Just give me a minute to start this load. Make yourself at home and I'll be right back."

Alex let Maisie off her leash and walked towards the kitchen, running her hand on the counter, touching the stainless steel refrigerator. She turned and leaned against the counter to look out at that glorious view of the mountains. She loved this cabin. If she could design herself a house, it would look just like this, with this view. And she could be happy here. She sighed. It wasn't an option.

"Sit down, sit!" Mary Louise exclaimed as she came back into the kitchen. "I've got some iced tea in the refrigerator. I'll pour us some and we can sit and have a visit."

Mary Louise not only got them tea in tall glasses, she produced a plate of snickerdoodle cookies.

Alex took one and bit into the sugary, cinnamon treat. "Umm, it's so good. I haven't had one of these for a long time."

"Well, help yourself, we have plenty." Mary Louise sat down and took one for herself. "Now, what's on your mind? Like I said, I'm surprised you aren't out hiking. Of course, you did find that body, that had to be scary. That would make me leery of going back out on the trail, that's for sure. Have you talked to Cole today? I haven't seen him, which is kind of surprising."

She stopped to take a breath and Alex jumped in. "No, I haven't seen him either, but I know he has to work, so I understand. I wanted to talk to you though, I need your advice."

She told Mary Louise about her trip to Laramie yesterday, meeting Marta, and being offered a job.

"Oh, that's just great, where are you going to work?" Mary Louise asked as she pushed her glasses up.

"It's called Hiking and Biking, have you heard of it?"

Mary Louise nodded. "Of course, why didn't I think of that? But they don't design their products, do they? You won't be able to design."

Alex explained the setup at the store to her, then sat back. Mary Louise sat for a few minutes, thinking.

"So, why don't you seem happy?" she asked at last.

"That's just it. I can't find a place to live and what's the point of having a job if I have no place to live? Even if the ranch had an extra cabin available, I couldn't afford to live here. I checked with a real estate agent in town, and I looked online to see if there was anything out there, but so far, no luck. I was hoping you knew of someone who had something to rent. Even a room would be okay."

"Hmm, let me think about it," Mary Louise replied as she looked around the room. "It's too bad you can't stay here."

Alex forced a laugh. "But then, where would Cole live?"

Mary Louise was silent. She was quiet so long that Alex started to feel uncomfortable.

"I suppose I'd better get going," Alex finally said. "Can you let me know if you hear of anything?"

"Oh, I'm sorry dear, of course I'll let you know, I have a couple of friends who might be willing to rent a room out, just let me talk to them."

Alex wandered over to the corral where Buck was working with the horses. Maisie sat at her feet as Alex hooked her arms on the fence to watch him. Buck led a saddled horse over to her. His coat was a beautiful golden color, shiny with a recent brushing and sporting a nearly white mane and tail.

"Do you ride?" Buck's voice was low and gentle.

Alex shook her head. "I haven't since I was young," she said, "and I'm not sure I can now. I broke my leg last summer."

Buck pushed his weathered cowboy hat up on his forehead. "Did they say you wouldn't be able to ride?"

"The subject never came up," Alex replied, "so I don't know."

"Only one way to find out." He walked the few steps to the gate and opened it. "Come on then, the dog can stay there for now though."

Alex didn't hesitate. She wasn't going to pass up this chance. It was just her and Buck, no one else to see if she fell off, and he was right, there was only one way to find out if she could even sit on a horse. She told Maisie to stay and followed Buck.

Buck led the horse over to a step and held it there. "It will be easier if you start from the step here, see how it goes, then we can see about mounting from the ground later."

Alex obediently stepped up on the step, which was actually two wooden crates, one taller than the other, sitting next to each other. It put her just high enough that she could step into the stirrup and swing her other leg over without having to boost herself up.

"Well, there, then, you're on," Buck said as he led the horse a step away and handed the reins to Alex. "How's that feel?"

Alex considered. She didn't remember horses being this tall and the ground looked a long ways away, but her legs adjusted to the saddle.

"It's good, I think, as long as he doesn't dump me on the ground."

"Good." Buck nodded and lifted one side of his mouth in a smile. "I don't think he'll dump you on the ground, will you Roger? Do you remember how to use the reins?"

When she nodded, he stepped away. "Why don't you walk him around a bit? I'll be right here if you need me."

Alex walked Roger...what a strange name for a horse...around the corral. She adjusted her seat to his gait and told herself she could do this. After several circuits around the fenced in area, Alex came back to Buck, who was leaning on the fence near Maisie. It looked like Maisie didn't know what to think, but she obediently sat on the other side of the fence.

"What do you think now?" Buck asked.

"I think I should try a ride sometime," Alex replied. "Assuming I can get off, I don't think there's any reason I can't ride a horse."

Buck nodded and walked back over to the step. "Getting off can stretch some muscles in your legs, but we can work on that." He held the reins while Alex dismounted.

"That was good," he said. "Come back again and we'll work on getting on and off without the step."

Alex thanked him and assured him she would be back, then went out the gate and to Maisie, who looked up at her with head cocked. She ruffled the dog's fur. "Right?" she asked Maisie. "Who thought I would be riding a horse today?"

As they walked back to their cabin, Alex realized she hadn't told Sandy and John about the opportunity to work in town, so she and Maisie took a detour over to their cabin. The lovely Alfie was still sitting there, along with John's vehicle. Alex was about to knock on the front door when she heard voices from behind the cabin. She walked around and found them sitting on their deck with Jackie and Steve.

"Just the woman we were waiting for?" Sandy called out.

Alex smiled. Why did everyone say that, she wondered briefly, but to be honest, they didn't look like they were waiting for anyone. The women had glasses of wine and the men each had a bottle of beer.

"What have you been up to today?" Jackie asked her as Alex and Maisie sat down on the top step of the deck. Alex leaned back so she could talk to everyone.

Alex laughed. "Believe it or not, I've been horseback riding, well, only in the corral with Buck, but I did it."

"Well, good for you," Steve said. "We went out the other day and there's nothing like it. We saw a golden eagle's nest and a pair of them."

"Wow," Alex replied. "Maybe I can go on a ride, but for now, we were checking to see if my legs would even allow me to ride a horse. Apparently, they will. Anyway, I was going to bring your artist's board back. I was able to buy myself one yesterday."

"That's fine dear, but there's no hurry," Sandy said, rising out of her chair. "I was going to come see you, and I hope this was okay, but we matted and framed the paintings you left with me. We took them into town to the gallery there and we sold one right off."

Alex was sure her jaw dropped to her knees. "You sold one? Really? One of my paintings?"

"I hope it was okay," Sandy repeated as she stepped over and handed Alex a check. "There's no charge for the matting and framing. Consider that my gift."

Alex looked at it, then at Sandy, then the others, who were all nodding. "Of course it's okay, but, really, you sold one painting for this much?" She looked at the check again. "I don't even know what to say. Wow. Thank you."

Sandy waved it off. "It was our pleasure," she said, "and the gallery will take more. The gallery owner was so impressed that he said he would buy outright anything you could get to him, no consigning necessary."

Alex was quiet for a few moments and her eyes filled with tears. She felt so blessed.

"Are you okay?" Sandy asked.

Alex blinked back the tears and smiled. "I'm wonderful, and I have more news. You'll never believe this, but I found a job."

"That's great," Jackie replied. "Where are you going to work?"

Alex laughed. "In Laramie," she said. "I found a place that designs and sells outdoor gear right here."

As expected, all four of them were surprised.

"That's great," Sandy said after congratulations were given. "I had no idea there was such a place here, but that works perfect with your art."

Alex nodded. "It does, and although it was never my intention to come out here and never leave, I think it's going to be good for me.

I really thought I was going to have to work in a larger city."

"How does Cole feel about this?" Sandy asked. "We've noticed you two have gotten pretty close in the last few weeks."

Alex felt the blush rise on her cheeks, even though she figured everyone here knew about her relationship with Cole. They had spent every moment together they were able to since Alex had gotten here.

"He doesn't know yet," Alex replied. "I haven't been able to find him. It's like he just disappeared."

"Did you ask Mary Louise?" Steve asked. "She almost always knows where he is."

"I did, but she hasn't heard from him either." Alex bit her lip. "I can only guess that he's been working with the sheriff on the details of the body we found."

"It's not like him to go off without telling Buck and Mary Louise," Jackie said. "It must have been very important."

Alex shrugged. "I suppose he'll turn up eventually. With no cell service here, it's not like it's easy to call people up here."

"Again, it's one of the best parts of being up here," John said. "We get to take the time to enjoy nature and each other, make new friends." He reached out and patted Sandy's hand. "Personally, I'm really glad Alfie broke down here."

Everyone laughed, and the subject of Cole's whereabouts was dropped.

Alex left a little while later and as she walked down the trail, she worried about Cole and where he could be, but there was nothing she could do about it. Alex fingered the check in her pocket and shook her head in disbelief. "Who knew I could paint, let alone sell a painting?" she asked Maisie. "I wish Cole would hurry up and get back, I have so much to tell him." Maisie woofed softly.

Alex was still thinking about the painting later that afternoon while she sketched. She and Maisie were sitting on the deck when Maisie suddenly raised her head, pulling Alex out of her thoughts. Her tail thumped on the decking. It still seemed odd that Merri and Anthony weren't next door. An older couple had moved into the cabin next door and although they were friendly, they weren't inclined to stop and have a visit.

Alex wasn't sure she and Cole were going to hunt for the treasure anymore, it felt like they had hiked the entire mountain range and were no closer to finding anything than they were the first day. And Cole had to work. He had a ranch to run, guests to tend to.

Maisie stood and walked over to the railing. "What is it, Maisie?" Alex asked. She set her can of soda on the table and was just about ready to stand up when Mary Louise came around the cabin.

"There you are sweetie," she greeted Alex. "I knocked at the front door and you didn't answer, so I thought you might be back here."

Alex smiled and stood up. "We spend a lot of time out here, it's so peaceful." She pulled a chair out from the table. "Come, join us."

"I can only stay a minute," Mary Louise said, standing at the bottom of the stairs. "I just wanted to invite you to dinner at our house this evening. Will you come? I'm making enchiladas, one of my favorites, and I make them from scratch, none of that frozen stuff."

Alex didn't hesitate. "I'd love that." Not only did she not have plans, but she also hadn't seen Cole all day. She didn't want to ask Mary Louise where he was, but the older woman must have read her mind.

"I finally heard from Cole," Mary Louise said. "He had to go home to Bishop's Hill last night. He got a call from his mom, and apparently his dad had a heart attack." She saw the sudden concern on Alex's face and quickly continued. "Cole finally called on the office phone a while ago, he said he couldn't through on anyone's cell phone. He says his dad's going to be okay, but he left right away to go to find out for certain. He's hoping to be back yet tonight, but it will probably be late."

"I thought you could do with a change of scenery and a good home-cooked meal, and I have a surprise too," Mary Louise continued.

"A surprise? What is it?"

"Oh, no, you don't." Mary Louise put her hands on her hips. "You have to wait until later for that. I've got to go, but I wrote down directions to our ranch, just come whenever you want. Buck and I are leaving in a few minutes, so we'll see you in a bit, okay?" She handed Alex a piece of paper.

The older woman moved surprisingly quick and was gone before Alex finished nodding. She was probably making sure Alex didn't have a chance to change her mind, Alex thought to herself.

CHAPTER NINETEEN

The Phelps ranch was beautiful. The grass was a luscious green, and trees with trailing branches lined a rock-strewn river, the water gurgling as it moved downstream. Alex noted several well-kept buildings, including a pretty red barn. Horses grazed in an adjacent pasture, surrounding by the same wooden fences as the ranch, and the house was surrounded by flower beds filled with brightly colored flowers.

The house was a two-story log cabin with a wrap-around deck on the south and west sides. The roof came to a peak above the deck, framing large windows.

"There you are, sweetie," Mary Louise said as she opened the door to Alex and Maisie. "Come in, come in, and welcome. Buck tells me you rode a horse today, isn't that great? I'm sure you enjoyed it." Mary Louise led her into the kitchen and when Alex turned, she was struck by the view. Beyond the kitchen island was the living room, and beyond that were those great big windows, much like Cole's, allowing light in as well as the view, and the view was spectacular. The valley stretched in front of the house and off to the southwest were mountains, not the spectacular white tips of the Snowy Range mountains, but still majestic.

"Isn't it great? Mary Louise asked. "I never get tired of the view, even when the outdoors is covered with snow."

"I love it," Alex said. "You can see the view while you're cooking,"

Mary Louise gave her a tour of the rest of the house, starting with the living room. A long dining table sat on one side of the room and the other side held sofas and chairs positioned so one could watch television or enjoy a fire in the fireplace that made one wall. A stairway led to the second story. There were three bedrooms upstairs and two bathrooms, and each of the bedrooms opened onto a balcony that overlooked the living room. Mary Louise showed her the two bedrooms on the first floor, including the master. It was decorated in the southwestern style of New Mexico with colorful accents in every room.

"I think I'd never want to leave here if this was my house," Alex exclaimed.

"It's a little large for us now that the kids have all grown, but it works for us. And when they all come home, we have lots of room for everyone," Mary Louise explained. "Oh, I forgot the best part, follow me." She led Alex outside and down a rock sidewalk to a cute little log cabin near the river.

"What's this?" Alex asked, looking at the windows adorned with green shutters, and a little deck. Large patio doors made up the front wall of the cabin, reminding Alex of the cabins at the ranch. Flowers bloomed in beds surrounding the deck and from hanging pots hanging under the eaves.

"It's a little studio apartment." Mary Louise opened the patio door. "Buck built it for me as a she-shed, but I decided I didn't like being out here by myself. I prefer the house and having someone to talk to."

Alex went through the doorway. It was smaller than the cabin at the ranch, but it had a sofa and chair, with a television mounted to one wall. There was a small kitchen area and a table with two chairs against the other wall. A short hallway led to a bedroom and small bathroom with a shower. A small alcove held a stacked washer and dryer. Like the big cabin, it was decorated in southwest colors and was bright and sunny.

"It's not very big and it only has one bedroom, but do you think it would work?" Mary Louise asked.

"It's beautiful," Alex breathed. "Work for what?'

"You, of course," Mary Louise answered. "When I told Buck you couldn't find a place to live, he said that if you liked, you could live here."

Alex looked around at the tidy space. "Me? Live here?"

"It's just sitting here empty," Mary Louise said, "so it may as well have someone living in it."

Alex was stunned. It was perfect. Better than perfect, whatever that was. And she could live here, thanks to the generosity of Mary Louise and Buck. "I would pay rent," Alex started to say.

Mary Louise laughed. "I thought you could live here free, but Buck said you would say no to that. We would include utilities and Wi-Fi since they come from the big house. Would it work for you?"

Alex took the two steps between them and hugged the older woman.

"Is that a yes?" Mary Louise asked as Alex finally let go." If you have your own furniture, you can use it if this doesn't suit you."

Alex spun around. "I love it and the furnishings are perfect. And the view!" She turned back to Mary Louise and her eyes lost their brightness. "Everything I own is in a storage unit in Kansas City and I don't even know what's in there since my parents packed my things from the apartment. James and I were going to buy a house after we got married so we didn't have a lot of furniture, and I think James' family kept most of it."

She looked around at the room. "This will work for me, but are you sure it will work for you and Buck?"

Mary Louise smiled. "It was Buck's idea and I agree with him. I don't know how you did it, but you've got a fan in Buck. He has only good things to say about you."

Alex doubted that, since he hardly had anything to say at all, but she wasn't going to argue. She loved Buck and Mary Louise.

"Good, it's settled then." Mary Louise turned to go. "Let's go have dinner then. Buck will be waiting."

As Alex suspected he would be, Buck was pretty quiet during dinner while Mary Louise chatted on about neighbors, and when they finished, he ambled off to the living room to watch television. "He loves his TV shows," Mary Louise explained. "After a hard day's work, he deserves to relax."

Alex helped Mary Louise clean up, then said her goodbyes.

"Yes, yes, you need to get back to the ranch before it gets dark," Mary L said. "There's a lot of wildlife out there at night, so you be careful."

Alex hugged her again and waved to Buck, who was still sitting in his chair. He lifted his head in acknowledgment. Mary Louise gave her the keys to the little cabin.

"You can move in whenever you like, and if you want to move your things out of storage, we have a shed here you can use for storage."

"That would be nice," Alex replied. "At some point I think I'm going to need my winter clothes." She paused. "Does Cole know I'm moving here?"

Mary Louise shook her head. "No, we just decided this afternoon to offer it to you. Does he even know you have a job and are staying?"

It was Alex's turn to shake her head. "No, I tried to find him yesterday when I got back, and then today, but I never had the chance to talk to him."

"Oh, well, you'll probably see him tomorrow, since he said he was coming home tonight, so you can tell him then."

Alex fetched Maisie from where she had been sleeping on the floor in front of Buck's chair, and they headed back to the mountains.

Cole's house was dark when they got back to the ranch, so Alex figured he was either asleep or not back yet. She was so excited with the developments in the last day or so, and wanted to share them with Cole, but Mary Louise was right. She could tell him tomorrow. Her last thought before she fell asleep was how grateful she was to Mary Louise and Buck for offering her a place to live.

Alex's cabin was dark, Cole noticed, when he turned the Jeep into the ranch's driveway. It was probably for the best, he thought, since he was dead tired. It had been a hectic couple of days, and stressful as well. His dad would be fine, but they had to do emergency surgery to put a stint in to keep him alive. He discovered that he wanted to talk to Alex, share the experience and explain why he hadn't called her. He realized that he didn't even have her phone number in his phone. Not that she had any service up here. Anyway, he would stop by first thing in the morning. Cole had talked to Buck on the phone and was assured that Buck could handle the horseback rides tomorrow. Danny and Noah had a couple of fly-fishing groups to take out on fishing excursions, but he wasn't needed for that.

He parked the Jeep and once inside, didn't even bother turning on any lights. He pulled off his shirt and jeans and fell into bed.

The next morning Cole finished the paperwork that wouldn't wait and set off for Alex's cabin. She was right where he expected, sitting on her deck with a cup of coffee in her hand. Maisie jumped up from her place on the deck and bounded over to him. A veteran now, Cole took her weight and let her give him kisses.

"It always amazes me how much she loves you," Alex said as Cole set the big dog's paws back on the ground.

"I'm telling you, women fall all over me," Cole said, shrugging. "It's a gift I have." Then he laughed. "You have any more of that coffee?"

Alex nodded and started to rise from her chair, but Cole waved her back down. "I can get it. I'll be back in a minute."

"I came to see if you were up for a hike today," Cole said as he came back out of the kitchen with a coffee mug.

Alex soaked in the sight of him sitting in the chair, baseball cap on his head. She had missed him more that she realized.

"I thought we were probably done looking for Anthony and Merri's treasure," Alex said.

"I thought so too, but I think we should keep looking, at least until we're satisfied we've covered all the places we marked on the map." He grinned. "And I have the day off."

"Then we should definitely go," Alex said. "They left all their maps and research with me if we need them. We didn't hike while you were gone. But wait, I almost forgot. I found a job."

Cole's gut felt like it had just gotten kicked by a horse. He didn't want her to leave.

"You did?" he asked, trying to keep his voice light and encouraging. "Where? Denver?"

Alex laughed and shook her head. "Here. I'm going to design for Hiking and Biking."

"Here?" He didn't want to hope. "As in Laramie here?"

"Here. I'm staying."

Cole jumped out of his chair and stood, then pulled Alex out of her chair. He picked her up in a hug and twirled her around.

"I start next week," she said when he set her down, "and there's more. Sandy took my paintings to a gallery in town and they want to sell them. They'll buy them outright and already bought one at full price, at the price Sandy asked for anyway, and she gave me a check."

"That's amazing," Cole said and scooped her up again. "I'm so proud of you." He set her down and held her at arm's length. "Where are you going to live? In town?"

Alex shook her head.

"With me?" he asked before she could say anything more.

Alex stopped with her mouth open. "Are you asking me to move in with you?"

Cole shook his head. "I would if I thought you would agree though, you know that."

"I thought I might have to do just that. Did you know there is no place in town to rent, or even buy? I even asked Mary Louise if she knew of any place and she said she would check around. She eventually came up with a solution."

"Really? What solution?" Cole wasn't sure this would be a good or a bad solution for him.

"Mary Louise and Buck said I could live in Mary Louise's she-shed."

"That's great." Cole picked her up a third time, then abruptly set her down. "Buck agreed to this?"

Alex looked at him, puzzled. "It was Buck's idea, according to Mary Louise. Maybe she was wrong?" Her face fell.

Cole considered it. "Buck's pretty private, so I'm just a little surprised he wants anyone living on the ranch."

"I don't know, but Mary Louise said it was okay, that Buck likes me."

Cole brushed the hair back from Alex's face. "He does like you, why wouldn't he? And he wouldn't have offered if he didn't mean it."

Alex suddenly smiled. "He let me ride a horse."

Cole looked around. "How long was I gone? A job? A place to live? Riding a horse? A lot happened while I was gone."

"Things have been moving pretty fast," Alex said, "and I only rode around in the corral. We were checking to see if my legs would let me ride a horse."

"And?"

Alex nodded. "I think I can do it. I used a step to get on and off, but Buck said we could work on mounting from the ground."

Cole tilted her chin. "You're amazing. And you're staying, really staying." He brought his lips to hers, then deepened the kiss. They were breathing hard when he finally lifted his head.

"You are so special," Cole told her, then put his finger to Alex's lips when she started to protest. "You are, and I'm so glad you're staying. Let's go for a hike."

"Is this even a road?" Alex was hanging on to the handle of the UTV for dear life as they bumped along a rocky and uneven path that Cole said would take them to the trailhead to hike to a place called Reservoir Lake.

Alex was sure they drove twenty miles of rough road in the Jeep, pulling the UTV on a trailer, before Cole announced it was time to switch to the UTV. She had no idea how far they had come since then, but there was no sign of life except for hawks flying above them and the occasional marmot peeking around a rock...no hikers here and no other traffic on what Cole termed a road.

"Technically, it's a road since we're allowed to drive on it," Cole replied, "but good news, we're here."

He parked in what loosely could be called a parking lot and pointed to a sign that announced the Lakes trail.

Alex sat and just admired the scenery. Imposing mountains, large boulders that looked as though they had been tossed there, and the sky that was so blue it took her breath away. They were high, high enough it seemed, to be on top of the world, with ripples of other mountains the only things on the horizon.

They were above the tree line, so the view was unbroken and absolutely breathtaking.

When they were ready to start hiking, Cole got out his binoculars and scanned the area.

"Anything?"

Cole shook his head and adjusted his pack. Alex knew he was looking for signs of Cash.

"This feels a long way from where the map showed the 'X'," Alex said as they skirted the edge of a small lake.

Cole nodded. "We're actually hiking back east. The lake we're hiking to is closer to the area marked on the map that it seems. We're just coming around from the backside because it's a shorter hike. We technically could hike around and back through the gap lakes area where we were the other day."

This way was fine with Alex, she decided, as she adjusted her floppy hat. Hiking along the gap lakes meant crossing the boulder field, an area covered with hundred of ways to break an ankle.

It didn't seem very long before they were at the lake and the area Cole wanted to explore. They searched for anything that looked out of the ordinary and found nothing.

"Lunchtime," Cole announced and found them a place to sit on a rock. Alex was positive she had sat on more rocks in the time she had been in Wyoming than in her entire life. She didn't mind though, the rocks were warm from the sun.

"We should have asked Mary Louise for another picnic lunch." Alex bit into her tortilla roll-up that was filled with peanut butter. "Why didn't we think of that?"

Cole considered his ham-and-cheese sandwich. "You're spoiled already," he said, laughing. "I try not to take advantage of Mary Louise, so today we're on our own. We only had one horse ride scheduled today. Buck took that and Danny and Noah are handling UTV rentals. We don't have a fishing trip today, which is the only reason I could get away. I was gone all day yesterday as it was."

Alex had just finished her apple slices and was putting her plastic trash baggie back in her pack when she spotted something.

"Look at that!" She pointed to several large bushes that were right in front of a boulder.

Cole looked and didn't see anything.

"I think it's a cave," she squealed happily, then left her pack sitting and rushed over to the bushes, disappeared into them.

CHAPTER TWENTY

"Alex." Cole grabbed their packs and Maisie's leash and followed her, ducking under the bush as well. It wasn't really a cave, more of a grouping of boulders that had made an indentation. It was large enough for the three of them, but that was about it. It offered shelter from the sun and possibly the elements on a bad day.

"You know there could have been a bear in here," Cole stated.

Alex cocked her head at him. "I thought bears didn't live above the tree line."

"They generally don't, but that doesn't stop them from foraging here," he explained, "and that wouldn't stop one from taking a little nap here."

"Okay, I'll give you that, I shouldn't have just rushed in here, but now that we're here, can we do a little exploring?" She started poking around in the dirt with her hiking pole.

Cole looked at the very small space. "By all means, let's look." It wouldn't take long. Alex was almost through the small area when her pole hit something. She looked up at Cole.

"It's probably just a rock," he predicted.

Alex stabbed a couple more times, a then a little harder and they heard the distinct sound of iron on iron. She looked up again, then knelt down on her good knee. Cole followed and pulled out his knife to move the dirt around away from the object.

"It's a metal box," Alex breathed. "Do you think it's our treasure?" She was so excited, she could hardly breathe.

"Our treasure, is it now?" He continued to dig.

Alex laughed. "You know what I mean."

"Yeah, I do."

Cole worked it loose and pulled it out, then shook his head. "It's not our treasure." He turned it around and brushed some dirt off. "It's an old army ammunition box. Probably World War Two era. He gently shook it, and it rattled.

Alex was disappointed, but still, they had found something.

"Can you open it?"

Cole pulled on the metal latch and the box popped open. He dumped the contents into Alex's cupped hands.

"I think it's a geo-cache."

"A what?"

"It's a hobby where people place a cache, a box like this, for others to find. You can take something out of it if you want, but you're supposed to leave something behind for the next person to find. I've never done it, but I know people who have."

Alex looked at the items from the box. A smooth red rock, a feather, a shot glass from Kentucky that promoted bourbon, three pennies and a few other trinkets. There was also a short pencil and a little notebook.

Alex opened it and found notes from people who had previously found it.

"How would you even find this?" Alex asked as she handed the notebook to Cole.

"The site would have GPS coordinates and have those listed on a geo-cache site on the internet. They're all over."

"And they're buried?"

Cole shook his head. "Not usually, but this one's been here a while. The dirt just blew over it and no one's found it for years."

"Should we sign it?"

"Absolutely." Cole handed the notebook back to her. After they added their notes and the date, they dug in their packs for something to leave behind. Alex found a carabiner and Cole added a whistle. They left the box behind but didn't rebury it. Cole set the GPS points on his watch.

"This way it'll be easier for the next people to find." They set off back in the direction of the UTV.

"I'm still excited we found something," Alex said as they came around a bend in the path. "If we can find this, then maybe there's a chance we can find the outlaw's treasure."

Cole didn't reply. He was fairly sure they were on a wild goose hunt and there was no treasure, but he wasn't going to voice that out loud. Looking for it was a good way to have another look for any trace of Cash and a great excuse to spend time with Alex. It was good for her too, he decided. Every day she got stronger and today she was hiking without having to stop and catch her breath.

He saw her look back at the imposing mountain they were leaving behind them. Cole knew it ate at her that she couldn't make it to the top. It was still on her list, he knew and he was going to help her make it, one way or another.

"Look, there's someone there." Alex stopped and gestured to a woman resting next to the trail. She had full gear, which meant she likely had spent at least one night out on the trail.

"Hi, how are you?" Alex asked.

"I think I'm lost," the woman said. She unfolded her trail map. "I should have been to Lewis Lake by now."

"Where did you start from?" Cole asked.

"I started at Lewis Lake and was taking this loop." She drew it out with her finger. It showed she should have gone south past the gap lakes. "I left my vehicle there, so I need to figure out a way to get back there."

Cole whistled. "That's a pretty long hike. We're right here, so you've gone way past where you should have turned south." He looked around. "Where's the rest of your group?"

"I'm by myself," she answered. "I've camped two nights out and thought I'd be back by now. I'm Melody Witlock, by the way."

"I'm Alex and this is Cole," Alex answered, and shook the woman's hand.

Cole also shook her hand, but said nothing. Alex could almost hear him thinking. He looked at the sky and then at the map, then to Melody. "You won't make it back before dark and going this way adds another nine miles to your hike, so you still won't get back before dark. It looks like a shower's coming as well."

"So it's too far to go back and too far to go on," Melody said. "I guess once I get to the tree line I can go ahead and camp again. I might be a little short on food, but I suppose it'll be okay."

Alex, who hadn't forgotten the many times Cole had lectured her about hiking by herself, looked up at him. His expression gave nothing away. She knew he wanted to say something, but he continued to look at the map.

"She could come with us though, right?" Alex asked. "We could give her a lift."

"Oh, I can't do that, I'll be fine, really," Melody protested. "I know where I'm at now, and I can get back."

"Alex is absolutely right," Cole said. "We have a UTV just up ahead at the trailhead. We can give you a ride over to your vehicle."

They finally convinced Melody to accept the ride and Alex was happy to sit in the back of the UTV with Maisie. Cole carefully worked his way back to the Jeep so she wouldn't be jostled more than necessary.

Although it didn't rain on them, the sun had already set behind the mountains by the time they got to the parking lot. They left Melody at her vehicle, waiting for her to unlock her door and put her pack inside. She waved as she drove away. Cole didn't say anything as they drove back to the ranch and Alex didn't push it. She waited until he stopped the Jeep in front of her cabin.

"You're angry, aren't you?"

Cole tapped his fingers on the steering wheel and stared straight ahead.

"It's not so much that I'm angry," he finally said, "but we both know first-hand how that could have gone wrong and ended in tragedy. Think about that body we found, that Mark Rutherford. There were people in his life affected by his death.

"Melody came out here by herself, didn't tell anyone where she was going and then took the wrong trail. Anything could have happened. She could have sprained an ankle or broke a leg, fallen and hit her head. She could have died out there and no one would even know until someone noticed the vehicle sitting in the parking lot. Even then, we wouldn't know where to look for her."

It was the exact situation Cole had found himself in with Cash, Alex realized, and it was hitting hard after finding Mark Rutherford dead only a few days ago. He sighed when Alex put her hand on his arm.

"I get it now. When I realized she was out there by herself, I saw what you saw, and I understood why you didn't want me to go alone. I could have been her."

Cole turned his head and looked straight into her eyes. "You could have been her. And it's not just the risk of falling or getting attacked by an animal, there are people in this world who prey on women. I couldn't stand the thought of anything like that happening to you, or Melody, for that matter.

"It's not just because you're women. I feel the same about men hiking alone. There's a lot of danger out there. I admit I've hiked by myself here, and I know most of this area like the back of my hand, but I don't do it anymore either. It's just not worth the chance you're taking."

"Do you think Cash just went out alone and something bad happened to him?"

"I don't know. If he did, I don't understand why he left Piper behind. We found a duffel with clothes in it in his pickup. His wallet and money were in the glove compartment. It was like he was leaving the area, but then why would he stop there? We found his hiking gear at his apartment.

"So, why would he hike out into the wilderness with nothing, even his dog? And if he's, well, if something happened to him, why haven't we been able to find anything, you know, like his body?" His voice, rough with emotion, drifted off to nothing. "It just doesn't make sense. Nothing about this makes sense."

Alex heard the pain in his voice and her heart broke for him. She caressed his arm.

"We'll find him Cole. I'll help you and we'll find him."

Cole shook his head. "I don't think we will. I've been looking for him for months. We've search everywhere. People who didn't even know him came out to help. We've posted flyers, offered a reward, posted information on the internet and we've gotten nothing. It seems like he's just disappeared, vanished into thin air."

"Do you think he left with someone? Got into another vehicle and left the area?" Alex's voice was gentle.

"We've considered it, and there were other tire marks at the trailhead, but that's not unusual. He didn't take his identification, and why leave Piper behind? I just can't believe he would leave Piper behind. Would you leave Maisie?"

Alex shook her head. "Never, even if I was dying. I just wouldn't, so I see what you mean."

She reached across the space between them to give him a brief hug. She hung on when he pulled her against him.

He eventually eased back. "Thanks for listening. That was a lot. I'd better get this UTV back before Buck fires me," he said in an apparent effort to lighten the mood.

Alex laughed, just as he hoped she would.

"I'm going to have to take a long hot shower, my legs are sore," Alex said.

"Hmm, I can think of a remedy for that."

Alex cocked her head. "Really? What did you have in mind?"

"Bring a swimsuit and meet me in an hour at my cabin," Cole said. "It'll be worth your while."

"Promise?" she asked as she got out of the Jeep. Maisie jumped out behind her.

"Promise."

Cole heard her laughing as he pulled away, but an hour later she was at his door.

The hot tub did wonders as Alex sat there, eyes closed, totally relaxed.

Well, not totally relaxed, she decided. Her muscles were relaxed, and her leg felt better, but spending time with a near-naked Cole had sent all of her senses into overdrive.

The hot tub was tucked away behind the house, out of sight from the Commons, and clearly for Cole's private use. As she had eased in, Cole was there, wearing only a pair of swimming trunks, to hold out an assisting hand. She hadn't brought a swimming suit, so she had improvised with a sports bra and a pair of shorts. Maisie opted to observe from the deck.

They had chatted and as the shadows deepened, the conversation and the mood became more intimate, more charged with growing emotions. It wasn't surprising then, that as Cole helped her out of the water, he drew her into his arms and, looking into her eyes, brought his mouth to hers. Alex didn't resist, and in fact, leaned into the kiss. His hands moved along her sides and down to her hips, then back again to allow one to rest lightly on her breast.

Alex's body reacted immediately, her nipples tightened and she could feel a tingling from there to her belly. His fingers teased the soft skin just below her breast and Alex stretched to get closer to him. Unexpectedly, he pulled her sports bra up and over her head, causing her to lose contact for a moment. Then he was back, and started a line of kisses from her neck to her breast.

Alex shivered, then sighed softly. Cole brought his lips back to hers, then lifted her and carried her into the cabin. He struggled for a moment to open the door, but Alex barely noticed. She was too busy absorbing all of the sensations she was feeling.

He set her down next to his bed and there was a bit of flurried movement as they tried to keep lips together and remove wet shorts. In a quick moment of sanity, Cole pulled the blankets out of the way and remembered supplies were in his nightstand.

They tumbled onto the bed and hot skin touched hot skin. Alex ran her hands down his chest, exploring hard muscles and hot flesh.

"You know you're going against your sleep with the guests policy, right?" she muttered.

"Umm, hmm," Cole mumbled. "Okay with that."

"I don't want to be the one..."

"Trust me, you're the one. Now stop talking."

"Are you up for another hike tomorrow?" Cole asked as they lay side by side on their backs, both panting from exertion.

Alex sighed. "I don't know, I'm pretty tired. I thought we could just stay here for a couple of days."

He nudged her in the ribs. "At some point, we're going to have to eat and Maisie will need to go out." Maisie, who had been sleeping next to the bed, raised her head and gave a soft woof.

"See?"

Alex rolled onto her side to look at him. "I thought you were the one who didn't think there really is a treasure, that all this looking is a waste of time."

Cole snugged her up against his side. "What I think is that searching for a treasure, real or not, is a good reason to spend a great summer's day with you," he said. "Plus, I'm always busy with the ranch, and I've seldom taken any days off just to enjoy myself."

"In that case, count me in." Alex kissed Cole's nose and rolled away from him. "Maisie and I had better get home and get some sleep."

"You could stay, go back in the morning."

She was tempted, she couldn't deny it. He looked so good lying there, all man. "Now, I need to go back now."

"Okay, okay." Cole rolled out of bed and started dressing.

"What are you doing?"

He looked up from fastening his jeans. "Getting dressed."

"I see that. Why?"

"So I can walk you home."

Alex put her hands on her hips. "I think Maisie and I can walk across the driveway by ourselves." Maisie thumped her tail.

"Still." he pulled his t-shirt on. "What if you run into Bigfoot one the way across the driveway?"

"What if you run into Bigfoot on the way back?"

"I can run faster than you can," Cole retorted as he pulled on a tennis shoe.

Alex laughed. She didn't doubt that.

CHAPTER TWENTY-ONE

Cole had told her they had a bit of a drive ahead of them, but Alex hadn't realized they were going quite this far. The white tips of Medicine Bow Peak seemed to be getting farther away, but Cole apparently knew where he was going. It was another beautiful day to be riding in a UTV, watching for wildlife, and splashing through washouts with water trickling through them. Maisie sat in the back with her tongue out, the wind blowing her fur back from her face.

Alex was also beginning to doubt there was any treasure out here, but she had to agree with Cole. They had a great time exploring, and Alex was positive she would not have seen any of these areas without Cole to go with her. She had been a little naive when she came out here, thinking she would just wander out into the wilderness, just her and Maisie, and nothing would happen to them. She shivered at the thought of that man falling down into a ravine with no one to help him.

She hadn't been watching where they were going, so when Cole turned tand started down a rocky road, she was sure he was lost. It was difficult to talk with helmets on, so she would have to wait to ask. It was a good thing she trusted him, Alex decided.

By the time he stopped, Alex felt like they were all alone in the world. There were no other cars in the trailhead parking area and no sounds except for the birds and the wind in the trees. They were in a wooded area where a tiny brook trickled along the rocks. Alex breathed deeply, could smell the pine trees. The whole area could have been a Christmas tree farm, she thought, but with very large Christmas trees.

Maisie jumped out and they gathered their backpacks, Alex put Maisie on her leash.

"You should think about getting a pack for Maisie," Cole said, "to help carry her water and dish, maybe some emergency food."

Alex looked at Maisie, and the big dog gazed back at her, like she knew they were talking about her. She woofed softly and Alex smiled. "I think she would actually like that, it would make her feel useful."

After Cole checked their GPS location and marked it, the three of them started up the trail. It obviously didn't get much use, but it was still visible. It was chilly out, but Alex knew from experience that as they walked, they would get warmer, just as the day would get warmer.

They came to a lake that Cole identified as Sand Lake and Alex knew she could sit on a rock and watch the water for hours. They walked along the shore and eventually the trail veered away from the lake.

Alex finally remembered the question she had for Cole.

"This seems awfully far away from where we were looking before, don't you think?"

Cole nodded. "I know it does, but we're trying to get just a little north of the 'X' on the map," he said. "It was easier and faster to come around from the north than it was to hike up from the south. Less steps and less time."

Alex couldn't argue with his logic. "Do you think there are more bears in this area, just because it's more remote?"

Cole considered the question. "I suppose there could be, but it's hard to know. They move based on the weather, how warm it is, and where they can forage. We'll be diligent and keep Maisie on the leash, keep an eye out for scat."

Finally, Cole said they were close to where the 'X' was marked on the map.

"As close as I can determine, anyway," he added.

"I feel like if I was hiding gold, I wouldn't go so far away from civilization," Alex said, looking around. "And if it took years to come back for it, would the landmarks be the same? I mean, all the rocks look the same, but trees grow, streams change course."

"All of that's true, but even the rocks can change, be split in half by the cold and heat," Cold replied. "Mines decay and are reduced to mounds of dirt, reclaimed by nature. But I have a feeling about this place. Maybe he chose it because it is so far away from every-thing."

"I hate to say it, I think we should be done looking. If there's a treasure here, someone either found it or it's hidden very well." Cole and Alex were walking around about the hundredth clearing they'd come across, poking with their walking sticks and pushing through brush. Maisie, on her leash, sniffed around everything, but was more likely looking for a ground squirrel or two than a treasure.

Alex sighed. "I think you're right. Maybe we misread the map and we're not even searching in the right area."

"That's a possibility, although it looked pretty promising." Cole inspected another stack of rocks. "Now that you're staying here and you have Merri and Anthony's research, we can go back and reread everything, see if we missed any details."

Just then, Maisie let out a yelp and dashed forward. Alex, who was only gently holding her leash, knowing she always stayed close to Cole regardless of the leash, let go. Maisie gave three or four deep barks and then was gone in a flash of fur around a clump of trees and rocks. Alex stood there frozen for just a second as Cole looked up from the rocks.

"What the hell?" He sprang into motion and went after the dog.

"Maisie, come back." Alex shouted and moved as quickly as she could after him. She didn't want to risk falling so she wouldn't run. She could only pray that Maisie hadn't smelled a bear and thought she needed to investigate. She shook her head. Maisie's behavior this trip was completely out of character. She didn't tackle people at home. She never went off leash. What was going on?

Cole paused for a minute and marked the GPS. They were no longer on the trail and he didn't want to get them lost chasing after a dog. He also didn't know which direction Maisie went, so he stopped for a moment while Alex caught up with him.

"Where is she?" Alex whispered.

"I don't know." He scouted the area and saw nothing. What had she heard? Or smelled?

A minute later, he heard several excited barks and took off on a jog in the direction he thought they were coming from. The barks stopped and Cole pulled his knife out of his pocket. He heard a couple of more barks and possibly a man's shout, then silence.

Oh no, Maisie was attacking someone, Cole thought. He glanced behind him to make sure Alex was with him and gestured to her to be quiet. They stood there, not hearing or seeing anything but rocks and trees.

They looked at each other when they heard a man's laughter,

coming from, where? They went forward together, quietly, towards the laughter. It appeared to be coming from a clump of bushes. Cole gestured for Alex to stay back while he pushed his way through the brush.

Maisie had a man pinned to the ground and wasn't biting him, she was furiously licking his face. The first thing Cole thought of was how Maisie had first greeted him, and wondered if Maisie knew him. The man was trying to ward her off with his hands, but it wasn't working. The big dog was lying spread-eagled on him, like he was a long-lost friend.

"Maisie, off!" Cole shouted.

The big dog stopped licking long enough to look around at Cole, but kept her oversized paws planted firmly on the man's chest.

Cole grabbed the leash and gently pulled. "Stop Maisie, this minute." Maisie finally obeyed and took her paws off of the man, then stepped aside and sat down next to him, tongue sticking out of her mouth and watching him like she was never letting him out of her sight. "What do you think you're doing?" he asked Maisie.

"Are you all right?" he asked the man while keeping his eyes on Maisie.

"I'm all right." The man didn't move from his place on the ground. His dark brown eyes widened, then closed. "I remember. Oh my God, I remember."

Cole finally looked at him, tall and thin, with a full dark beard and wavy, deep brown hair. He stopped and stared. The man on the ground opened his eyes and looked at Cole.

Alex came up behind him and stopped as well. She let out her breath in relief that it wasn't a bear. She added her own words of scolding. "That's not what we do, Maisie, we've talked about this. You don't get to tackle people, especially ones we don't know." She trailed off as she looked from one man to the other. Both were frozen in time, neither moving or saying anything.

"Cole?" The man on the ground raised up on one elbow. "Cole? Oh my God, I remember you."

"Cash?"

"Cash?" Alex repeated.

"Cole." He looked at the dog, still waiting to be allowed to continue giving the man kisses. "That's not Piper then?"

"Maisie. She's Alex's dog." Cole gestured to Alex. "Cash? It's really you?" He crouched down beside his brother. "You're all right?"

"It's really me and I think I'm okay. Maisie, right?" He put his hand up to pet Maisie's head. "She packs a pretty good punch, snuck up on me."

As Cash raised himself to stand, Cole pulled him into his arms for a hug. He could barely believe it. Cash was alive. And well. And here. He was here.

The hug only lasted a moment, then Cole pushed away and shoved his brother backwards. "What the hell? You were here the whole time? We've searched everywhere for you, you ass." An unusual anger filled him. "What kind of game are you playing, pretending to be missing, not letting anyone know you're okay? My God, Mom and Dad, all of us, have been frantic. We thought you were dead."

Alex cleared her throat. "Maybe you could let him tell you, Cole."

"I need to sit down. I have a headache." Cash sank to the ground. Maisie nudged up against him and he rubbed his hand into her fur.

Alex sat down next to him, and Cole squatted, looking him over. "You're not okay."

"I am. I'm just, well, it's hard to explain. I had forgotten every-thing, who I was, what I had been doing. All I could remember was someone was trying to kill me."

"Someone tried to kill you?" Alex asked, startled. Of all the things that she might have thought happened to Cole's brother, that wasn't one of them.

"You've had amnesia?" Cole asked. "But you know who I am now."

Cash ran his hand through his hair and nodded. "As soon as you spoke, I recognized your voice. And the dog. I recognized the dog." Cash looked at Maisie, still obediently sitting next to him. "I thought she was Piper." He looked at Cole and rubbed his forehead as if it hurt. "Piper was with me, is she okay?"

Cole nodded. "We found your truck at a trailhead parking lot," Cole said, "and Piper was in it. She's with Mom and Dad at the ranch. We're a long way from that trailhead."

"I'm not sure I could find it again, I pretty much ran as far away from that trailhead as I could, and when I found this overhang and got settled here, I stayed. Surprisingly, it works well to keep rain and snow off me."

Cole looked around and realized they were under a huge rock overhang, not a cave, but the overhang gave it the appearance of a small cave. It wasn't large, but large enough for a tent. Cash had made a bench out of a log and several more logs were positioned near the back of the overhang as shelves. They were lined with sup-plies, from a camp stove to a bear barrel filled with packaged food.

"You have a tent?" Cole asked with surprise in his voice. "It looks like a sporting good store in here. How did you get all this?"

Cash shrugged and smiled for the first time. "I have a lot of things. I've foraged and picked up things hikers and campers left behind. You'd be surprised what people leave out here."

Cole saw the humor in that. "We would not," he said, grinning. "Alex and I have been hiking out here for a few weeks now and we've found some pretty interesting things."

"I'm Alex, by the way." Alex extended her hand and Cash shook it. He cocked one eyebrow at Cole.

Cole nodded. "Alex is staying at the ranch, on vacation, but now she's staying permanently. She found a job in Laramie."

"You're living together?" Cash's voice held surprise.

"Not yet," Cole replied. "I'm working on that." He smiled at Alex. "Just so you know." He turned back to Cash. "But she's rented Mary Louise's she-shed."

Alex sat dumbfounded for a moment. He really wanted her to live with him? How had she not picked up on that? And what was that little question between the brothers? She would think about that later, she decided. The men were talking again.

"So, what happened? How did you end up here?" Cole asked Cash.

"I wasn't sure until just a little while ago," Cash said. He reached over to pet Maisie. "When I woke up and was lying on the ground and all I knew was I had to get away. My eye was almost swollen shut, and I was sure my nose was broken. Possibly my ribs as well. I had a horrible headache, but I ran for awhile until I thought I was going pass out...My head and ribs hurt so much. I had to sit and rest, then I just kept going."

"But it was cold up here and there weren't many hikers out here at that time of year." Cole let Cash rest a moment. "And I think we had a snowstorm several days later, I thought for sure you froze to death if you were out here. How did you manage?"

"I got lucky," Cash replied. "The first day, while I was still walking, I found two backpacks that were fully supplied. I heard a man and woman arguing and the woman was mad. She said this was the stupidest idea he had ever had. I remember that clearly. She grabbed one of two packs off the ground and threw it down a hill and stomped back down the trail. The man looked at it for a moment and then turned and followed her, leaving the second pack there as well.

"I waited and they never came back for them, so I took both. Then I hiked up here where I knew there were fewer hikers," Cash continued. "I got lucky again and found this overhang. I was so tired by the time I got here, I had to sleep. I likely had a concussion and sleep was the last thing I should have done, but I couldn't help it. My last thought was no one was ever going to find me, I would die here and that would be it."

Cole rubbed Cash's arm. "But you didn't die, and we've found you. Anyway, go on."

"The only thing I could remember was that someone had tried to kill me. I could only see misty clouds of thoughts and couldn't get any of it to come into focus. I saw the helicopters and knew people were searching for something, but I couldn't risk showing myself since I couldn't remember who the threat was. Or maybe I had tried to kill someone. I couldn't be sure until I could get my memory back."

Cash went on to explain that he had foraged, picked up things hikers left behind. He had a big break when he found a fishing pole, so he could have fresh meat.

"Everything else was pretty much packaged, mostly freeze-dried," he continued. "I couldn't risk starting a fire, didn't want to be noticed or start the forest on fire. Luckily, that couple had a cute little camp stove and enough fuel to get me by until I found some more."

Cash looked at Cole. "So, I pretty much stayed out of sight,

Whenever anyone came along, I just stayed in here until they went away. Apparently, this dog wasn't going to let that happen." He scratched Maisie's head.

"So, now, do you remember what happened that night?" Cole's tone was soothing.

Cash took a deep breath. He recalled meeting a woman at a bar one night in Laramie. Her name was Hailey and she was so sweet. Petite, blonde, big blue eyes. They hit it off immediately and spent the night dancing.

"She said she had just broken it off with her boyfriend and was ready to move on. Whenever she mentioned him, she looked around to see if he was there. I got the feeling she was just a little afraid of him."

They started seeing each other after that, but mostly at his house. She said she didn't want her ex to find out she was seeing someone else. The ex-boyfriend was a bit of a thorn in Cash's side, but they managed to make it work. She would come over after she got off her shift at the hospital where she was a nurse, but she usually had a friend drop her off and pick her up, so her car wouldn't be at his house.

"I should've seen that as a red flag and backed out of the relationship, but I really thought it was temporary." Cash shook his head. "I should've known better." He had a thought. "Did she come forward after I went missing?"

"Not that I know of," Cole said. "Do you know her last name? Or the friend's name?"

"Her last name was Johnson, Hailey Johnson. And her friend was Rachel, I think, or something like that." Cash ran his hand through his hair. "It's all back. I worked so hard to remember and I didn't have anything for so long. It's a bit overwhelming.My head is throbbing."

"Take a minute, I know this is a lot, especially since you just remembered everything," Cole said. He reached into his pack for his first-aid kit and dug out two pain relievers, gave them to Cash. Alex handed him her water bottle.

"Thanks," Cash replied. He swallowed the pills and handed the water bottle back to Alex, then continued his story.

"We decided to go away for the weekend and meet up here so her ex wouldn't know," Cash said. "Man, I was so stupid. One of her friends was going to bring her up here so the guy wouldn't follow her. Instead, when I got here, he was waiting for me." He paused for a minute. "Big dude, and mean. Duke Richards, I think his name was. And another guy, also big. They grabbed me by the neck and dragged me down the trail, then proceeded to beat me up. He shoved me and I fell back, must have hit my head on a rock, because when I came to, they were gone and I couldn't remember anything except that my life was in danger. Until today, that is."

He scratched Maisie's head again. "When this dog jumped me, it was exactly what Piper used to do. I immediately remembered her and then the rest came flooding back. And then there was you. I am so glad to see you."

Cole and Alex digested that information.

"I never gave up looking for you."

Cash jumped up and started pacing. "I knew people were looking for me. I did. I knew I must have family out there who was worried. But frankly, I was afraid of that unknown threat of someone out there looking for me."

"He probably thought he did kill you since no one ever came forward with any information about your disappearance."

"I didn't even remember Piper."

Cole nodded. "She was in the truck with your duffle and wallet and wouldn't get out even to pee. She stayed in the truck until we got back to the ranch. I kept her there thinking we could go look for you together, but she wasn't happy. She whined and would only sit on the porch looking for you." It was Cole's turn to run his hand through his hair. "She was losing so much weight, we were afraid she might die, so Mom and Dad took her back to the ranch. She's better, but they say she runs to the lane every time she hears a truck."

Cash shook his head. "I feel so bad about that. I left her in the pickup because I thought I was only going to be gone a second." He looked at Cole and Alex. "I have another question for you, Cole."

"Go ahead," Cole invited.

"What are you guys doing all the way out here? It's pretty far off the beaten path."

Alex and Cole laughed, then Alex answered. "You're not going to believe this, but we were looking for a buried treasure."

Cash looked at one and then the other. "Nah, you guys are pulling my leg. There's no treasure out here, I feel like I would have found something like that."

"Maybe, if you were looking for it," Cole said. "You've had the time."

"Agreed," Cash replied. "I was just concentrating on staying alive and trying to remember who I was."

"This is a great place to do that," Cole said, looking around. Alex did the same. This was almost exactly like the place they had found near Reservoir Lake. She wondered what they might find if they did some digging, but she didn't say anything.

Alex and Cole shared a look.

"What?' Cash asked.

"Nothing important, we can talk about it later, but first, did you have a plan or were you just going to stay out here forever?"

Cash shook his head. "It's easy to lose track of time out here, but I know it's summer. Not July yet because I haven't heard fireworks. I also know there would be very little chance of me making it through a winter. I wouldn't have been able to collect enough food. I can fish, but I can't hunt, and when the lakes freeze over and the snow falls, I won't be able to get any food. I would have had to make a decision when it started to get cold even if my memory didn't come back."

"Are you ready to get back to civilization?" Cole asked. "It's a bit of a hike, but we have a UTV on the other side of the big lake to the north."

Cash looked around at the little area that had been his home for months and was silent.

"Is there anything here you want to take with you?" Cole said as the silence grew longer. "We don't have enough room for all of it, but we can take some things now if you want."

In the end, Cash filled a backpack with the packaged food that wasn't in the bear barrel and a few other things to take along. They dismantled the tent and packed it behind one of the logs so it wouldn't blow out into the open. Cole marked the site's GPS with his watch.

The three of them pushed through the brush with Maisie right beside them, and Cash stopped to sweep their footprints from the area. He looked up to see Alex and Cole watching him.

"Sorry," he said, shrugging, "force of habit."

"You did a good job staying undetected," Cole said as they started walking. "You know, we looked for you with infrared cameras, never saw you at all, but we wouldn't have if you were under this rock."

They walked out and back to the UTV, catching up on family

matters. Alex sat in the back with Maisie for the ride back, she had insisted, and she got the feeling that Cole didn't want to let Cash out of his sight. Alex didn't blame him, and she knew that now they had found Cash, Cole wasn't going to lose him again.

When they got back to the ranch, Alex and Maisie walked back to their cabin while Cole and Cash went to Cole's cabin to call the authorities to let them know Cash had been found. She wasn't surprised that she could hear Mary Louise's squeal of excitement when the men went inside.

CHAPTER TWENTY-TWO

Alex sat on the back step, looking at the lake. She didn't know what time it was, only that the sun was in the west sky, and she was sitting in the shade. Maisie laid next to her, head on paws, sleeping peacefully. The events of the day ran through her mind. How amazing that they had found Cole's brother alive and well.

He was every bit as handsome as Cole, the dark, wavy hair that fell to just above his shoulders made him look very sexy, as did the beard. Strangely though, he didn't make Alex's heart race when she was around him. She sighed. What was she going to do with herself? Alex was sure they would be busy for days sorting out the events that led to Cash's disappearance in the first place and she hoped they would be able to find the men responsible for beating up Cash.

Alex heard the Jeep head out of the driveway and figured they had gone to Laramie to meet with law enforcement. She supposed their parents would meet them or they would go home, but she wasn't sure.

So here she sat, at loose ends for nearly the first time since she got here. Alex sighed again, then rose to go inside and find something to eat. They had hiked a long way today and her legs were tired. Not hurting, but tired, and she was definitely hungry. Maybe after dinner she would come back out and work on some sketches, do some painting in the morning.

Alex paused at the patio door. It was so peaceful here, she thought for about the millionth time. Birds chirped, the wind blew through the trees.

Alex went for her morning walk around the lake with Maisie and wondered what Cole was doing. She wandered over to the office, but Mary Louise must have been busy cleaning cabins because she didn't see her. Even Buck was gone, out on a horseback ride, she supposed, since the horses were gone.

"Well, Maisie, it looks like we have the day to ourselves, what shall we do?"

Maisie gave a soft woof. "I'd like to do a longer hike too, but we'll wait until Cole's back for that. Maybe I'll paint for a little bit."

Her painting time took her all the way to lunchtime, but she only stopped for a few minutes to find something to eat and open a soda to drink. Maisie sat at the patio door looking outside as Alex ate her lunch.

"I know, it's a beautiful day and we should be outside," Alex told her. "How about a compromise? Let me get my stuff together and we can sit outside while I paint."

She moved her operation to the patio table and was so engrossed in the painting she was working on that she didn't hear anyone coming. Maisie stood and woofed softly so that Alex looked up. It was Jackie and Sandy. They were carrying several glasses and a bottle of wine.

Alex stretched her shoulders. "Come on up, we could use a

break.”

The ladies settled into chairs and Sandy poured them each a glass of wine. “The guys went fishing today and we were going to go shopping. We decided we were feeling lazy, so we detoured over here. It looks like you’ve been busy,” she observed. “Can we look?”

“I love these,” Jackie said after she set the last one down. She looked at Sandy and Alex. “It’s interesting how good you both are, but your styles are different.”

Both women laughed. “That’s a good thing,” Sandy said, “or I might be out of a job.”

“I’m not sure I have a style,” Alex added. “I’m just painting and trying to improve my technique.”

“Well, you’re doing fine,” Sandy said, patting Alex’s hand. “Now, we want to know, is it true that you found a body?”

Alex nodded, suddenly serious. “Technically, Cole found the body, but yes, I was there.” She leaned in. “Merri and Anthony were positive they had seen a bear in that same spot some time before. I think when Cole and Maisie went over that way, they were sure he was going to find a dead bear.”

“Do you think it was murder?” Jackie asked.

“Oh, no, the sheriff told Cole it was just an accident. The man had altitude sickness and apparently lost his balance.”

“And is it true you found a missing person just yesterday?” Sandy asked.

“You two have been busy.” Alex laughed.

“Well, to tell the truth, we ran into Mary Louise as we were getting ready to leave for town,” Jackie explained, “but she talks really fast, you know, so we only managed to get part of the story.” She stopped to sip from her glass. “We were pretty sure you would know all the details.”

"Got it." Alex explained about finding Cash when they were out hiking and that the guys had gone to see the sheriff yesterday.

"But Cole hasn't come back yet, has he?" Sandy asked.

Alex shook her head. "I expect they went to their parents' house. I don't know if Cash even has a place to live or a job. Anyway, I doubt Cole will be back before this evening."

"Where's Alex?"

Mary Louise looked up from the carrot she was chopping. There was no smile on her face.

"She left."

"What do you mean, she left?" Cole was confused as much by Mary Louise's demeanor as her words. She never said anything in just two words. This was serious.

"She left. She checked out this morning. Last night was her last reserved night and we couldn't extend her reservation. We've got new guests coming in this afternoon who need that cabin."

Cole ran his fingers through his hair. "Wasn't she going to your ranch? I thought when she left here, she was moving in at your place."

Mary Louise nodded. "I thought that was the plan, but I met her at the corner this morning when I was driving here and I saw her turn and go west on the highway. Why would she go that way? Our ranch is the other way."

Cole had no idea. He thought she was supposed to start working in Laramie in a day or two, but he had to acknowledge he hadn't talked to her much about that. With the excitement of finding Cash, thoughts of his future with Alex had been put on hold. He and Cash had gone straight to the sheriff's office, and after several hours of giving statements and going over events, he had driven Cash to their parents' ranch.

Cole had called them from Laramie, so they were prepared, but it was chaos when they got there, as all of their brothers and sisters had gathered to welcome Cash home. It was already dark when they got there, so Cole had agreed to stay the night.

One night turned into two, Cole had finally gotten away early this morning. Cash had wanted to come back with him, but Ben had suggested he stay at Bishop's Hill until they had apprehended the men who had attacked him.

Mary Louise pointed at him with her knife. "You've been so excited about finding Cash alive and so busy with him, no don't interrupt," she added as Cole opened his mouth to speak. "You know you've pushed her to the side. Have you even talked to her the last couple of days?"

Cole shook his head. Mary Louise was right. He and Cash had hurried off to Laramie, he hadn't even stopped over at her cabin to tell her where he was going, and he hadn't tried to call, hadn't seen the need, and would she have gotten the call? He knew cell phone service here was non-existent.

He slumped into the chair opposite Mary Louise. "What am I going to do? I've got to find her."

Mary Louise shook her head. "I don't know. There's always the possibility she changed her mind and decided to go somewhere else."

Cole shook his head again. No, he wouldn't believe that. Cole straightened, then stood and gave Mary Louise a kiss on the cheek.

"Do you know where she went?" the older woman asked with a hopeful look.

"I don't, but I know how to find out," he called back as the door slammed behind him.

Cole found the Coopers along with John and Sandy on the Coopers' deck. "Have you seen Alex?" he asked without offering any greetings.

"Why, hello Cole. No, we haven't seen her recently." Jackie answered for the group. "She said something about going to Medicine Bow Peak, but that was a couple of hours ago."

"She said she had something she wanted to do," Sandy added. She trailed off as Cole left in a flash of jeans and flannel shirt.

"Well, what do you suppose that was about?" Steve asked. "He was in a pretty big hurry."

Jackie shrugged at her husband. "Young love, maybe?"

The others chuckled as they returned to their visiting.

Alex sat on a bench just beyond the parking lot at the trailhead for Medicine Bow Peak, Maisie at her feet. She looked up, admiring the imposing mountain. White stone jutted towards the sky, blue with fluffy white clouds moving over the peak. One of her goals when she came to Wyoming was to hike to the top of the mountain. She had tried and failed when she first got here, and now she wondered why it had seemed so important.

This trip had been an amazing experience, even without the hike that had brought her here. She had hiked, grown strong, made friends, found a new job and a new hobby. 'Side gig,' Alex amended, but mostly a hobby. She had a place to live, and she had found Cole. She had slept with him, the only man she'd ever had besides James. And James. She had let him go along the way, found her peace with his death. She was able to look towards the future and she hoped that future still included Cole.

Alex hadn't heard from him since they parted at the office the other day. She couldn't really blame him since he had his hands full. She understood how important his brother was and she was so glad they had found him alive and well. She supposed they were done looking for the treasure, now that Cash was back and she was starting a job, there wouldn't be any time to search.

She sighed and pulled her sketch book out of her backpack. She sketched for a few minutes and decided the angle wasn't quite right, so she shrugged into the pack and she and Maisie started walking. She only needed to go about thirty yards, Alex determined, but hadn't quite gotten that far when she heard her name behind her. Maisie immediately stopped and turned around to go back.

As Alex also turned, she saw Cole jogging towards them.

"Oh, you're back." Alex greeted him with a smile. "How are things with Cash?"

Cole ignored her question. "What do you think you're doing?"

Alex opened her mouth to open to answer but didn't get the chance.

"After all we've been through and here you are," he said, clearly upset. "I thought you had learned by now. I mean, of all the stupid things to do, this is it."

Alex felt her eyes fill with tears at the unexpected attack and blinked to stop them. She squared her shoulders. Maybe a few weeks ago she would have cried, but not now.

"I don't know what you're talking about and I'm not sure I care, but I'm an adult, you know, and I can do what I want. I don't need you or anyone else telling me what I can and can't do." She ignored Maisie's soft whines at her raised voice.

Cole started to speak, then just stood there and watched the unfamiliar fury in her eyes.

Alex poked him in the chest. "Are you listening to me?"

Cole put his hands up to ward off another attack and lowered his voice. "I'm listening, something you're not doing."

"How did you even find me?" Alex asked. "Were you following me?" Her heart nearly stopped at the thought. No, he hadn't followed her, she immediately knew that was something he wouldn't do, but what was going on with him?

Cole put out his hands to encompass the area. "I didn't follow you, well, I did, but only because I was scared for you. The Coopers told me where you went. After all we've been through, how could you even think about hiking to the top of this peak by yourself?"

Alex's eyes went wide. "Is that what you're thinking, that I came out here to hike to the peak, try again? By myself?"

Cole nodded. "Isn't that what you're doing?"

Alex poked him again. "No, and even if I was, it's not your business. I just wanted to make a couple of sketches of the mountain, and I wanted a better angle, so I was just walking up to that rock there." She turned around and pointed to a rock about ten feet behind them. "I can still see the parking lot from here, I saw no harm in going this far. I don't even have my hiking pole."

Cole was silent.

"This is where you apologize." Alex put her hands on her hips.

Cole inwardly groaned. Damn, she was right.

"I apologize."

"From the bottom of your heart for not trusting me and my judgment."

"From the bottom of my heart," Cole said. "I should have trusted you. I do trust you. I was just so scared. I don't want to lose you."

"Like you almost lost Cash." She understood, she really did. They had rescued four people and found one body in the short time she had been here, but she had told him she wouldn't hike by herself, and she didn't.

He stepped up and took her into his arms, tipped her face up. "Please come back to the ranch, move in with me." He continued before she could protest. "I know, you were planning to move to Mary Louise's little cabin, but I'd like you to stay at the ranch. I have enough room and we could set up one bedroom as a place for you to design, or paint, or whatever you want."

"You really mean that?" Alex asked. He had mentioned it before, but she hadn't really taken him seriously.

Cole nodded. "I never want to lose you, I want to wake up every morning to you," he whispered. "I love you."

"Wait, what? You love me?" Alex's voice squeaked a little as she realized what he actually said, and she backed up a step. "We've only known each other for a few weeks. Are you sure?"

He gently pulled her back to him and brushed her hair from her cheek. "I know, but I also knew the minute you opened your door that I had been waiting for you. Only you."

"You've never been in love before?"

"No." He shrugged. "I dated, but I swear, every time I thought things could get serious, I closed my eyes and saw you. I knew that one day you would show up in person. I just didn't know where or when. So I waited."

"How could that be? You mean, you had some sort of vision?"

She felt his chuckle before she heard it.

"I don't think I have visions, and I know it sounds crazy, but here we are."

He was in love with her, after only a few weeks. She and James had been classmates all though school, then friends and eventually that had grown into love and respect. It hadn't been the immediate attraction that she felt with Cole. But a few weeks? It seemed far-fetched.

She thought about her own feelings. Why couldn't he have fallen in love with her this quickly? She fell in love with him in the same amount of time.

"Are you there?" he asked after she was quiet for a few minutes.

He felt her nod. "I am, and I love you too." She lifted her face to his and met his lips. He was everything she needed and wanted.

"Let's go home?" he asked.

"Let's go home," Alex replied. Maisie agreed with a soft woof.

****

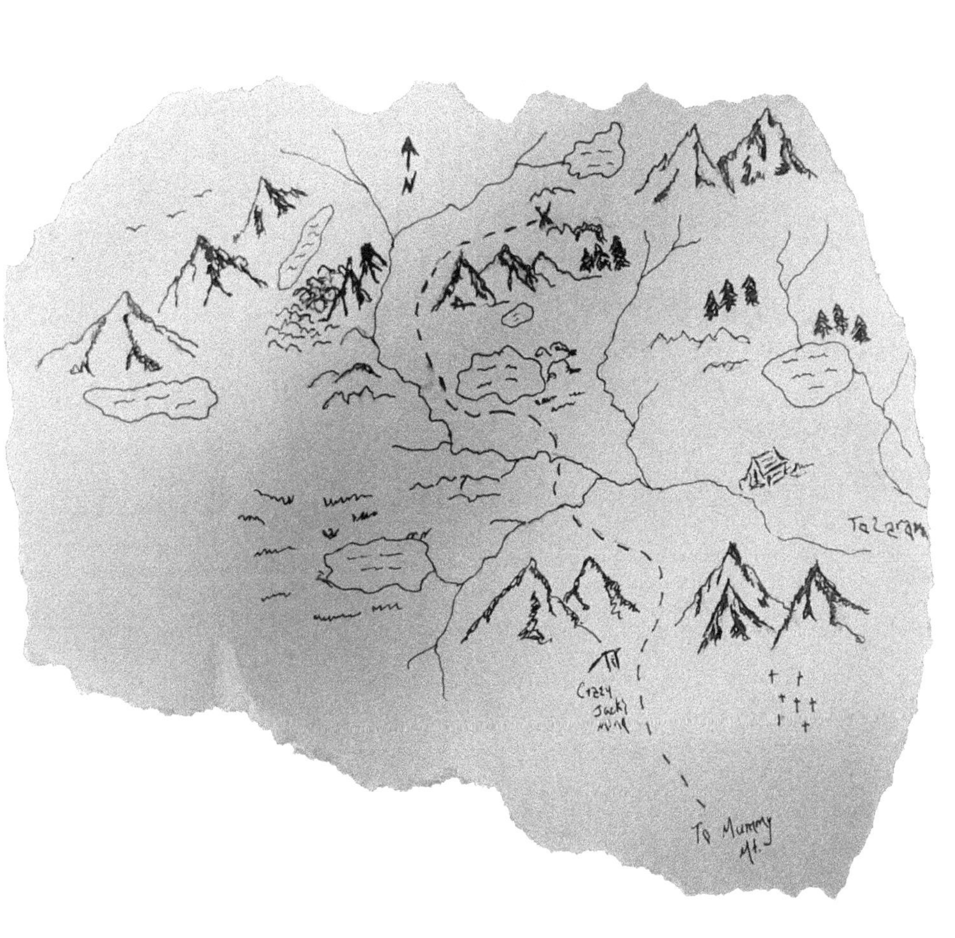

Crazy Jacky Hill
Talaram
To Mummy Mt.